Frozen: a ~~Para~~Normal Mystery

by Christine Amsden

Twilight Times Books
Kingsport Tennessee

Frozen: a ~~Para~~Normal Mystery

Paladin Timeless Books, an imprint of
Twilight Times Books
P O Box 3340
Kingsport TN 37664
http://twilighttimesbooks.com/

First Edition, July 2018

ISBN: 978-1-60619-287-0

Library of Congress Control Number: 2018939157

Cover art © 2018 by Lou Harper, CoverAffairs.com

Printed in the United States of America.

For everyone who has fallen in love with Cassie, as I have.
Thank you for your support; this one is for you!

Chapter 1

APPARENTLY, LIFE DOESN'T END WHEN YOU GET MARRIED. I SUPPOSE THAT'S obvious, but it's hard to tell from the way Happily Ever After stories dominate our culture. At any rate, marriage seemed like such a solid conclusion to the stories I had to tell that I ended my first four memoirs the day I married Evan Blackwood.

If only I'd known then that all hell was about to break loose.

My name is Cassandra Morgan Ursula Margaret Blackwood, and if you think that's a mouthful, go ahead and call me Cassie. Most of my friends still do, although I no longer feel unworthy of the full appellation.

To be fair to my younger self, eager to share her journey of self-discovery with the world in the wake of some powerful events, things were quiet for almost two years. More happened to my two best friends than to me during that time. Oh sure, I consulted with the sheriff's department here and there on cases that mystified them. I also worked with my husband and a dozen others to form and support the White Guard, an organization attempting to unify and protect the magical world. We made some big gains when Matthew was able to convince most of the magical world that his nemesis was using blood magic to control people's minds – including mine and my husband's.

It was a sobering moment for us.

But mostly during that time, I grew a baby and took care of her. I always wanted children, maybe because I'm the oldest of nine and having kids around seemed natural.

Anastasia Blackwood turned one in mid-December, right around the time my youngest siblings, Michael and Maya, both turned two. Honestly, I would have preferred to have two separate parties – or even three – to give each child his or her due attention, but my mom wasn't up to it. She wasn't up to much anymore, including party planning, so it fell to me and Juliana, seventeen now and pretty much already an adult. The last two years had aged her, as the responsibility for raising Michael and Maya fell heavily upon her shoulders.

The day started normally enough. Juliana, with Michael and Maya in tow, arrived at my place several hours before the party to decorate. My two best friends, Madison and Kaitlin, came to help too, the latter with a one-year-old son of her own. Madison, pregnant but not showing just yet, volunteered to keep the toddlers out of trouble. "For practice," she said, although we all knew she was doing us a favor. I'd return that favor as soon as she realized how badly moms need breaks sometimes.

Yeah, I know, babies and birthday parties and maybe life really does end when you get married. Or at least loses its sex appeal. Although for the record, I still found Evan as sexy as ever. I mean, the man could drive me to orgasm with a single, magical kiss.

Damn, but it was addictive.

Speaking of Evan, he wasn't invited to the setup party. Officially, because it was a ladies' only event, but unofficially, because he wanted a Star Wars theme and I didn't. I humored him by hanging a banner reading "May the Force Be With You" under the banner reading "Happy Birthday" in bright, colorful letters.

Once our large living room was more or less ready for the party, I left Kaitlin and Madison blowing up balloons while Juliana and I disappeared into the kitchen to finish decorating the cakes. Yes, cakes. If they couldn't each have their own party, they would at least get their own cake.

Anastasia's cake was done already – a three-dimensional fairy tale castle complete with turrets and flags and a fire-breathing dragon wrapped around one of the towers. The fire breath was an illusion, compliments of Scott Lee, Evan's cousin and Madison's soon-to-be husband. Real fire would have melted the icing.

"You put a moat monster in!" Juliana exclaimed when she saw it. The moat, constructed of blue jello, did indeed contain a gummy worm "monster."

I nodded, then glanced guiltily at the two undecorated sheet cakes I had baked "just in case." Mom had sworn she would make cakes for the twins, but I couldn't trust her these days.

"Did Mom bake a cake?" I asked.

"I don't know." Juliana bit her lip. "She said she would; I reminded her when I left that she needed to make the cakes, but it was a bad morning."

"What happened?" I asked, almost afraid of hearing the answer.

"She was drunk."

"I thought you threw out all the alcohol!"

"We did. We either missed some, or she's brewing it in her potions lab."

"Damn." I stared at the plain sheet cakes, then looked at the castle that had taken me many, many hours to complete. Compared to the works of art my mom had created for us on our birthdays growing up, it probably looked pathetic, but it would be awe-inspiring next to a flat rectangle with icing.

"Do you have more icing prepared?" Juliana asked.

"I bought plenty of extra ingredients, so I can make more. That'll give us a chance to think up decorating schemes." I moved toward my oversized stainless-steel refrigerator as I spoke and pulled out three bowls of icing, each topped with a cold, damp towel. Then I started pulling bags and tips out of the decorating drawer.

"Do you think—" I started, then stopped myself. It was a horrible thought, one I couldn't possibly give voice to.

"Do I think she's coming at all?" Juliana asked, apparently reading my mind. Some sorcerers can do that, but not Juliana. Her gift is healing. "The thought crossed my mind. But Nicolas and Isaac said they'd drag her here if they had to."

Nicolas was my next youngest sibling, currently twenty, and Isaac was just after Juliana, currently fourteen. With Nicolas and me out of the house – me married with a child of my own and Nicolas neck-deep in an intense apprenticeship – a lot of responsibility had fallen on both Juliana's and Isaac's shoulders. For that matter, Elena, eleven, Adam, eight, and Christina, five, were all growing up faster than they should have to. But as the two oldest at home, it was worst for Juliana and Isaac. My understanding was that Juliana took care of the kids, while Isaac took care of Mom.

Mom had simply never recovered from the blow of losing her husband, my father, almost two years earlier. His death had profoundly impacted all of us; I still thought about him and missed him. Making things particularly hard was the fact that we had unfinished business between us. What would he say if he knew I had married Evan, for instance? But the worst thing for me was knowing that the last words I said to my father were, "I hate you."

I didn't mean it. I wanted to tell him that, desperately.

"I swear she was getting better for a while," Juliana said, tucking a long strand of dark hair behind an ear. She looked more like Dad, while I resembled Mom, but nobody had trouble believing we were sisters.

"You mentioned that." I didn't want to talk about Mom anymore, though. The day would be hard enough without churning up all the old hurt and betrayal. At one point, I thought I'd forgiven my mom, but sometime during her decline I'd changed my mind. Somehow, her refusal to pull herself together for the sake of two helpless babies was worse than anything she'd ever done to me – and she'd once magically disowned me.

Dad had gone along with her plans; that was part of the unfinished business. But for now, I had to focus on those he left behind.

"So Maya and Michael," I said, eager to change the subject. "What are they into?" I'm afraid I didn't spend much time with my youngest brother and sister, not even when I visited the rest of the family. I usually spent those visits dealing with Mom.

"Well, Maya's a summoner and Michael's a fire starter," Juliana said.

"We did gifts for their first birthday," I pointed out. "And we've known Michael was a fire starter since before he was born."

Technically, we didn't know for sure Michael was the fire starter until after he was born – we didn't even know there were twins – but the fact that Mom had set things on fire while she was pregnant confirmed the existence of a fire starter in her womb. Pregnant moms often channel their unborn baby's gifts. Anastasia had saved my life before I even knew she was there.

"Believe me, I still know Michael's a fire starter every day. His gift keeps slipping its binding; it used to be every few months, but lately it's just about weekly. I'm terrified the house is going to burn down around us."

"Have you asked Nicolas for help?"

"He did the last binding himself. Clark Eagle even helped, although Nicolas is getting really good after two years of study."

"We might need to call a full circle," I said. "I know Evan would help."

Juliana shook her head. She never said it outright, but I often got the impression she didn't approve of Evan. Almost two years after the feud between our families had officially ended, was it possible she still harbored some kind of resentment for them? Of course, they had cursed her bald – apparently permanently. Months of research and experiments had failed to undo that nasty bit of magic, compliments of Amanda Lee, who had never shared her secret. Juliana currently wore an excellent wig that matched her old hair so perfectly it was hard to remember it wasn't real. At least for me. Might be easier for her, all things considered.

I glanced at my watch. We had about an hour and a half to get the two cakes ready. "Okay, gifts it is. But we need to come up with a better concept for summoning than Mom did last year. Most people thought the girl surrounded by toys represented greed."

"And then they thought the fire was wrath." Juliana chuckled. "Okay, let's just do Dora and Diego."

"Are you sure?"

"Yeah. It's their favorite show. They watch it every day."

We set to work, using pictures from the Internet, skills honed from years of cake decorating, and a bit of magic – provided by Juliana. I still didn't have a drop of magic, although I channeled some of Anastasia's because she was nursing. I didn't use it, though. That had been a hard decision, but Mom's breakdown had made it easier. She'd spent her life having child after child, making sure she was either pregnant or nursing, so she could continue to channel the magic that had been stolen from her as a teen. While she hadn't been a bad mom until recently, she had always chosen to have children for the wrong reasons.

I would not become my mother. Not on this. So I didn't use magic, even when I had it available. I did some ritual meditation to keep it from building up and overpowering me, and that was it.

As we worked, I kept sensing Juliana wanted to say something. After the third time she paused, opened her mouth slightly, then shook her head, I asked her what was going on.

"Nothing," she mumbled.

"Juliana. Something's going on. You can tell me anything."

She bit her lip and looked up from her work. For a moment, I wasn't sure she would tell me, and I felt a pang somewhere in the region of my heart. Had I been such a bad big sister that she couldn't even talk to me? I knew I wasn't around as much as I used to be, but I was married and had a baby of my own. And she never asked for more. Never. If she did... well, I'd find a way.

"I'm worried about Maya," Juliana said suddenly.

I glanced at the Dora cake, which was nearly done. It only needed the birthday message artfully applied across the top.

"Why?" I asked.

"She screams whenever she's separated from Michael, even for a moment. It's weird, and it can't be healthy. It doesn't even matter who else is with her, not even me." Juliana's voice was full of hurt and bewilderment; she clearly saw herself as the twins' mom. Maybe in some ways she was, but I wondered if the twins had a healthy, secure attachment to anyone.

I didn't say any of that to Juliana. It wouldn't help.

"She loves her brother," I said carefully. "I'm sure it's just a phase."

"Maybe."

But I could tell Juliana wasn't convinced. Neither was I. Having recently read every book on parenting I could get my hands on, I thought it very likely that the whole family was having some serious emotional fallout from Dad's death and Mom's subsequent depression.

Maya didn't have a parent; Juliana might want to fill that role, but maybe she couldn't.

We finished the cakes just as the first guest arrived – Evan's mom, Laura Blackwood, who didn't like me but who doted on her granddaughter. Soon, the house was full of guests, mostly from the Blackwood side of the family.

"Where's Mom?" I murmured to Juliana after thirty minutes.

Juliana was on her phone, thumbs working overtime. "Elena says Isaac and Nicolas are trying to revive her. She passed out." Juliana glanced at the twins, then at me, and I could tell she was torn between going to help and staying for her twins.

"Stay," I said. "Nicolas and Isaac can handle it."

Juliana nodded doubtfully, then pasted a smile to her face and went to lift Michael into her arms. Maya let out a shriek that threatened to turn violent before Juliana scooped her up too. Huh. That was a bit extreme. How had I never noticed before?

Two strong arms came around me from behind, pinning me against a hard, warm, familiar chest. I melted against it, letting myself find strength and comfort in a loving embrace.

"Nice party," Evan murmured in my ear. "What's wrong?"

"Mom's passed out drunk."

He cursed under his breath.

"Do you think the Blairs could help her somehow?" I asked. The Blairs were a family of mind mages, and it was a mark of desperation that I mentioned them at all. I didn't trust mind mages, and I already owed Matthew ten years of service for a favor he'd done.

"I don't know, but let's try to think of something else first. Come on, it's time to cut the cake."

We went through the motions of the party: cutting cake, singing songs, opening presents, and playing games. Nicolas arrived an hour late, with the rest of my brothers and sisters, but without Mom. Nobody said anything, but there was tension in the air. Everyone noticed.

The party lasted for three hours, well past the kids' nap times. The adults simply went on without them until finally, everyone had left except for my siblings and two best friends. I sensed that none of them wanted to go home, and I didn't push them.

Finally, shortly before dinnertime, the doorbell rang. My heart leapt, thinking that Mom had shaken off her stupor and come after all. I dashed to the front door and flung it open, trying to decide if I should shake my mom or strangle her.

Sheriff David Adams stood on the other side of the threshold, hands in his pockets, a familiar look of tension on his face. I'd seen that expression before – he wore it when a situation made him feel he was in over his head.

"We've got a big problem down by the lake," he said without pre-amble. "I need you."

Chapter 2

IHAVE TO ADMIT, "I NEED YOU" ARE JUST ABOUT MY FAVORITE WORDS IN THE English language. I'm not sure what that says about me, but there it is. The words were especially welcome at that moment, when my mom had utterly failed her youngest children and, in so doing, failed most of the rest as well. Now, the sheriff needed me, and I needed a distraction. I was all set to go.

"I just need to grab my purse and let Evan know I'm leaving." I turned my back to him and started across the foyer.

"You might want to bring Evan too."

I stopped and tried not to feel hurt. Evan and I had an agreement – I was free to do all the investigating I wanted as long as I called him when there was danger. Now, the thing about "danger" is it's subjective, and I'll give you one guess as to whose definition was broader.

Whenever Evan joined me on a case, I felt overshadowed. It didn't matter that he never made me feel less than himself, it didn't matter that I did have skills to contribute, and it didn't even matter that I'd set most of my old insecurities about not having magic in a magical world behind me. It was just how I felt. Less.

I guess in real life, self-actualization is a never-ending process rather than the dramatic culmination of a series of events. It does make for a handy conclusion to a memoir, though.

Evan appeared in the entrance to the living room, at the end of the hallway. He looked at me, then past me to the sheriff.

"What's going on?" he asked.

"The sheriff needs me," I said. Then, grudgingly, "He suggests that you might want to come along."

Evan raised his eyebrows for a moment, then nodded, wiping all emotion from his face. His neutral expression was one I called his "game face" and it was nearly flawless – except with me. I could almost always tell what he was feeling.

Like right now, Evan was wondering how bad the situation had to be for the sheriff to suggest he come along and whether or not that meant I should stay behind.

"Maybe I should check things out first," Evan said. Yeah, like I said...

"I don't know how long the scene will stay put," Sheriff Adams said from behind me. "I'd like Cassie to get a look."

"Stay put?" I asked. Then I shook off the question. Actually, I didn't want him to tell me what he thought until after I'd seen whatever it was. I wanted to form my own conclusions.

"See if Madison will stay with Ana," I told Evan. "I just need to take care of a couple things and we can go."

By "a couple things" I meant taking some breast milk out of the freezer in case Ana needed it and sneaking into her room to whisper "I love you," even though she was down for her nap and couldn't hear me. It was more for me than her.

We were ready to go within five minutes, but the sheriff was tapping his foot impatiently when we returned to the foyer.

"Took you long enough." The sheriff glanced at his watch.

"You're lucky we had someone over to watch the baby, or it would have been longer," I said. "What's the big hurry? No wait, don't answer that."

The sheriff tapped the rim of his brown hat and gazed at me with something unfathomable in his weary blue eyes. He was in his late thirties but looked at least a decade older. Signs of stress, perhaps, from all the cases that had him way out of his depth? He didn't even have a wife or lover to help him unwind at the end of the day. The last relationship he'd been in, as far as I knew, was with a witch named Belinda Hewitt who'd put him under a love spell. Maybe that had soured him on the whole idea of love. I hoped not, for his sake.

He somehow looked older than the last time I'd seen him, which had only been a few days ago. A strange mist or fog had been lingering around the lake for months, and he'd wanted to know why. So did the White Guard, but I hadn't told him that part; I'd only said that it didn't seem to be hurting anyone so I'd look into it, but it wasn't a priority. Which was, after all, exactly what the White Guard had decided.

"You'll want to bring some winter gear — a heavy coat, hat, gloves, scarves." The sheriff turned his back to us and headed for his SUV, parked right out front.

"Coat?" I glanced at Evan, then out the front door. The trees just visible in the deepening twilight had long since lost their leaves, but there wasn't a hint of frost in the air. "How about a light jacket? It's fifty degrees."

"Not where we're going," he said cryptically.

Evan opened the coat closet, grabbed two heavy coats and the bag where we stowed our winter gear, and gestured for me to precede him out the door. He still had his game face on, but I could sense the underlying confusion there. Or maybe I was projecting my own confusion onto him.

We took Evan's new car, a green Tesla Model X, with him behind the wheel — one of marriage's many compromises. There's really a lot that goes on behind the "Happily Ever After," when you think about it. Who sleeps on which side of the bed? Do you squeeze your toothpaste from the bottom or the top? Who's going to cook? Do the laundry? Mow the lawn? The list goes on and on.

I like to drive, but Evan loves to drive. More importantly, he hates feeling out of control (i.e., being in the passenger seat). So I let him drive whenever it's the two of us. It's not weakness, even if it is a gender-conforming stereotype; it's just more important to him.

I got a princess theme at Ana's first birthday party. And not Princess Leia. It's all about compromise.

Evan followed the sheriff's SUV down Lakeshore Drive heading east, toward the resorts and away from what I liked to call "Sorcerer's Row." Basically, the sorcerers all tried to live as close as they could to the node under Table Rock Lake, which was slightly west of Eagle Rock. To the east, lakefront property went to private industries, hotels, cabins, and condos. There were also marinas and public beaches that way. And, lately, a persistent fog.

"The cake was beautiful, in case I forgot to say," Evan said after a few minutes of silence. It was usually my job to fill the silence, but my mom had me on edge. Unfortunately, thinking of the cake reminded me of her. She had always made such beautiful cakes.

"Thanks." I stared out the window, watching tendrils of mist wind through the trees dotting the lake shore. Above us, the sky was clear and cloudless and I had the sudden impression that the clouds had simply fallen to the ground.

"Do you want to talk about it?"

"No."

"Must be bad then."

I sighed. I usually did like to talk things through, but I didn't see how talking would help now. I'd known Juliana had been doing most of the work with the twins, but today it had hit me: my youngest brother and sister were being raised by a seventeen-year-old. If my mom couldn't do it, if she couldn't be a parent, shouldn't I be the one to step in? But if I did that, it couldn't stop with Michael and Maya. I had five other brothers and sisters between the ages of five and seventeen who were parenting themselves right now. The situation wasn't fair to any of them.

So what was the answer? Take them away? Should I be the one to raise them? I had a baby myself now, but I sure didn't feel old enough to parent teens. I was only twenty-three.

Besides, it wasn't fair to me either. I wanted more kids. Evan had been hinting about trying again for the past three months, and I thought I might finally be ready. How could I have another baby and raise my seven siblings, not to mention Ana?

And how bad was it, really? Bad enough to even be thinking along these lines? Taking the kids away from home would be traumatic all by itself; it just wasn't something to do – or even consider – lightly.

What I really wanted was my mom back. Wasn't it bad enough that I had lost my dad?

The sheriff surprised me by driving past the resorts and the cabins without stopping. Leaning forward in my seat, I began to pay closer attention to where we were headed. Eagle Rock itself was pretty small, but the sheriff's department protected the whole county, including broad swaths of forests and farmland.

I tried to remember if I'd ever been out this far past the resorts, even when I'd been a deputy, but I didn't think I had. The resorts gave way rather abruptly to forest, right around the time Lakeshore Drive went from a four-lane road to a two-lane road. After another half mile or so, the road veered away from the lake, and ramshackle homes began to dot the landscape, making me wonder if Lakeshore Drive had changed names. These homes were set further north, well away from the water.

The sheriff slowed and put on his turn signal. Evan slowed too, and I noted the fog stopped abruptly at the edge of a dirt driveway just up ahead. The sheriff's SUV turned onto that driveway and Evan followed without comment, giving me a chance to take in the scenery.

A ramshackle, ranch-style home was set so far from the road that it looked no bigger than a shoebox. The yard was huge, though, assuming the surrounding acres went with the house. And someone had done a good job of keeping those many acres looking neat and tidy. There was nothing fancy here, no flower beds or gardens or hedges, but the lawn was neatly mowed. Back through a few sparse trees, I spotted an old shed and a well-loved riding lawn mower.

As the house loomed larger, I spotted a patrol car parked in the grass near the drive. Something glinted off the windshield, and I realized with a jolt of surprise that it was iced over. I spotted Frank Gibbons standing guard just outside the front door to the little ranch house. He rubbed gloved hands together and blew on them just as I became aware of a chill in the air. I didn't see his partner.

"Is the heater on?" I answered my own question with a quick glance at the temperature controls. It was on, albeit low.

The sheriff parked his car and Evan pulled in next to it. Grabbing my coat from the backseat, I slid out of the car... and instantly wished I'd put the coat on before leaving.

"It's freezing!" I quickly bundled up, ducking back inside for the hat and gloves Evan passed my way.

"Where's Jim?" The sheriff had emerged from his SUV, also bundled up, and was approaching the front door, his hands buried deeply in his coat pockets for warmth.

"We're taking turns to get out of the arctic circle." Frank lifted a hand and pointed to the east. "He went that way this time, keeping his eye out for anything suspicious. The freeze loses intensity about a hundred yards out, and disappears completely after another hundred or so."

"All right." The sheriff nodded toward the door. "Things still frozen in there?"

"Yes sir. Hard to say if it's easing off." Frank waved at me and smiled. "Hi, Cassie. Nice to see you on this one." His smile faded as he nodded at my husband. "Evan."

"Frank," Evan replied tonelessly. My husband had cultivated a bit of a bad boy reputation in his youth. Some would say more than a bit. He made most of the locals nervous; the rest were terrified.

I shoved my gloved hands into my pockets for added warmth and started for the house, ready to take a look at whatever had the sheriff so on edge. He was already ahead of me, going up the steps to the front porch where he stopped beside Frank and waited for us to join them.

The cold grew more intense with every step I took toward the house. My ears grew cold, despite the hat I had pulled down low around them, and I lifted my gloved hands to cup them.

"The temperature is measuring zero degrees out here," Frank said. "That's ten degrees higher than it was when you left, but it's not getting warmer as fast as you thought it would."

The sheriff seemed to relax slightly at those words. "How about inside?"

"You think I've gone back in there? I'm not crazy!"

The sheriff only grunted his response.

"Hang on." Evan's voice came from behind me, sharp and commanding. I turned to see a look of intense concentration on his face. "There's magic in the air... but it's odd."

"Dangerous?" I asked.

He hesitated. "Odd. But... I think I can dispel the cold."

"No," Sheriff Adams cut in. "Not until Cassie has seen what's inside."

"I'll be fine," I told Evan. Clearly, someone had already gone in the house and come out alive. I could handle the cold.

"I can't cast a warming spell," Evan said, but I didn't let myself worry about that. Heat magic wasn't his forte.

"Maybe we should have brought Nicolas instead," I said.

Evan grunted. He and my brother, Nicolas, only got along grudgingly, for my sake.

"When you go inside," the sheriff was saying, making me shift my attention back to him, "you'll get hit with a cold so fierce you think you'll freeze to death. Might not be as bad as it was thirty minutes ago, but it's bad. Get in, take a look around, and get out. Don't risk lingering too long. Okay?"

"Okay." I hesitated. Evan had joined me, sliding a gloved hand into mine and tucking me close to his side, providing much-needed warmth and that familiar sensation of being cherished. I squeezed his hand, and he squeezed back, telling me without words that he would let no harm come to me.

I stepped past the sheriff and, with my free hand, twisted the doorknob. It was a good thing I was wearing gloves, because if I hadn't the chilled metal probably would have frozen my fingers off. I twisted and pushed, shoving the door inward, and stepped into hell frozen over.

Chapter 3

THE COMBINATION LIVING ROOM AND KITCHEN WERE HIDDEN BENEATH thick layers of ice from ceiling to floor. Frost coated every surface, and ice crystals seemed suspended in midair. Cold tore at me through layers of clothing as I stepped inside, plunging me into temperatures beyond anything I had ever experienced in my life. Someone from Alaska might have known this sort of cold, but here in Missouri we had no point of reference for it. My "heavy winter gear" was totally inadequate, and I instantly understood why the sheriff had warned me to get in and out quickly. If I stayed here, I would become part of the frozen landscape.

Much like the couple frozen to the couch, arms locked around one another in a fierce embrace, faces etched with terror.

Drawing in a lungful of frigid air, I crossed the modest living room to get a closer look at the couple. Fairly young. About my age. In fact, the woman looked familiar.

"Nadine," I whispered as the name popped into my head. She'd been a couple years ahead of me in school and I hadn't known her well, but we'd been on the cheerleading team together.

She didn't look dead. Part of me itched to take my glove off and search for a pulse. Her face was so animated, so full of life. Maybe she was just being held in some sort of cryogenic suspension. It was a desperate hope, but I'd seen some bizarre things happen with magic. Impossible wasn't a word I liked to throw around too much.

"Has this scene been processed at all?" I asked through the still-open front door.

"No," Frank replied. "Can't stay in there long enough. You might want to back out."

I flexed my fingers, which were starting to turn numb. I didn't want to leave yet. I hadn't ID'd the man, and I hadn't gotten a good look around.

I took that look around now, before Evan forced me out – as I knew he would in about sixty seconds. I wasn't sure if this was Nadine's house or the unknown man's or both, but it was very well loved.

There were things everywhere, buried in the ice – knickknacks and crafts and pictures on the wall, some clearly homemade – but it was all neatly organized and immaculately cared for. In another person's hands, this space would have been cluttered, but these two had made the place look cozy and welcoming. The kitchen, separated from the living room by nothing more than a counter, was neat and tidy, not a dish or cup in sight. Across from the frozen couple, a small flatscreen TV hung from the wall, a crack marring the once-smooth surface.

"Let's go," Evan said.

I didn't argue. Backing out, I joined the sheriff and his deputy on the porch and closed the door behind me.

"So," the sheriff said, "who can work ice magic like that?"

"Nobody," I replied.

He looked at me skeptically, but after a quick glance at Evan to confirm what I already felt certain about, I repeated, "Nobody. I've never heard of a gift like this."

"A gift." The sheriff rubbed his gloved hands together. "But there's more to magic than gifts. Haven't you always said so?"

There *was* more to magic than gifts. In fact, there was some debate as to whether or not a gift counted as magic, since it was instinctive and automatic, tied to a person's soul in a way nobody understood. Someone with a gift, like Evan's gift of telekinesis, could use it all day without growing tired, as effortlessly as breathing.

I had a gift too, though I'd only discovered it around the time Ana was conceived and I still couldn't use it very well. My gift was called dreaming – I saw possible futures in my dreams. Trouble was, I didn't often remember my dreams. Which was a lot more than I'd been able to say two years ago, when I could *never* remember my dreams.

Magical talent, on the other hand, was tied to the blood and it drew on energy from nature, beginning with the self. Pockets of energy, such as the node beneath Table Rock Lake, magnified magical ability, which was why so many sorcerers lived near the lake. But using magic, with or without a node, could sap a person's strength and if taken too far, could burn them out.

It had happened to Matthew Blair recently. He still hoped to regain some small use of his magic, but so far if he had, he wasn't saying.

Magical energy could be shaped into almost anything, though, given the right circumstances and will. It could technically be shaped into intense cold. But the sheer power it would take to create this sort of lingering effect... it was hard to fathom.

And I stood by what I'd said. Nobody in town, so far as I knew, specialized in cold.

"What about your own family?" Sheriff Adams asked.

"What about them?"

"Your brother's a fire starter. Your dad was. Isn't cold basically heat in reverse?"

I hesitated. I supposed you could look at it that way, but I had never known my brother or my father, before he died, to use cold magic. Only heat.

"Can we walk away from the house a bit to talk?" I asked. My teeth were chattering; when I got home, I was going to light a fire and roast my hands over it.

The sheriff, Frank, Evan, and I all walked along the dirt path back toward the road. The cold eased up noticeably a few yards past the cars, which wasn't quite as far out as Frank had indicated earlier.

"It's warming up." Frank turned to look around. "I wonder where Jim is; he hasn't checked in recently."

I glanced to the east where Frank was looking, but didn't see anyone. I was about to suggest the walkie when Frank pulled his out, stepped a few yards away, and tried to raise Jim.

I turned to the sheriff. "Okay, spill. What do you know? Who called this in?"

The sheriff cleared his throat. "We got a 911 call from some missionary group that was traveling door to door. Frank and Jim took the call, then called me.

"They hadn't gone in by the time I arrived. It was too cold and it's a nice day; they only had light jackets. When we got here, the place was sub-zero. My car registered an external temperature of fifty below. Inside that house... I can't even imagine. It was an hour, at least, before we went inside. I let Frank go to pick up some winter gear. By the time he got back, it was closer to twenty below out here, and we risked a quick look inside the house. Saw what you saw, but couldn't stay. Not for longer than thirty seconds. My fingers were already blue. That's when I went to consult you."

"So the temperature is going up by, what, twenty to thirty degrees an hour?" I asked.

"Sounds about right. I figure in an hour, those two will thaw out."

I shook my head, trying to think. But I had a sudden, sharp idea what it felt like to be the sheriff. I was totally in over my head here. He'd come to me for answers, but I had none to give. I knew of no practitioner who could cause cold like that.

"Your family—" Sheriff Adams persisted.

"No, they don't do this kind of magic." I shook my head. "I'm not sure they could; Nicolas's gift is instinctive and always, always hot."

"All it takes is one person to see it differently," the sheriff said.

I shrugged. I thought he was on the wrong track, but maybe it was better to humor the possibility for now.

"You have an ID on one of the vics?" the sheriff asked.

"Nadine… can't remember her last name off the top of my head. Who owns the house?"

"Jared Wilks, who we're assuming is the male vic but we won't know for sure until we can get in there for longer than a minute."

The name didn't ring a bell, but I didn't know the name of every last person in town, especially the more mundane residents. As far as I knew, Nadine had no connection to magic. Then again, lots of seemingly normal people in the area could trace their family trees to a sorcerer if they looked far enough back. You just never knew.

"I still can't reach Jim." Frank returned to our huddle, though his eyes remained on the horizon, apparently looking for Jim. The sun had nearly set and it would be dark in the trees. "Should I go looking, do you think?"

As if the question had conjured his partner, the man stumbled out of the trees ahead. Literally, stumbled. Something was definitely wrong.

Both Frank and Sheriff Adams rushed toward Jim. I started to go after them, but a familiar tug of magic held me back. I struggled against the gentle but unbreakable force for a moment before glaring over my shoulder at Evan, who stood firm and unapologetic for his heavy-handed tactics.

"Let me go! Damn it, Evan, we talked about this."

Evan didn't answer. He was too busy rushing past me, yelling for Frank and the sheriff to stop.

That's when I saw it – the thing that had scared Evan. It was... a dog, maybe? But massive. As black as night. And with red, glowing eyes. If it weren't for the eyes, I might have mistaken it for a werewolf. Well, that, and the fact that the moon hadn't risen. Wolves didn't turn when the sun went down, only when the moon rose. It wasn't even the full moon; I would never have left Ana with Scott if it were.

The monstrous thing lunged for Jim, a thirty-something man in very good shape who couldn't seem to outrun it. It tore at the backs of his legs, drawing blood and sending Jim sprawling to the ground on hands and knees.

I couldn't move, and not because Evan's power still held me. That thing was about two seconds from eating Jim, a man I happened to like and who I knew had a wife and two kids at home.

A strangled yell emerged from Jim's throat. Guns blazed – I hadn't even noticed Frank and Sheriff Adams drawing their weapons. The beast growled, momentarily losing interest in Jim as it fixed those demon eyes on the two men trying to fill it with lead.

Then, suddenly, it was in the air, flying backwards through the trees and out of sight.

The guns went quiet but the sheriff and his deputy continued to run toward their fallen comrade. Evan stood stock still, staring into the woods, arms raised and waiting. Listening.

Suddenly, the sound of a canine howling filled the air.

"Move!" Evan shouted. "It's coming back!"

I itched to go to them, but I knew that if I did, it would only focus Evan's attention on me instead of where it needed to be – on helping

Jim. So instead, I dashed for the car – Evan's car – threw myself inside and started the engine.

Meanwhile, Evan was lifting Jim with his power, trying to be both fast and careful, which wasn't easy for him. I could see the strain on his face as Jim's body hovered in midair for a moment, then flew far too quickly in my general direction. He was going to crash into the car!

I had a moment in which to think to jump out and open the back door before Jim was hurled rather unceremoniously in through the gap, head and arms smacking the door with such force that it shook the car. Evan ran after him; Frank and the sheriff ran for their own vehicles.

The black dog thing emerged from the trees, its low growl piercing my skull like a thousand sharp knives. It sat there for a moment while fear, icier than the bitter cold, threatened to overwhelm me.

Move! I told myself.

"Get in the car!" Evan shouted.

He didn't need to tell me once. I was already sliding behind the steering wheel, leaving the back door open for Evan to duck inside. Behind me, I heard Jim screaming in pain, his cries competing with those of the black dog, but there was nothing I could do for him except get him the hell out of there.

The second Evan was in the car, my foot hit the gas and we were tearing down the dirt drive. Glancing in my rearview mirror, I saw both Sheriff Adams and Frank get to their cars, the latter a mere body length ahead of the dog-thing. It slammed into his car as the driver's door shut, with enough force to rock the vehicle.

"Come on, Frank," I whispered, trying to keep one eye on the road ahead of me, one on the rearview mirror to check on his progress. I heard more than saw his engine roar to life, then dust flew as he peeled out.

By that time, I was already hanging a right onto Lakeshore Drive – or whatever it was called this far east – accelerating to seventy miles per hour before my heart stilled enough for me to back off the accelerator.

Jim had stopped screaming. He wasn't making any sounds at all. That couldn't be a good thing.

"Hospital?" I tried to look at Jim in the rearview mirror to check his condition, but the angle was wrong. Actually, all the mirrors were positioned for Evan's much taller height.

"He won't make it if we take him there. Home."

I shuddered, but said nothing. Evan had already begun muttering incantations designed to keep Jim's body in stasis until he could get to the seat of his power, his familiar spell circle tied directly to the node, his potions, and his books.

Evan didn't go around doling out magic to save people. For one thing, he couldn't save everyone. For another, sorcerers tend to be very secretive. Almost to a fault. And to top all that off, if Evan saved Jim's life, then Jim would owe Evan a huge debt.

I'd once owed Evan a debt like that. I had been literally unable to deny him anything he asked of me directly. He had to be careful when he spoke to me, because if he phrased something as an order, I had to obey it. It had also been difficult to deny him anything I knew he wanted, whether or not he asked for it.

In other words, if Jim lived, it would be at a high price. Of course, he had kids. He had to pay it, if he could. He had no choice.

Two SUVs followed me all the way back home, but thankfully I saw no sign of a black monster from hell. My head was still pounding, I realized after I'd pulled into our driveway and parked the car. I drew in several deep, shaking breaths, smelling the metallic tang of blood in the air as I did so.

I looked behind me. Jim's face was deathly pale, and there was blood everywhere. The dog had apparently torn an artery in the back of his leg. Evan had stopped the bleeding with his stasis spell, but it was no wonder he'd said Jim would die if he went to a hospital. There wouldn't have been time.

"I'll take care of Jim," Evan said. "Keep those two out of my way."

I nodded and started to unbuckle my seat belt before realizing I hadn't fastened it. Wow, I really must have been terrified.

Getting out of the car, I met Frank and the sheriff. The former looked frightened, the latter furious. I held my hand up to both, trying to indicate to them that they needed to stop.

Frank stopped. Sheriff Adams came right at me, putting himself in my face.

"Why didn't you take him to the hospital?" the sheriff demanded. "I know how debt works. Is Evan collecting them now?"

I placed a hand on his chest, attempting to still him and push him back. "Jim's almost dead. Evan's the only chance he's got."

"I want to see for myself."

It hurt that the sheriff didn't trust me, but I stood my ground. "When Evan gets him safely in the house, you can take a look at how much blood is in the backseat."

The sheriff wasn't looking at me anymore. His gaze had gone over my shoulder. I glanced back to see Evan backing out, the still form of Jim hovering just ahead of him. Jim looked dead. And there didn't seem to be an inch of his tan deputy's uniform that wasn't covered in blood.

"Oh my God." The sheriff's face went suddenly ashen.

"Let Evan work." I repeated.

The sheriff had already backed down. Taking two full steps away from me, he went to confer with Frank, the two men whispering so I couldn't overhear them.

Meanwhile, Evan had gotten Jim out of the car and was levitating him slowly up the front steps. Not being in mortal danger this time, he was able to take more care. The front door opened as Evan and Jim approached, then the two disappeared inside, the door closing behind them.

"Will he live?" Frank asked.

"I don't know. But if anyone can heal him, Evan can."

"What the hell was that thing?" Sheriff Adams asked.

"That," I said, "is a very good question."

Chapter 4

J IM HAD BEEN MY PARTNER ONCE, YEARS AGO, DURING MY BRIEF AND INFA-
mous time working directly for the sheriff's department. He lasted
longer than any of my other partners and for once, I had run out on
him rather than the other way around. He wasn't the sort of man to
scare easily and tended to be pretty laid back, which wasn't the same
as saying he didn't care about things. He took his duty to protect and
serve seriously.

I invited Sheriff Adams and Frank inside to wait for news. The
sheriff immediately slipped into the dining room for privacy as he
performed the unhappy task of calling Jim's wife. I didn't envy him
that call.

Frank, meanwhile, settled into the den, where Madison and her
mate, Scott, were watching TV. Scott grabbed the remote as soon as
he spotted us, turned the TV off, and looked up expectantly. "What's
with the heavy coats?"

I'd forgotten I was still wearing one. Silently, I slid the coat off my
shoulders and let it fall to the floor, along with my gloves and hat.

"Is Ana okay?" I asked, needing an update on my child before anything else. There was no reason to suspect a problem, but there was
something about terror and the adrenaline crash afterward that made
me want to check in on my loved ones.

"She's still upstairs." Madison cast a quick glance at the baby monitor at her elbow before looking back at me. "She's been talking to herself for about twenty minutes, and you said to let her if she's happy.
We were just thinking about interrupting her for dinner."

"I'll get her." I turned and dashed up the stairs without another
word, heading for the room next to the master bedroom. There were
eight bedrooms in our three-story house, which Evan had designed
himself, and he said he could add more if necessary. He claimed to
share my desire to fill it with children, but I wondered if he knew
what he was in for. Growing up as an only child, he couldn't imagine
the chaos. In some ways, I knew, he was trying to make up for the

loneliness of his own upbringing, but that upbringing had shaped him as much as mine had shaped me.

Ana's eyes were open when I looked in on her, bright and full of intelligence. She was, as Madison had said, happily chatting in baby babble. I'd listened to her do just that for a whole hour once, although she usually got fussy after fifteen minutes. Today, she had her feet in her fists and when I walked in, she giggled.

"Hello, happy girl." I picked her up and spun in a circle, eliciting a squeal of delight. "I don't know what I did to deserve such a happy baby, but I'm a lucky mommy."

"Ma!" Ana grabbed my breast, making me wonder, yet again, if she thought *mommy* meant me or my boobs. "Ma."

I could take a hint. Retreating to the rocking chair by the large picture window, which was currently blocked by thick purple drapes, I gave Ana what she and I both needed – a connection.

I've often heard women say that nursing is a bonding experience, and it is. For me, especially, the connection between us was a living thing. I'd felt magic stir in my blood for the first time when I was pregnant, and I continued to feel that magic connect us every time she nursed. It didn't work if I pumped and someone else fed her from a bottle, it only worked when we were skin to skin. Sometimes, I felt a ghost of that connection when we weren't nursing, just touching and cuddling.

It was fading. The magic had filled my blood during pregnancy, giving me the power, I was sure, to rival any sorcerer in town. Except perhaps Evan, who, after all, had about twice as much magic as he should. He had mine, siphoned away before we were born as a result of a nasty feud and a nastier spell.

He'd offered to give it back, but I'd turned him down. A lot of people don't understand why I made that choice, but I stand by it. I love him.

Which wasn't the same as saying it was easy to let go. It had actually been easier when I'd first turned him down. He'd given me a gift that day, one more precious than the magic he offered. He'd given me his love in an irrefutable way. I could only do the same. But at that time, I had never felt the magic. I didn't really know what I was missing.

Now, I did feel the magic. It stirred in my blood; a warmth, a tingle, a reassuring presence. A drug I was slowly weaning off, one that would become addictive if I ever truly used it.

The magic called to me. Every day, though I never said it out loud, I heard it whisper in my mind. *I'm here. Embrace me. Feel the power. Before it's too late.*

I shook my head, denying the voice. Mom had caved. Mom had embraced the power and it had driven her crazy in the end. She'd had babies until she couldn't anymore, until her husband had died. I sometimes wondered if she'd be pregnant again had he lived. She was only twenty years older than me, after all, and could theoretically keep going. Feeding the craving for magic she could get only one way.

Ana pushed away from me and I switched her to the other breast, trying to shift my thoughts away from the dark path they'd traveled. The room was dark; I hadn't turned on the light and the only source of illumination was a nightlight by her crib. I wished I had thought to open the drapes before sitting down, at least. Then I could look out into the twilit sky.

You can do that from here, the magic whispered. *You know the spell. You know the theory. You watched your dad teach it to Nicolas and Juliana and Isaac. It just takes a whisper of the power you're wasting, siphoning off during meditation to serve no purpose at all. Just a whisper. A flicker. Look at the curtain. Look at it, and make it move.*

The corner of the heavy drape twitched before I tore my eyes away, shifting my body as I did. This apparently annoyed Ana, who slapped her free hand onto my other nipple and squeezed.

"Ouch! We talked about that." Gently, I pried her hand away.

Ana popped up, apparently deciding she was done, and I had a moment of regret at the abrupt end to our connection. There was still magic within me, but these days it was never so powerful as when Ana was actively nursing, which she only did about four times a day. How often would it be in a year?

When would I be ready to quit entirely?

Evan would usually poke his head in around this time, watching us together as if he, too, could feel the connection. Maybe he could.

Tonight, of course, he had a critical task to complete. He was probably upstairs, in his lab, where he had a permanent casting circle etched into the floor and all the materials he needed at his fingertips.

I knew the underlying principles of most healing spells too. I could help, take some of the burden away from him.

Shaking my head, I got my clothes back in place and headed downstairs with Ana on my hip. The magic was seductive, but it lied. Evan didn't need me, and if he needed help, he had his powerful cousin right downstairs.

Speaking of Scott Lee...

A pair of raised, angry voices carried all the way to the top of the stairs. Tucking Ana more securely against my hip and letting my free hand slide along the curved wooden banister, I rushed downstairs, wondering what could have happened.

The door to the den stood wide open and inside, the sheriff and Scott stood practically nose to nose, staring each other down. Madison sat, wide-eyed, on the leather sofa. She hadn't moved since I'd come in. Frank remained on his feet, but had edged away from the squabbling pair to stand near the wet bar.

"Just because it looks like a dog doesn't make it a werewolf!" Scott's fists were balled into fists and his posture was rigid. In his face, I saw something of the monster that lived inside him, coming out at the full moon each month. Something of the wolf. He got that look when he was angry.

If he had looked at me like that, I'd have backed off. Sheriff Adams wasn't even flinching.

"It had glowing eyes. I'm not stupid. No normal animal has eyes that color." The sheriff jabbed his finger at Scott's chest. "I heard rumors of a place running experiments on werewolves and I know her brother" – he jabbed his finger at Madison – "is half wolf all the time. You can't tell me they weren't working on a way to let you shift outside the full moon."

Madison winced. She was very sensitive about what had happened to her brother. Scott, perhaps sensing his mate in pain, growled, the sound low and menacing.

Ana began to scream.

"Stop!" I told the two men. "Please, stop. We need to talk about this rationally, and this posturing isn't helping. You're just upsetting Ana."

Both men glanced at me and Ana, then looked away. They did, at least, have the sense to look chagrined.

"You," I said to Scott, "sit over there by Madison. And you," I said to the sheriff, "go sit over there." I pointed at a recliner on the other side of the room.

There was a moment in which I wasn't sure if they would listen. Ana's increasingly high-pitched shrieks filled the ensuing silence, forcing me to back down from my own rigid stance to do the baby dance. I thought it would undermine my credibility, but strangely, it didn't. At the time, I had no idea why. I've since come to understand that the angry mama glare has a lot of power.

"Sheriff, what's eating you?" I asked when he'd settled himself in the offered seat.

"What do you mean?"

"You've been acting off since you came here asking for help. And it's more than this one case, however horrible it is. There was no reason, none at all, to think there was so much danger that Evan needed to come with me. The cold was bizarre and the deaths ..." I trailed off, images of Nadine and Jared flashing before my mind's eye. I saw again the fear in their faces, and the way they'd clung to one another in their panic. They must have been in love.

Rallying, I continued, "If you think I'm too stupid to come in out of the freezing cold, then you don't need my help on this case at all."

"It's a damn good thing Evan came." Sheriff Adams heaved a sigh and took off his broad-brimmed hat, running his fingers through his thinning hair.

"It *was* a good thing he came. It might even save Jim's life." I did a bit more baby bouncing; Ana's cries were decreasing in volume, but

I had the sense that she was gearing up for another assault. "But why did you think he needed to be there?"

"It's not the first werewolf I've seen outside the full moon," Sheriff Adams said.

"It can't be a werewolf!" Scott growled.

"It wasn't a werewolf." I shot Scott a look I hoped conveyed the idea that I could handle this. Then I turned back to the sheriff. "It had red eyes, not yellow eyes. Werewolves have yellow eyes. They also look much less like dogs or wolves, despite the name."

Scott growled. Ana shrieked.

"Scott, calm down," Madison rubbed her hand along his rigid forearm.

"You'd think the sheriff might believe a werewolf about what a werewolf's like," Scott snarled. "Cassie's never even seen one!"

"Never want to," I added, shooting a rueful look at Madison. She had seen Scott transform twice, and both experiences had been hellish. She still had nightmares.

"That thing bit Jim," Sheriff Adams said. "I need to know if my deputy is going to turn into a monster."

I hadn't thought about that. Just because this thing wasn't a werewolf, didn't mean it couldn't reproduce the same way. Werewolves made new werewolves by biting. Vampires made new vampires by biting. There was plenty of precedent in the magical world for concern.

Unfortunately, I was having trouble thinking with Ana shrieking in my ear. I bounced, I shushed, I swung and swayed and tried to remember the other S's.

"Let me take her." Madison got to her feet and crossed the room, putting her arms out for Ana. I hesitated. I didn't want to let her go. On the other hand, I couldn't think.

Sighing, I let Ana slide from me to Madison's outstretched arms. She screamed harder, tears falling down her face as she shot me a look of utter betrayal.

"I'll get her some dinner." With that, Madison swept Ana from the room, closing the door behind her. Ana's screams gradually faded with distance, until, finally, I couldn't hear them at all.

It didn't help. I knew she was crying and still felt guilty.

"You said you've seen these things before?" I asked the sheriff.

"Twice. First time was a couple months ago when little Craig Jenner went missing."

I remembered that. I'd been about to suggest that Evan do a scrying spell for the missing six-year-old when the search teams said they'd found him in the woods. He'd gotten lost and spent two nights there, beating the odds against coming out alive.

"I was the one who found the boy," Sheriff Adams continued. "Found him just after sunset, like tonight, sleeping at the base of an old oak tree. When I approached him, I heard this growling noise and I turned to see a dog like the one we saw tonight, with glowing red eyes. I thought he was going to attack, but then Craig woke up, spotted me, and flung his arms around me. When I looked back, the dog was gone."

I frowned. "Some kind of guardian spirit? But who summoned it? Craig Jenner doesn't come from a family of strong practitioners."

"The other one I saw was prowling outside your mom's house when I stopped by to check on her last week." My head snapped up. "Mom's house? What?"

"I spotted it when I pulled up the driveway. It was prowling the edge of the house and when it saw me, it stopped and growled. Again, I thought it would attack. When I got out of the car, it growled louder. I ended up getting right back in and speeding off."

"But it didn't attack." I looked at Scott, not because I thought the thing was a werewolf, but because a werewolf might understand the mind of a predator. But Scott, too, looked confused.

"I feel something in the air." The sheriff stared at me. "Can't you feel it? The mist over the lake that never seems to dissipate. Everyone's a little more on edge, a little more depressed, or a little angrier. It's subtle; I didn't notice it all at once, but tonight when I saw those two young people frozen in ice, I knew something else was going to happen. I could feel it."

"Intuition," Scott said. He wasn't growling anymore, but looked pensive. "Evan's often wondered if you have it."

"All good cops develop instincts," Sheriff Adams said dismissively.

"If you say so. I've felt the pull of intuition. I know what it's like. That bone-deep certainty you can't explain. And maybe later you can logic it out, put the pieces together, but maybe you never do. And in that moment all you have is a choice: Listen to your gut or suffer the consequences."

"What does your intuition tell you now, Sheriff?" I asked. "Is Scott telling the truth? Is it a werewolf?"

He looked away. "Probably not. But for all the weird stuff that happens around here, there have never been many magical creatures. Made me think that kind of stuff was made up."

"It usually is," I said, but I caught Scott's eyes and stopped, wondering if I'd made the classic mistake of assuming I knew more than I really did.

Chapter 5

THE SOUND OF THE DOORBELL RINGING KEPT ME FROM FORMULATING other questions. Glancing at the three men standing around the room, half-angry, half-scared, and half-confused (yes, I know that's three halves), I decided a warning was in order. "Behave yourselves. I'll be right back."

Slipping out of the room, I left the door ajar so I could hear the men if they started at each other again. The house was quiet; Madison must have settled Ana. I stopped just outside the front door and checked the video feed, not wanting to be surprised this time. Then again, I had no idea who might be there.

A middle-aged, middle-height woman stood on the front porch, staring around nervously as she wrung her hands over and over again. When her gaze slid by the camera, I got a good look at her face and recognized her. Sarah. Jim's wife. Of course she'd come.

I opened the door. She looked up, staring at me with red, swollen eyes. Her makeup was smeared and her hair was mussed.

"Sarah, come in." I opened my arms in a sign of welcome and she flung herself into them, seeking comfort. "It's okay," I whispered as I patted her on the back. "Jim's going to be okay."

"That's not what David said." Sarah backed off, putting a foot or two of space between us. "He said Jim might die."

David was Sheriff David Adams, but I never called him that. I couldn't make myself think of him by his first name, probably because I'd started at the sheriff's department when I was so young. Sarah was much closer to his age than to mine.

"Evan can save him." I injected all the confidence I felt into my voice. Yes, Jim's injuries were serious. He wouldn't have survived a trip to the hospital. But Evan had saved me from worse. A vampire had once ripped out all of my intestines and Evan had painstakingly put them back. Or possibly regrown some. I didn't like to linger over the details. The point was, he'd done it.

Sarah buried her face in her hands and let out a strangled sob.

"Why? Why is he willing to save my Jim? Your kind doesn't usually…
that is to say, I've never… why?"

"Rumors of my husband's dark nature are highly exaggerated." I
gestured for her to step over the threshold, which she seemed afraid
to do. "Come in. Seriously. You can wait in the den with Frank and
the sheriff."

Tentatively, she stepped over the threshold and allowed me to
close the door behind her. I led her to the den, where she immediately went to Frank's side and exchanged a tight hug with the younger
man. Only when she disentangled from him did she pause to take in
the other occupants of the room. She smiled at the sheriff, but her
face froze when she spotted Scott.

Pretty much everyone in town knew he was a werewolf. Even
the mundane population, or at least the ones who believed in magic,
knew the rumors.

"You said a werewolf attacked Jim." Sarah's words were for the
sheriff, but her eyes never left Scott.

"That was a misunderstanding." I put my body between Sarah and
Scott, not wanting to stir that up again. "We're still trying to figure
out what it was, but it was definitely not a werewolf."

"So he won't – he won't turn into a monster if he lives?" Sarah
asked.

I hesitated. How could I say anything at all about the potential
consequences of this attack when I had no idea what had attacked
him?

"What aren't you telling me?" Sarah asked, misinterpreting my
hesitation.

"Nothing. Look, why don't you three stay in here? Scott, come
help me in the kitchen. We can put together some leftovers from the
party for people to munch on."

"When can I see Jim?" Sarah asked. "How long will… how long
will it take?"

I glanced at my watch. Evan had already been working for about
forty-five minutes. Since he didn't have to replace intestines, it
shouldn't take too much longer. The blood replenishment potion

took twenty-four hours to brew, but I'd mixed up a batch last month so we'd have it on hand if we needed it. Evan would just have to stir in some magic. He'd probably finish any minute now, although Jim would need a good night's sleep followed by a ton of food and water. With good rest and proper nutrition, he'd reach full health in twenty-four to forty-eight hours.

"I expect we'll have news soon," was all I said. "I'll be back in a few minutes with some food."

Sarah didn't ask further questions as we slid out of the den and across the darkened first floor to the kitchen – the only other room with lights on. Madison had Ana in a highchair, happily playing with banana and avocado. Some of it even went into her mouth.

"Who's here?" Madison moved to her mate's side and gave him a quick hug, as if it had been hours rather than minutes since she'd last seen him.

"Jim's wife," I said.

"Is everything okay?" Madison asked.

"Fine. We're just here for food."

Scott nodded. "I talked the sheriff down. It wasn't a werewolf."

"Are you sure?" Madison asked. "I didn't want to say anything in front of the sheriff, but he did have a point. They were running some nasty experiments. Look at what happened to Clinton."

Clinton was Madison's younger brother. Half brother, actually, on her mom's side. She had another half brother, though she'd only discovered his identity two years ago: Evan.

Clinton had been bitten by a werewolf last May, kicking off a series of events that had resulted in his being kidnapped, experimented on, and ultimately turned into something that wasn't quite a werewolf. And wasn't quite human. He had fur on much of his body at all times, plus the yellow eyes. At the full moon, he retained his human hands and his human intelligence. The other wolves in his pack didn't trust him, which made the full moons dangerous for him.

Worst of all, he had lost the ability to speak. He was completely dependent upon sign language and notepads for communication these days.

If that could happen to Clinton, then what else could happen?

Scott put his arm around Madison's shoulders and rubbed his hand on her upper arm. She leaned into him and I looked away, giving them a moment of privacy while I raided the refrigerator. We still had sandwich trays left over from the party, plus more fruit, vegetables, chips, and dip. We even had more cake, although the castle looked far less impressive with big chunks missing from its once strong fortifications.

"Tell me it's not all starting again," Madison said. "Things were just settling down. We're about to get married, and we have a baby coming in a few months."

"We'll be fine. I don't think this thing is a werewolf."

I pulled out a head of cauliflower and began chopping it, placing the pieces on a large vegetable tray around a bowl of ranch dipping sauce.

"You have a thought about what it is, though, don't you?" I said to Scott as I continued to work.

He blew out a breath. "There were other things at that lab besides werewolves. There were a few vampires, but that wasn't it either. Some of the other creatures, I didn't have the experience to describe. There was this guy with black, leathery wings... he helped us escape, but I never found out who or what he was. And there were cages full of animals that weren't quite animals. I've often wondered if these things were experiments, or something else. There are all kinds of stories from the old world about magical creatures, but if they ever really existed, then most were exterminated by sorcerers centuries ago."

"So only werewolves and vampires survived?" I asked dubiously.

"Vampires reproduce insanely quickly, and werewolves can pass as humans most of the time." Scott shrugged. "I'm not a magical historian."

"Who is?"

"I'd try Henry Wolf."

Of course. Henry Wolf, my husband's old mentor, was the oldest man in town. I sometimes thought by a huge margin. He was a bit kooky, living in a small cabin by the lake with no running water or electricity. He seemed to think that modern technology interfered with magic, although I'd never noticed anyone else having that problem.

"Let me help with those trays." Madison was by my side then, chopping vegetables and arranging them on the largest tray. A smaller tray contained grapes, apple slices, and miniature oranges.

When we finished, Scott carried both the fruit and vegetable trays to the den, while Madison took the sandwiches. I cleaned Ana and brought her along a few minutes later.

Evan was coming down the stairs just as I entered the front hall. His hair was wet, suggesting he'd stopped to shower, which was a good thing considering how much blood there had been. If he'd walked into the den covered in Jim's blood, Sarah would have flipped.

He smiled when he saw me, weary but victorious. I returned the smile, fleetingly, and Ana chimed in with a squeal as she tried to jump out of my arms into Evan's.

"Jim's going to make it?" I asked, just to make sure.

"Yeah. He'll be fine. Got any food?"

"In the den, but you're going to have to convince Jim's wife he's alive first."

Evan reached the bottom of the stairs and took an eager Ana from my arms. Then he threw his free arm around me in a quick family hug.

"How quickly can you shoo everyone away?" Evan whispered in my ear. His tone hinted at what, exactly, he wanted to do with me and an empty house, though we also had to get Ana to bed first.

"I'll do my best. Sarah's going to want to see her husband, though."

Evan nodded, then led the way into the den to join the rest of the group. The low hum of noise emanating from the room stopped abruptly at his entry, but Evan pretended not to notice. He went straight to his favorite spot on a reclining love seat, cradling Ana close to his chest, and summoned a bottle of water from the wet bar. It glided sedately across the room to hover by Evan's side for a moment before he closed his hand around it.

Sarah and Frank flinched. Which I knew was the point. Evan was tired, badly in need of food, water, and rest, yet he wanted to prove to the near strangers in the room that he was as powerful as ever.

Sighing, I set to work putting a plate of food together. When I finished, I traded the food for Ana, who protested loudly until I sat next to Evan and settled her in the thin space between us.

"Jim should make a full recovery in a day or two," Evan said.

Sarah, who still had not found a seat, collapsed into a nearby chair. "Are you sure? Can I see him?"

"He's sleeping soundly. Don't wake him."

Sarah nodded. "I won't. I just need to see him."

"Madison," Evan said, "can you take her upstairs to the yellow room?"

Madison looked momentarily surprised at the request, but I saw the dawning comprehension in her eyes. We needed to talk, and Sarah was in the way. Madison didn't really need to be here, but she did know the house well enough to take Sarah to the room we had designed specifically for healing. Yellow has healing properties, and the east-facing room on the third floor also got morning sunlight, which was potent for good health.

When Madison led Sarah away, Frank and Sheriff Adams finally chose to sit, both taking opposite ends of the leather sofa. Scott continued to stand, arms crossed over his chest, looking ready for battle.

"We still need to know what that creature was," Sheriff Adams said. "And how to kill it."

"It's a hell hound," Evan said.

Everyone stared at him.

He shrugged and took a bite of sandwich, chewing slowly and swallowing before continuing. "What else could it be? The glowing red eyes were a pretty big giveaway."

"The sheriff thought it might be a werewolf," Scott said.

Evan rolled his eyes. "I bet you loved that. No, it's a hell hound. I've seen pictures."

"Where?" just about everyone asked at the same time.

"Master Wolf's got some fun books at his place. Old. Hand-copied with hand-drawn pictures. Anyway, they're fierce and very difficult to kill. But they're also supposed to be extinct."

"What else do you know about them?" Sheriff Adams asked.

"That's about all I remember. I can visit Master Wolf tomorrow to find out more. In the meantime, we need to keep people away from that house."

"There are two dead bodies in that house!" Sheriff Adams glared at Evan. "I've got to get back in there and process the scene."

Evan raised one eyebrow, his expression utterly calm. "Okay, but there seems to be a hell hound lurking nearby."

"We should set up a police barricade," Frank said. "Yellow tape across the driveway and issue an emergency alert to the community."

"That sounds like just the sort of thing that would attract curiosity-seekers." I shook my head. "We'd be better off doing nothing at all."

"What happens when Jared's parents or brother drop by for a visit?" Sheriff Adams started shaking his head too. "There's got to be something we can do, even if we can't get in to process the scene."

"A pretty simple ward would keep anyone from entering the property," I said.

Actually, the most basic ward was something like a brick wall, keeping anyone and everyone from entering or leaving a home. It was a sledgehammer, not at all elegant and usually not useful. It was a primer spell, one kids learned as a foundation for other, more useful spells. But in this case, it was all we needed.

I could do it. I could drive over there right now, find my quiet place, focus the magic, and wham! Sledgehammer. It didn't even need practice or refinement.

And after all, Evan was worn out. He didn't look exhausted or drained yet, but there was no reason for him to push it. Not when all I had to do was...

"I'll do it." Scott was pacing back and forth behind the love seat where Evan and I sat. I'd almost forgotten he was there.

"I don't want to incur more debt." The sheriff looked from Scott to Evan to me. "I don't entirely understand how it works, which is why

I rarely ask Evan along for magical consults. But he saved one of my men tonight."

It suddenly struck me why the sheriff had been so angry earlier. I closed my eyes, drew in a breath, then slowly let it out. Of course! He'd been afraid. He'd decided that Jim didn't owe Evan the life debt – that he did. He was, after all, the sheriff. He was responsible for his men. And he'd asked Evan to come in the first place.

He might not be wrong.

I glanced at Evan, who had finished his sandwich and was busy working on his apple slices. Ana had an apple slice in her fist and was gnawing on it, oblivious to the tension in the room.

"It's complicated," Evan said after a long moment of silence. "Ultimately, it's up to you to take the burden of the debt from your deputy. If you feel that obligation, then it's yours. But the debt is not so great as you might suppose. You're a public servant, and helping you helps the community, which comes back to benefit me. In fact, if you make sure to follow your instincts and tell me whenever you think there's a possibility that Cassie is in danger, I'll consider us even."

"I'm not sure that's necess-" I began.

"Done," the sheriff interrupted.

"Done," Evan echoed.

I sighed. The men in my life were always trying to protect me. Some things never changed. At least this lifted the burden of magical debt, which is serious business. So was the sheriff's promise to keep Evan in the loop, or it would never have served as effective repayment.

"What about asking Scott to cast a spell for me?" the sheriff asked.

"It's not for you; it's for my pack. All I need is for some fool to get torn to pieces by a hell hound and end up with an angry mob going after my werewolves."

The sheriff removed his hat, brushed his hand through his hair, then slammed the hat back on. "This is all semantics."

"It's not *all* semantics," I said, glancing sideways at Evan. "It can be very, very real. You're right to be cautious."

"All right, then. I'll drive you out there." The sheriff stood and started for the door. "I don't want too many people along in case things go wrong."

Scott nodded and wordlessly followed Sheriff Adams from the room.

"Um," Frank began.

"Go home," I said.

"Thanks." He was up and out so quickly I thought I saw skid marks. Clearly, all the magic talk had scared him.

"Alone at last." Evan sighed and visibly let himself relax into the leather, kicking up the recliner to Ana's delight. She climbed off the sofa and proceeded to try to lower the footrest – one of her favorite games.

"Madison, Sarah, and Jim are still upstairs," I reminded him.

He groaned. Then he looked longingly at his empty plate.

"I got it." I stood and refilled the plate, returning to hand it wordlessly back to him. I plucked a half-chewed apple slice from the love seat before retaking my place next to him.

"Thanks. Are you going to eat?"

"I snacked all afternoon." *Out of nerves*, I didn't add. Mom's absence from the party triggered all my overeating instincts.

"Hey, this is no big deal, but just for the record," Evan began, and I braced myself. Sentences that began like that didn't end well. "The blood replenishment potion actually works better if you stir in the magic just before use."

I froze. I hadn't – I couldn't have infused magic into a potion by accident, could I?

"I said it's no big deal." Evan brushed his hand over my upper arm. "Some potions work better when the magic has time to settle and really sink into the base liquids, but in this case the base liquids are designed to become the blood and when that sits on a shelf for a few weeks... well, it's not ideal. We should mix up a new batch when we get a chance."

"Sure." I stared at Ana, still busily trying to get Evan's footstool to lower.

"You're allowed to use the magic you're channeling." Evan's hand continued to make patterns on my upper arm, creating a tingling warmth wherever he touched. "It's a survival mechanism, designed to help you protect your children while they're still young. It doesn't make you like your mother."

The sound of Madison's laughter and her footfalls on the stairs kept me from having to answer. Which was a very good thing, because I knew he was wrong. If I wasn't careful, I could end up exactly like my mother.

Chapter 6

EVAN AND I MADE LOVE THAT NIGHT, ONCE THE GUESTS HAD LEFT AND Ana fell asleep. As much as I had needed a connection with my child, I also needed one with my husband. He was tired, and I was on edge, so we came together quickly in an encounter that was no less precious for its simplicity.

He fell asleep immediately while I lay awake, staring at the high, vaulted ceiling of our master bedroom. It didn't matter how often I saw it, death left a mark. And this death... they'd looked so scared. Nadine and Jared had been clutching one another, perhaps knowing death was imminent. And then it was over.

Death is, perhaps, the only real ending to anyone's story.

I drifted into restless sleep and, as usual, caught only bits and pieces of dreams: Dense fog. A feeling of panic. A child's face.

None of it meant anything, though I would dutifully write it all down in my dream journal. Sometimes when I flipped back to see what I wrote last month or last year, I had an impression of what it really meant. Six months ago, I'd written about seeing Madison glowing from within – now she was pregnant. Around the same time, I'd dreamed of blood. Then Matthew uncovered Alexander DuPris's use of blood magic.

The images meant nothing to me before the fact, and probably wouldn't as long as I could only catch glimpses. True dreaming was meant to show me far more than snapshots; I should be able to see vast possibilities and let my sleeping mind fathom complex contingencies.

The worst thing was that I'd gotten a taste of it, back when I'd first discovered my gift. I'd seen enough to warn Kaitlin not to go with Jason – not that she'd listened. I'd seen other things too, mostly with the help of a dream catcher allowing only pleasant images to fill my mind at night. Too bad the future isn't entirely full of pleasant images.

Abigail Hastings, a gifted seer who had only begun to mentor me, died before she could finish imparting her wisdom. She'd died before she even knew for sure that I was a dreamer, though looking back, I think she suspected. Now it seemed everyone – or at least everyone who knew I was a dreamer – had some advice about how to recall my dreams, usually something along the lines of, "Relax, meditate before bed, and use these scents." White Guard meetings were the worst; I knew they wanted me to truly be their seer, but the more they pressed, the worse things got.

I woke the next morning to find Ana tugging up my nightshirt, plopping down sideways on the bed next to me, and helping herself. Evan crawled into bed behind me and the three of us lay like that for a few minutes, until Ana suddenly decided she was done.

"I'd like to come with you to see Mr. Wolf today," I told Evan as we dressed for the day. He usually visited his old master alone, but he didn't usually go with an objective in mind.

"I figured. Mom's coming to babysit."

"Great." I didn't like to say bad things about his mother in front of him, but she gave me the creeps. I had to keep reminding myself that Evan turned out great, so surely I could trust her with my daughter for a few hours.

It was two hours before we arrived at Henry Wolf's house. First Jim had to be woken, fed, and reassured. He was much better, though he had only scattered memories of what had happened to him. His wife arrived during breakfast to fuss over him before she took him home. Then we had to wait for Laura Blackwood, who had apparently overslept. She arrived for babysitting wearing a pencil skirt and silk blouse. I didn't say anything. Sometimes, you just gotta let things go.

Finally, we made it to the two-bedroom cabin near Table Rock Lake, tucked neatly away down a dirt road. It was a sturdy building, but nothing connected it to the outside world. No phone lines. No power lines. No satellite dish. No plumbing. I still had trouble imagining Evan living here for three years, completely cut off from civilization, but he said it had been good for him. That the experience had allowed him to focus on his magic in a way nothing else could have.

Mr. Wolf sat on a rocking chair on the front porch when we arrived, obviously expecting us. He had wards set miles away to alert him to any visitors – wanted or unwanted.

He didn't smile when we walked up the two wooden steps to the porch. He just kept rocking, staring at Evan.

"Do I know you?" he asked.

Evan sighed. "I'm sorry I haven't visited in a while."

"Heh. Don't know if I believe you. A man who's sorry for not visitin' someone don't wait 'til he needs something."

"What makes you think I need something?" Evan asked.

"Mornin', Cassie." Mr. Wolf smiled at me. "Always nice to see you. You could come with Evan for a visit. Bring the baby."

"We invited you to the birthday party yesterday," I said, although I started to feel a little guilty myself. I knew Mr. Wolf didn't like crowds or parties.

"Had to stay. Trainin' up a new youngun."

"You got a new apprentice?" Evan straightened and I tried not to look too interested. Henry Wolf hadn't taken on an apprentice since Evan had left him two and a half years ago.

"Yep. He's out checkin' the wards. Told him we had intruders."

"I said I was sorry." Evan sighed. "I should have made time for you; I know it. The White Guard keeps me busy, especially lately, since Matthew got back from Pennsylvania with proof that Alexander was using blood magic. We've got a flood of new recruits now, and just as many fights. It's crazy."

"It's crazy, but not just cuz of blood magic." Mr. Wolf stopped rocking and leaned forward. "If you'd come to see me, I'd told you so."

"What's going on?" I asked before Evan had the chance. "Does it have something to do with why a hell hound attacked a deputy last night?"

Mr. Wolf didn't look remotely surprised by this news. "I 'spect so. There's more magic in the air than usual. Can't you feel it?"

"I don't know." Evan looked at me. "What do you think?"

"How would I know?" I didn't meet his eyes. We hadn't finished our conversation from the night before and I didn't want to get into it here, in front of Mr. Wolf.

"You been dreamin' lately?" Mr. Wolf turned his wizened eyes to me, letting me feel the force of fathomless decades of power in the form of wisdom. No one knew how old Mr. Wolf was, but I suspected the answer would shock me.

"I-I still don't remember my dreams very often. Sometimes we use the dream catcher, but then I only see good things, which doesn't tell me a lot. I haven't bothered with that in a few months." I paused; I'd gotten too much advice over the last couple of years, but never from Mr. Wolf. Maybe he knew something the others didn't. "Do you know a spell to help me remember my dreams?"

"Yep. It's a little thing I like to call confidence."

Evan chuckled. I glared at him.

"What?" he asked. "I've been telling you the same thing."

He had, and it hadn't helped in the least.

"We could do the mind reading spell again," I offered. We'd done that a few times; Evan would read my mind while I slept then tell me what I dreamed.

Mr. Wolf shook his head. "You gotta be able to guide the dreams. Try the catcher. Better 'n nothin'."

"Okay." I looked him in the eyes and nodded. I would do it. I respected Mr. Wolf more than just about any other practitioner in town, even if he was a bit kooky. He always seemed to have his heart in the right place.

"So hell hounds …?" Evan began.

"What about 'em?"

"I can't remember much from that book you showed me all those years ago. What can you tell me?"

"They're s'posed to be extinct."

"They're not." Evan shoved his hands into his jeans pockets and plopped down onto a wooden bench across from Mr. Wolf. Apparently, he'd decided to take it upon himself to sit down, since his master hadn't extended the invitation.

For my part, I decided to lean against a post where I'd have the advantage of height.

"What are hell hounds?" I asked Mr. Wolf, deciding that Evan's clipped comment wasn't getting us anywhere. "Where do they come from? How did they supposedly die out?"

"Not sure where they come from." Mr. Wolf reached beside him to grab an old wooden pipe, which he proceeded to light up before continuing. "Never were too many, far as I know. Never 'round here. Old stories put 'em in France and Germany back in the Dark Ages."

"You have books about them," Evan said.

"I got books about a lot of things. The hell hounds don't fill a whole book. You saw 'em in *A History of Medieval Witchcraft*, which mostly talks about witch trials. They made out everything they didn't understand as evil. Talked about the devil a lot. Pacts with the devil. Demons. The dogs, which have red eyes and are fierce strong, got called hell hounds."

"So what you're saying is, the name is a misnomer?" I asked.

Mr. Wolf shrugged and blew out a lungful of pipe smoke. "Never believed in hell myself, but who knows? Point is, I don't think the people who wrote out that book knew much about the creatures. Too scared to think straight, I reckon. Can't trust a man too scared to think straight."

"So the book didn't have much to say about them at all?" Evan asked. He sounded disappointed.

"Nope. Just said they're black, got red eyes, are fierce strong, only come out at night—"

"They only come out at night?" I interrupted. "You mean if we went back now, they wouldn't bother us?"

"That's what the book says." Henry Wolf shrugged. "It is six hundred years old. Almost as old as I am." He chuckled, and I wondered if he was joking.

"How do you kill a hell hound?" Evan asked. "They fired dozens of bullets at it last night, but it didn't make a dent."

"Underbelly," Mr. Wolf said. "You gotta get to them from underneath. Rest of the hide's real thick, like armor."

"Thanks." Evan started to stand, but apparently changed his mind. "Who's your new apprentice, by the way?"

"Pat Malloren."

"Pat?" Evan stared at his old master as if the man had finally lost his mind, but I nodded thoughtfully. True, the Mallorens were generally a bad bunch, but I had reason to think that maybe Pat wasn't as bad as the rest. Given a chance, he might even grow into a decent man.

He was also Evan's cousin, but Evan didn't like to be reminded of that.

"Kid's got heart." Mr. Wolf nodded, as if that was that. Maybe it was.

"We really do have to get going," I said. "I'm sorry to run off, but now that we know the hell hound's not going to attack during the daytime, we need to go back to the scene and try to find out who killed two people."

"I get it. You just be sure to stop by soon for a real visit. The both of you. I want to know how the dreamin's going."

"We will." Evan stood and offered to shake Mr. Wolf's hand, but the old man got to his feet and caught Evan up in a fierce hug instead.

We were halfway back to the car when I thought to ask Mr. Wolf something else. "Hey, do you know anyone in town who could cause a sudden and powerful freeze?"

"Freeze? You mean cold?" Mr. Wolf stared at me with an expression I'd never seen on his face before. "That what happened to whoever died?"

I nodded.

"Heh. That's… a very unusual power. Human body don't create cold."

"Are you saying whoever did it isn't human?" I asked.

"Nope." But he didn't elaborate.

80CB

I called the sheriff as Evan drove us back to Jared's house. He met us there twenty minutes later and waited with me while Evan unmade the ward Scott had put up the night before.

"What did you learn?" the sheriff asked.

"Not much." Briefly, I told him what we did know. "The important thing is that we should be safe during the daytime."

"But Evan's still here."

"He needed to take down the ward." That wasn't entirely true, though. I had the feeling that Evan was going to stick by my side during this one, especially after what Mr. Wolf had said about the human body not generating cold. His words kept echoing through my mind, but I had no better idea what they meant now than I had half an hour ago.

We'd brought our winter gear with us, but we didn't end up needing it. As soon as I stepped out of the car, I could tell that whatever cold had descended upon this place, it had evaporated. The air temperature was a brisk forty-five degrees, the same as it was across most of the countryside. I put on my light jacket and headed for the house, braced for what I would see there.

Death has a smell. It's hard to put into words, but when you've experienced it, you never forget. Any fleeting hope I had that Nadine and Jared might have thawed out disappeared the second I opened the front door and caught the scent in the air.

Their bodies had slumped together since the first time I'd seen them. I tried not to look; that was the sheriff's duty, not mine. My job was to take a look around this house and find some clue as to what had happened here yesterday.

"I got a team coming to dust for prints." Sheriff Adams handed me a pair of latex gloves. "In case you have to touch something."

I took the gloves and put them on absently, searching the room for clues as to what had happened. I more than half expected to see evidence of a casting circle, despite not having noticed one the night before. I'd had less than a minute, after all, and I didn't get much past the front door. But the house was neat. Orderly. Almost too neat and orderly.

I walked through the living room to the attached kitchen, noting the absence of so much as a single cup for water. Even organized people had to drink.

The kitchen trash contained an empty two-liter bottle; I had to restrain myself from putting it in the recycle bin instead. Come to think of it, there was a blue recycle bin not two feet from the trash. Why hadn't they recycled the two-liter?

Pushing the bottle aside, I peered inside for a closer look at the trash, knowing that such things could be a veritable fountain of information. Aside from the two-liter, there were a few pizza crusts. I glanced around for a take-out box, but didn't see one.

"I'm going to look for a trash bin outside," I told the sheriff. I went through the front door even though I suspected the bin would be in back, so as not to disturb more of the scene than I had to.

Evan stood sentry outside, leaning against his car. He arched his eyebrows when he saw me, but I just shook my head before walking around back.

They had two large, round metal trash cans. One was empty, the other only half-full, suggesting they'd had a trash pickup in the last couple of days.

Resting on top of the other debris, I found the pizza boxes – one large, one personal size.

"Who else was here?" I whispered to myself. Returning to the house, I told the sheriff what I'd found.

"There are a bunch of toys in one of the bedrooms, but I don't think they have kids."

"Why not?"

"Didn't come up on the background search and anyway, there's no bed. Just the toys."

I decided to have a look for myself and indeed, in the first bedroom on the left, I found a neatly laid out playroom. There was a shelf full of books and games, bins of carefully stacked and labeled toys, and a closet with more of the same. There were also a few rolled mats and stacked blankets that I assumed could be used for naptime.

"They didn't have a license to run a daycare, did they?" I asked. It all looked a bit too well organized for casual babysitting.

"I'll get Janie to check into it." He went outside to make the call, leaving me to continue my inspection of the house.

There was a bathroom across the hall from the playroom. Again, it was immaculate, with a pump bottle full of liquid soap the only thing near the sink. No toothbrushes, I noted. I checked under the sink, where I found a few spare toothbrushes and toothpaste, but none had been opened.

Moving along, the second door on the left turned out to contain a treadmill, an exercise bike, a set of weights, a yoga mat, and various other equipment. A small TV hung from the wall, much like in the living room.

If they had kids, they wouldn't have the space in this small house for a dedicated workout room. Yet they definitely had kids over regularly enough to have a dedicated playroom.

I moved to the last room in the house, the master bedroom, directly across from the workout room. Here, I found the first signs of clutter. The bed was unmade, a few clothes were on the floor, and a basket of clean, unfolded laundry lay on the bed. The attached bathroom contained toothbrushes, hairbrushes, razors, and hair care products.

I didn't touch more than I had to. At some point, I might return for a more detailed search, but the forensics team needed as clean a scene as possible. Mostly, I had been looking for evidence of magic use – candles, books, potion ingredients, or even just some herbs. I found nothing of the sort. Not even a basil plant on the windowsill.

Returning to the living room, I let my eyes do one last sweep of the room. They fell on a DVD case half sticking out from under the couch where Nadine and Jared still embraced one another. I hesitated, not wanting to get close to them, but needing to see that DVD case.

Finally, holding my breath, I ducked to my hands and knees and pulled it out as quickly as I could, managing not to touch either of the poor souls in the process.

The case was light, suggesting the DVD had been removed. But it was the title that captured my attention: *Frozen.*

Sheriff Adams walked back in through the front door. "What'd you find?"

I held up the case, absolutely unable to speak. It was a movie, just a movie. A cartoon, for crying out loud! And yet, some part of it had come to life in this house with devastating consequences.

Sheriff Adams walked over to the DVD player and pushed the eject button. The missing DVD popped out.

"What does this mean?" Sheriff Adams asked.

"I have no idea. Maybe it's just a coincidence." But I didn't believe it and, I could tell, neither did he.

Chapter 7

NADINE AND JARED DID RUN A DAYCARE OUT OF THEIR HOUSE, WE DIS-covered as we began the laborious process of uncovering the secrets of the victims' lives. It was not, however, licensed. Their nearest neighbor provided that tidbit almost gloatingly, and Nadine's mom confirmed it through sobs that threatened to tear her apart.

"They just got engaged." Mrs. Young buried her face in her husband's chest, refusing to look at me or the sheriff. "They needed the money and she was so good with kids and the state only lets you take care of four kids at a time."

"Do you know the names of the kids she was taking care of?" Sheriff Adams asked.

"Can you ask your questions later?" Mr. Young asked, putting an arm around his sobbing wife and drawing her close to his ample chest. "You just told us we lost our daughter. Have a heart."

"I understand, and I can't tell you how sorry I am for your loss. But there might still be a danger."

"From preschoolers?" Mr. Young asked, and I could see tears glistening in his eyes too, though he fought to hold them back.

"From somebody with serious power." Sheriff Adams stared into those glistening eyes and did not back down. "You know what kind of power I mean?"

Mr. Young's eyes flickered to me briefly, betraying fear. "We don't… we never… not in our family. My wife and I moved to this area thirty years ago during the tourism boom, thinking to open a little antique shop."

Downtown Eagle Rock was full of antique shops, but as far as I knew, this couple didn't own one. I had to assume that their dream hadn't come true and judging by the ramshackle condition of their small, dilapidated home, they had fallen on hard times.

"How did she die?" Mrs. Young's voice was so small, I barely heard it. It wasn't even a whisper, more a croak.

"We don't have an official report from the medical examiner yet," Sheriff Adams said diplomatically.

"But you know," Mrs. Young said, again in that croaky almost whisper.

"It was magic." I stepped in, sensing that we'd get further by being direct. I watched both Mr. and Mrs. Young carefully for a reaction, and was somewhat disappointed at not getting much of one.

"Not in our family," Mr. Young repeated. "Jared's, maybe."

We didn't get anything more from the grieving parents, and after a few short minutes I encouraged the sheriff to back off. We'd be back later, when they had a chance to process. I couldn't even imagine what it must feel like to lose a daughter. I thought of Ana and my heart clenched with dread.

Evan had gone back home, much to my relief. If he'd been there, I don't think the Youngs would have said anything at all. I rode along with the sheriff as he went from place to place, questioning neighbors, family, and friends. After the first hour, we no longer had to tell people about the murders. They already knew. The upside and the downside of living in a small town.

By the time we tracked down Jared's dad (his mom was dead), the man was more than halfway drunk. Mr. Turner looked a lot like his son – tall and thin, with dark hair and thick eyebrows. In Mr. Turner's case, the hair was starting to go gray. He sat in a camp chair by the fog-shrouded lake, a fishing pole lying forgotten by his side as he took a pull from yet another can of beer. At least eight cans were strewn about him, crushed and empty.

A neighbor had told us he'd gone fishing. The neighbor hadn't mentioned that he'd phoned Mr. Turner to share the news.

I stared out over the misty water, remembering what the sheriff had said about there being something in the air. Standing this close to the shoreline, closer than I'd stood in many months, now that I thought about it, I could almost sense what he meant. I shuddered, then turned my attention to Mr. Turner.

"If you came to say my boy's dead, I already know." He didn't stand. Or even look at us.

"We came to ask you when you saw him last." Sheriff Adams kicked at a couple of the beer cans as he drew nearer, then motioned me closer.

I wrinkled my nose in disgust, but got within smelling distance. It reminded me a little bit of my mom, though she tended to get drunk on wine.

"Seen him last week. We go fishing together every Sunday. Never showed today." Mr. Turner finished off the beer he was holding, crushed the can, and tossed it to the side before reaching into the cooler beside his chair to grab another.

"Maybe you should go easy on that," Sheriff Adams said.

"What for? My boy's dead. You got kids, sheriff?"

"No, sir. Never had that pleasure."

Mr. Turner laughed, mirthlessly. "Pleasure, is it? Doesn't seem pleasant right now." He finally looked up, and spotted me for the first time. "What's she doing here?"

"She's consulting on this case."

"Consulting? Word is she only consults when something weird is happening. Something weird happening, Sheriff?"

"Possibly. You got any practitioners in your family?"

Mr. Turner didn't answer right away. He was too busy staring at me, especially at my chest, and in a way that made me feel distinctly uncomfortable. Nobody had looked at me like that since I'd married Evan. No one sane would dare.

"My daughter's mixed up in that occult nonsense." Mr. Turner took another pull on his beer and then belched loudly. I turned my head away, unable to hide my disgust.

"What do you mean, mixed up in the occult?" Sheriff Adams asked.

"You know. She calls herself a witch. Chants nonsense and burns incense. Hangs out with her witchy crowd. Disappears at the full moon, probably dancing naked or something. We don't talk about it much."

The sheriff glanced at me as if inviting me to ask questions, but I shook my head. This man was either too drunk or too ignorant or both to tell us anything. The daughter, on the other hand, might be worth talking to.

"What's your daughter's name?" I asked.

"Jessica. Little Jessie." He belched again, the smell noxious.

"Where can we find her?" Sheriff Adams asked.

"On a Sunday? Sleepin' it off."

ಬಂ೦ೞ

It was late afternoon by the time we arrived at Jessica Turner's small ranch house in a quiet residential area of Eagle Rock. The place wasn't far from a home I'd once lived in, back when I'd chosen to room with Madison and Kaitlin. In fact, the floor plan was probably identical. She even had similar pots full of ivy, a plant often used for protection, hanging from her front porch.

The sheriff knocked. He rang the doorbell. I glanced at the open car park nearby, seeing a bright red pickup truck. Somebody was home.

"When he said she was sleeping it off, I didn't think he meant all afternoon," I said.

The sheriff grunted and rang the doorbell several more times. Finally, I spotted a flutter of movement through a front window, heard a sound almost like a snarl, and the front door burst open.

She looked feral, her blue eyes flashing with undisguised anger. I got the instant impression she wanted to bite. She wore nothing but a blue housecoat loosely tied around her waist. It fell to mid-thigh, revealing long, lean legs. Her red, obviously dyed hair hung in matted clumps to the middle of her back.

"Ms. Turner?" Sheriff Adams asked.

"What are you doing here at this indecent hour?" She flung some of her red hair back over her shoulder, letting the lapel of her housecoat fall open slightly to reveal the swell of one pale breast.

"It's four o'clock in the afternoon, ma'am." The sheriff tipped his hat. "I am sorry to have to wake you, but I've got some bad news. Your brother is dead."

For a moment, her angry, feral expression remained. Then shock replaced it. Followed by anger once again. "How?"

"That's what we're trying to figure out. Your father seemed to think you might be a witch. Is that true?"

She snorted, an indelicate sound. Then she seemed to notice me for the first time, standing a few feet behind the sheriff. "Well, well, little Cassie Scot."

"Do I know you?" I asked.

"I know you." And with that, she turned slightly to give the sheriff her full attention, effectively dismissing me. Well, then. If that wasn't a clear sign of what she thought of me …

"Were you and your brother close?" Sheriff Adams asked.

Jessica hesitated, and once again her feral expression slipped. "Sometimes."

"I don't know what that means," Sheriff Adams said. "Ma'am—"

"I'm twenty-five years old. I'm no ma'am."

"Would you prefer I call you miss?"

She looked him up and down and then very slowly, very deliberately, licked her lips. I couldn't believe the nerve of her, and I was about to say something when I saw the sheriff shift slightly, in obvious discomfort.

Seriously?

"I'd prefer you call me Jessie," she said. "That's what my friends call me."

The sheriff cleared his throat and, I noted, kept his back to me. "Well, Jessie, what do you mean by saying you were sometimes close to your brother?"

She shrugged, the movement revealing more of that breast. "We were close as kids. Then again, a few years ago, when… things happened to change my life. But not lately. No, not lately." Her eyes flickered downward for just a moment before going back up, and it struck me that she was struggling to keep herself put together. As if she feared any crack in her facade, even due to something as natural as grief, might hurt her.

"Do you practice witchcraft?" Sheriff Adams asked, bluntly.

"Not anymore."

"But you did?"

"Yes." She gestured at some ivies hanging from the ceiling of her front porch. "I still employ a few tricks I learned along the way."

"But you're not involved with magic any longer? Do you have any contact with practitioners? Is there anyone who would want to harm you or your family?"

Jessica looked at me, finally. "There's only one practitioner out there with a grudge against me, but he wouldn't go after my family."

"Who is it?" I couldn't help asking.

"Scott Lee."

I sucked in my breath, and the answer hit me like a sledgehammer. That feral look in her eyes, the snarl …. "You're a werewolf."

She curved her lips upwards, but I can't say it was a smile. "For five years now."

"Why doesn't your alpha like you?" I asked, bluntly. Scott was fiercely loyal to those he considered his, especially his pack.

She shrugged. "I tried to eat his mate."

"Madison?" Now it was my turn to dislike her. She'd been off-putting before, but I, too, was fiercely loyal to those I considered mine. And Madison was one of mine.

"Oh, don't look at me like that. The bitch–" And here she laughed. "Well, not a bitch, is she? He bit her, and she didn't even turn. She's not wolf enough for him."

"She's my friend." I said it as a warning, but Jessica only laughed and tossed her mane of red hair around.

"This is getting us nowhere," Sheriff Adams said, stepping to the side to put his body between us. "Did your brother ever practice magic?"

"No. He didn't believe in it until I was bitten, and after that, it scared him." That seemed like the first totally honest thing she'd said.

"What about Nadine?" I asked.

"What about her?" Jessica sidestepped to try to get a look at me, but the sheriff kept blocking. "Did something happen to Nadine?"

"She's dead too."

"No!" And here, finally, was a true emotional reaction. Interesting.

"Did you know her?" I asked.

"We were best friends. How did she die? How did they die?"

"Frozen to death," Sheriff Adams supplied. "As if by magic."

"Did Nadine ever explore witchcraft with you?" I asked, suspecting the truth.

"Yes, but she – she gave it up after what happened to me. We never really knew anything. We were so stupid. Playing with powers we didn't understand. Couldn't understand."

"Did anyone teach you?" I asked, already knowing the answer. No one would teach ordinary people magic.

She shook her head. "Sheriff, why don't you come back in a few hours? I need to... pull myself together."

Sheriff Adams glanced at his watch, hesitated, then nodded. "All right."

"And come alone." With that, Jessica closed the door in his face.

Chapter 8

EVAN WAS HOME BY THE TIME I GOT BACK, WHICH MEANT HIS MOTHER WAS gone and I didn't have to deal with her. Breathing a small sigh of relief, I nursed Ana before helping Evan get dinner ready. I told him what I'd learned – what little there was.

"You should ask Scott about Jessica," Evan said. "He's told me things… whatever she says, it's easy to believe she crossed paths with the wrong person."

"And her brother got killed for it?" I shook my head. I'd talk to Scott, because I followed up on my leads, but I wanted to talk to the families Nadine babysat for more. We hadn't learned any of their names by the end of the day, but several deputies were still casing the area, and I suspected they'd have some names soon.

We chatted about the White Guard over dinner. Apparently, Matthew thought some new human predators might be active in the area. That often meant Evan would be gone, sometimes for days. I didn't begrudge him what he had to do, but I missed him.

We prepared for bed in silence, but when I slid my pregnancy protection ring on my finger, Evan came up behind me and lay his hand on mine to stop me. "Leave it off tonight."

My heart skipped a beat. We'd talked, sure, but it had only been talk. We hadn't really decided to have another baby yet.

"I'm ready. You're ready. Ana needs a brother or sister."

"Maybe." I thought of my mom, and of my brothers and sisters. I'd let the murder be an excuse to stay away today, but that wouldn't last. Tomorrow, probably, I'd need to check on them. I dreaded what I'd find.

"I'd like to dream first," I said.

"To find out when you're most fertile?" Evan asked. "I don't mind just trying every day. It's a burden, but it's one I'm willing to bear."

I laughed. "No, it's not that. It's my family. I just… I'm worried about them and I think I need to know what's going on before I make serious plans for the future."

"All right." Evan's hands dropped away from me, leaving me feeling empty.

"Don't be like that. Things are complicated right now."

"They're only complicated if you make them that way." He sighed, and I could tell I'd upset him. But I couldn't back down.

"I might have to take in seven kids. Have you thought about that?"

He stiffened. Apparently, he hadn't.

"Overnight, I would go from having a certain amount of freedom to being a soccer mom."

"Who plays soccer?"

"That's not the point."

"Then what is?" Evan turned me to face him, placing a hand under my chin to lift it slightly. He loomed over me, which I normally loved about him. But not just now. "You're already a mom. And someday, Ana's going to need to go to sports games and dance recitals and whatever else. It's already happening."

"Yeah, but this way I'm easing into it a bit. You can't tell me I can go from one child to eight without feeling overwhelmed. Without making sacrifices."

"Of course not, but we'll have help. Assuming the worst happens. And either way, I want another baby. I hated being an only child."

"I know." I wanted more babies too, and he knew that. Two days ago, I had nearly said yes, but now...

"So let's leave it off." He took my hand in his and began to loosen the ring.

"Not tonight." I withdrew my hand.

"Fine." Evan backed away from me. "I'll get the dream catcher hung up for you." He disappeared into our large walk-in closet, coming out a minute later with a beautiful, colorful tool for peaceful sleep. There was already a hook on the tall ceiling above the bed, so Evan simply had to guide the dream catcher there with his gift.

"I'm going to watch TV," Evan said when he'd finished.

"Evan—"

"Good night." And with that, he left the room, closing me in by myself.

I hadn't gone to sleep alone since our marriage, except when he'd been away. I stared at the closed door, wondering if I should relent, but I couldn't. This wasn't a decision he could make on his own. I wasn't ready; he didn't have to agree with my reasons, only respect them.

He would come around. He didn't like not getting his way. And he still wasn't used to not getting his way, not even after a couple years of marriage. He easily deferred to me when it wasn't important, but I suddenly wondered if I'd let him make all the truly important decisions without even realizing it.

A humbling thought.

Not going after him wasn't easy, but I did it. I crawled into bed and lay there for a very long time, staring up at the red and gold dream catcher, sparkling slightly in the moonlight. I breathed deeply, working through several meditation exercises before sleep finally overtook me.

₧₨

I dreamed of a child. Another little girl, although she looked remarkably like Evan. Abigail – named for my old mentor – was more sober and serious than her big sister, who she idolized, and absolutely brilliant. I saw her life running forward, skipping ahead like an avid reader peeking at the last page of a novel. She graduated with honors. Apprenticed with Master Wolf – the first girl he'd ever taught but she was too tenacious for him to turn down. Together, they studied the new magic.

Going back, I saw her prom date, a shy boy she completely intimidated but who beamed at the honor. I saw her mastering spellwork with her father, years ahead of where she should have been. Her first day of school. Her first steps. Her first word – nose. Her birth. Her conception. It happens in two days, though I won't be fertile for five.

₧₨

I woke smiling. Evan had come to bed sometime in the night, and was snoring softly, his entire body curled around mine. I disentangled myself reluctantly, then reached for my dream diary. I had to write everything down before I forgot.

Two days. I wasn't sure how prepared I was for it, but having seen my daughter, having glimpsed her life, my arguments against trying again melted away. I couldn't not bring Abigail into the world, now that I'd met her. It would break my heart.

"Good morning." Evan came up behind me and started kissing my neck. Apparently, he wasn't upset anymore.

"Good morning." Not much into morning. Ana hadn't even woken us yet, and she never slept past six thirty.

"Interesting dream?"

"Amazing." I glanced at my notebook, at the pages of details I had carefully transcribed, and frowned. "What's the new magic?"

"Hm?"

"Abigail is going to study the new magic. I saw it. I remember it quite clearly, but I didn't have any context to understand it. It was like… it was like the rules as we know them are about to change."

"Really?"

"No, not really. More like …" I tried to put things into words. "Maybe it's more like our understanding of magic is going to develop so much and so fast that it's going to feel like the rules have changed. But really, we're just learning that things aren't the way we think they are."

"I don't know. Maybe it's a wait and see thing?"

"Maybe."

"So, another girl?" Evan asked. "What's she like?"

"You."

"Me?" He smiled.

"Yes, just like you. Absolutely determined to get her way."

Evan caught me around the waist and tossed me onto the bed. My notebook went flying and I made a weak protest, which I doubt he heard since I was laughing so hard. He came down over me, and lowered his head until his lips hovered millimeters above mine.

My breath hitched. I still loved his kisses.

"I'm pretty determined to get my way now," he said.

"Prove it."

His lips touched mine and the world turned upside down. My thoughts exploded and my vision blurred as my body was forced into an instant climax. Wave after wave, contraction after contraction, rippled through me until I thought I would die from the pleasure of it all.

When I surfaced, Evan was still leaning over me, staring at me, a look of smug satisfaction on his face. He did that sometimes – kiss me with the full force of his gift, inducing an intense orgasm just to prove he could.

"Think we have time for more before Ana wakes up?" I asked.

As if she'd been listening, Ana chose that moment to start crying. Evan dropped his forehead so it rested against mine, his disappointment almost palpable.

"Are you sure we're going to have another baby?" he asked.

"I'm sure. And she's going to be amazing."

ഇരു

I left Ana with Evan when I went to visit my mom that morning. I'd checked in with the sheriff, but he still didn't have the names of the kids Nadine had cared for so there wasn't a lot for me to do on the case. If I were a deputy, I'd still be out chasing every flimsy lead, but as a consultant I let the department handle most of the legwork while I handled the magic.

Which meant I had no reason not to visit my mother.

It was still early when I pulled up in front of the castle I'd once called home. The kids would be at breakfast now, getting ready to leave for school in about thirty minutes. Even Christina was old enough to be in kindergarten, leaving only the twins home alone with mom all day.

I glanced nervously around when I stepped out of my car, recalling that the sheriff had seen a hell hound around here a week or so ago. I still wasn't sure what that was about, though I planned to mention it to Mom, among other things.

The door swung open to admit me as it had done when I still lived here. Nicolas powered the wards these days, and he kept them keyed to me. Not to Evan, but to me.

Baby steps. At least our families weren't actively trying to kill one another anymore.

The living room was a mess. I paused in the entryway, staring at the huge room designed to comfortably accommodate ten people. The once immaculate space bore signs of obvious neglect. There were dirty dishes everywhere, crumbs and bits of food on the furniture and floor. Pillows and blankets were strewn about too, making me wrinkle my nose in distaste at the idea of using them. It all needed washing.

The room was empty. I followed the sound of low voices to the dining room, where I found five-year-old Christina trying to pour her own milk into her cereal. She was alone – the voices were coming from the kitchen, beyond the dining room.

"Let me help," I said, taking the nearly full jug from her small hands and drenching her cereal. When she smiled at me, I knew I'd recalled right that she liked to drown her mini wheats.

"Did you come to see me?" Christina asked.

"I came to see everyone."

"Oh." Her face fell. "Sometime, can you come to see me? No one comes to see me."

My heart cracked a bit as I swept her into a big hug. I'd once under-stood that Elena had gotten caught in the middle, but I guess I'd left before realizing the same thing was happening to Christina. She'd been the baby until the twins had come to usurp that role.

"Of course I will. Can Ana come to see you too? She and I will take you out to lunch. Maybe the first day of Christmas break?"

Christina smiled and nodded. "Then can we go to McClellan's store?"

I froze. McClellan's sold dark magic artifacts. The former owner, David, had been killed when he'd tried to steal Madison's soul but his brother, Cormack, continued the tradition. The White Guard was breathing down his neck a bit, making him tow the line more than his brother had, but I still wouldn't set foot in that place.

"How do you even know that store?"

"It's got a big sign, silly. And it's not far from the Main Street Cafe. Jules takes us there after school all the time." Jules was Juliana. Mostly, we didn't shorten one another's names, but Christina had only recently begun talking at all well and still referred to most of us by the shortened names she'd invented.

"But why would you want to go in there?" I glanced at the door to the kitchen. I still heard voices – Juliana's and maybe Isaac's. "Sweetie, they sell evil things."

"I know. There's a fairy trapped inside who needs our help."

"I see." I didn't see. Not remotely. Maybe she'd been watching Peter Pan? "Do we all just have to say that we believe in fairies and clap our hands?"

Christina looked at me as if I'd lost my mind. "No, we need to sneak in the back and let her out of the cage they put her in."

"Okay. Well, that sounds like a plan." Not a very good one, but hopefully she would forget this story in the next week. It struck me that she might be making up imaginary friends to compensate for some real lack.

"Do you think she'll be okay until we get there?" Christina was toying with her cereal, not really eating it. She seemed to be look-ing at something far away and I wondered, not for the first time, if she was looking through time or space – foresight or farsight. Her verbalization skills had been too weak for us to understand what she was seeing for so long, but she'd been speaking far more clearly since kindergarten started.

"What are you looking at?" I asked.

"The fairy."

"In McClellan's store?"

"Yeah. In her cage. She's sad. And oh… the big man is coming now." Christina shook her head and looked at me. "I don't like the big man. I can't watch when he hurts her."

"What does he do to her?"

Christina shook her head. "I don't know. But she hurts so bad."

Was is possible that there was… well, not a fairy, but someone being held prisoner in McClellan's store?

"Christina, what's Evan doing right now?" I asked suddenly. She could talk now; I could discover the truth behind her gift, with a few well-chosen questions.

"Talking on the phone."

"To who?"

"His cousin."

I took my cell phone out of my purse and tapped Evan's face. It rang several times before he answered. "What's up?"

"Were you just talking to Scott?"

"Yeah. How did you know?"

"Christina told me."

"Did she? Finally learning to master farsight? You thought she had it for years – that or foresight."

"Yeah. Looks like it. But she says someone's being held in a cage in the back of McClellan's store."

Evan went silent for a moment. "I'll look into that."

"Thanks. Love you."

"Love you too."

Christina was looking at me expectantly when I ended the call. "Well, Evan's going to see about your friend at McClellan's store."

She frowned. "Evan?"

"Yeah, Evan. My husband."

"Why him?"

"Well, he's got lots and lots of magic."

"I know. But he makes you cry."

"What are you talking about?"

"At night, he makes you cry at night."

I shook my head, but a horrible idea was forming.

"And this morning. He made you cry this morning. And scream."

I felt my cheeks burn and I turned away slightly, unable to meet her innocent gaze any longer. *Note to self: Look into blocking farsight. Preferably before scarring five-year-old for life. Or me, for that matter.*

"I need to talk to Juliana now," I said.

"Okay." Christina went back to eating her cereal, but her eyes were once again unfocused and, I suspected, looking at something far away.

Juliana and Isaac were indeed in the kitchen, as were Elena and Adam. They glanced at me when I walked in, but none of them greeted me. Not even Adam, who had once wound himself around my legs every time I walked in the house. Of course, he was older now. Two years older physically and who knew how many years older emotionally?

"Why is Christina eating alone?" I asked.

"I didn't want to worry her," Juliana said. "She's too young."

I glanced at eight-year-old Adam, leaning against the counter and picking at a bagel.

"About what?" I asked.

"The lady who's been watching the twins while we're at school died over the weekend."

"Why isn't Mom watching them?" Then the full import of what she'd said sank in and I stared. "Nadine?"

"You know her?"

"You know her?" I shot back. Oh crap, I'd just stumbled upon the connection between Nadine and magic – and it was much, much closer to home than I ever could have guessed. The sheriff had even asked if a fire starter could have done it; he was wrong, Michael couldn't have done it. I stood by what I said. Still…

"Cassie?" Juliana asked. "You don't look okay."

"Who else does she watch? We've been trying to find out, but it's an unregistered, unlicensed daycare and nobody's talking. Like they're afraid she's going to get in more trouble than dead if somebody finds out."

"Um, well, she's got six kids altogether. Or, she had." Juliana looked at her watch. "We have to leave for school soon and nobody's ready. Can we talk later?"

"Now." I glanced at Isaac, Adam, and Elena in turn. "Get ready for school. I'll take care of the twins today."

"But don't you have a job right now?"

"Yes, but Evan can watch them. Or his mom. They can play with Ana."

Juliana shook her head and I stared at her, dumbfounded at her refusal of what seemed like a perfectly reasonable solution. No, the only solution. The others scattered.

"What's going on?" I asked slowly. "Why don't you call me for help more often? I'm over here twice a week but you never invite me. I always sort of barge in."

"You're always welcome." Juliana shifted sideways, not meeting my eyes.

"That's not the same thing and you know it. I didn't know for sure Christina had farsight. Did you?"

"Yes."

"Why didn't you say something?"

She shrugged. "A lot's going on, and we always sort of knew."

"How long has Mom been so far gone she couldn't watch the twins while you were at school?"

"A few months." Juliana put her hands up defensively. "You can't watch them regularly; you already leave Ana with your mother-in-law half the time. But never with Mom."

No, I never left Ana with Mom. I didn't trust her, and wasn't that telling?

"Maybe I can't watch the twins every day," I said, shoving down my guilt, "but you could have asked me for help. It's not like I don't have my own baby to worry about. I've got resources."

"Nadine needed the money."

"This isn't about Nadine. Not today. Who else are you going to call?"

"Uncle John?" Juliana asked.

I threw up my hands in disgust. Uncle John had tried to steal our family's legacy after our father — his brother — had died. We didn't have much to do with him anymore.

"Why didn't you call me the moment you knew there was a problem?"

She wouldn't look at me, and I was fighting a growing certainty that I wasn't going to like her reason at all.

"Juliana!"

"Cassie!"

"What's wrong with you?"

"I don't want *that man* watching the twins."

I closed my eyes. This was what I'd feared, but clearly it was even worse than I'd imagined. "You mean my husband?"

"I mean *that man*. Look, I get it. You love him. Blah blah blah. And I haven't said a word against him since you got married. It was too late anyway. But he's not getting anywhere near Michael or Maya unless I'm there too."

"I didn't realize you hated him so much."

Juliana glanced at her watch. "I really do have to get to school. I'm about to fail math. And maybe history too."

"I'll ask Kaitlin to watch the twins," I said. She hadn't gone back to work since returning to Eagle Rock. At the moment, she was living with Matthew Blair, which I thought should count more against her than Evan should count against me. I'd take her word for it that there was good in him, but old grudges die hard. And he had once tried to force me to marry him.

"That would be great," Juliana said.

I hesitated. "And as soon as you get off school, you and I need to talk."

She mumbled something under her breath.

"Now, who else did Nadine babysit?"

Chapter 9

Nᴏɴᴇ ᴏꜰ ᴛʜᴇ ᴏᴛʜᴇʀ ᴋɪᴅs ᴏɴ Jᴜʟɪᴀɴᴀ's ʟɪsᴛ ᴄᴀᴍᴇ ꜰʀᴏᴍ ᴍᴀɢɪᴄᴀʟ ꜰᴀᴍɪ-lies. That struck me as ominous, somehow, but I set to work with determination and an open mind. I still had no idea what had happened, or how, which meant asking questions until something finally clicked into place.

Sheriff Adams insisted on accompanying me when we went to interview the families of the children in care. He looked strange when we met at the sheriff's department. Different. There wasn't anything I could put my finger on, exactly. No one had suddenly slipped him a hair regrowth potion. He hadn't suddenly lost weight, or gained it.

Was he standing straighter, perhaps? Or was it something in his eyes?

"Ready to go?" he asked crisply.

"Sure. What happened to you?"

"I don't know what you mean."

Behind him, seated at the reception desk, Janie snorted.

"You know something?" I asked.

"I just said the same thing to him when he came in. I think he got laid, but he won't admit it."

"Really?" I thought back to the day before, then frowned. "Not Jessica Turner?"

The sheriff's cheeks went a little pink, which I took as confirmation. I wasn't sure what to say. If it had been anyone else, congratulations might have been in order, but Jessica...

"You didn't get slipped another love potion, did you?" I asked.

"I am not having this discussion. You said you have names. Where are we going?"

Janie snickered. I took out my cell phone and called up the note I'd taken earlier.

"Four kids, two families. That's three kids from one family and one from the other. The one with three kids is the Pruitts – Mark and Kathy. They've got a four-year-old son, a two-year-old son, and a six-month-old daughter. The other family is the Bakers. They've just got a three-year-old daughter."

"Pruitts first?" Sheriff headed toward the door without waiting for my response, suggesting it hadn't really been a question.

I followed him to his squad car, once again getting in the passenger seat and letting someone else drive. I'm not sure why I suddenly resented that position, especially since we were on official police business, it made sense to go in a police car, and it wasn't my car. But something was eating at me, and it was more than riding shotgun.

I hadn't seen my mom that morning. In the end, I'd simply collected the twins and dropped them at Matthew and Kaitlin's place without looking in on Mom at all.

"How's your mom?" Sheriff Adams asked, not for the first time making me think he was a mind reader. He wasn't, but I was as sure as I could be that he possessed strong intuition.

"She has good days. She has bad days." Although lately, she'd only had bad days. I couldn't remember a time in the last six months when she'd had a good day.

"Do you ever think maybe ..."

I waited for the sheriff to finish, but when a full minute passed without him saying anything, I prompted him, "Do I ever think maybe what?"

"So vampires feed off blood. But I've read books, and sometimes in books that's not the only thing they feed off of. Some feed off emotions."

"I've never heard of something like that in real life. People are creative. They make up all kinds of things. Just this morning, my sister was telling me about a trapped fairy."

"Now see, that's a good point too. There are fairy stories, myths and legends. Maybe some of them are real."

"Maybe." I wasn't sure where he was going with this, but I played along. "Scott Lee thinks anything is possible through magic, and that it's ultimately all a product of our will to believe in it. If that's the case, anything could be true."

"But you disagree?"

"I wouldn't go that far. I just… I don't like the idea that there isn't at least some sense in the world. How can we do what we do, try to figure out what happened to two people frozen to death in their homes, if there aren't some rules to govern it all?"

"Maybe there are rules, but we don't understand them yet."

"Maybe. As for myths and legends… talking to Mr. Wolf yesterday made me think that more things were possible once upon a time, and we lost touch with it all."

"Like vampires who feed on emotions?"

"I suppose. What's your point?" I turned fully to face him, though he kept his eyes firmly fixed on the road ahead of him. In profile, his features looked sharper, and his nose was a bit crooked from this angle.

"I told you the other day that I thought people were just more depressed than they used to be. It's not just your mom, although she's one of the worst. I've gotten calls on three suicides and seven attempted suicides in the last six months alone. That's insane. I've never seen the like, not around here. We got the attempted suicides taken to the county hospital and I talked to the nurses there, who said they're overwhelmed with patients. They don't have room for them all. They're having to release them before they're ready to go."

"I didn't realize …" I must have been living in my own little world not to have noticed something like that. But if my mom were being attacked, wouldn't I have noticed? It wasn't like she hadn't been depressed pretty much since Dad died. She'd checked out longer than six months ago.

But she had been getting better. Not as quickly or as dramatically as some of us would have liked, but she had come to my birthday party back in May and even managed a smile. Once.

"We kept it quiet," the sheriff said, interrupting my train of thought. "The three suicides made the papers, but the attempts didn't need the whole town knowing what they'd done – or almost done. And I didn't think it had anything to do with magic."

"But now you do?"

"Now I'm reevaluating. It's not right to blame everything on magic, but just because these people weren't frozen in blocks of ice doesn't mean something magical isn't going on."

We finished the drive in silence, me mulling over what the sheriff had just said. He had good instincts, and I needed to trust them. Which had me thinking it was time to call a White Guard meeting. If something was stirring in the magical world, they'd be the first to know.

The Pruitts lived in a comfortable two-story house near the resort they managed. Mrs. Pruitt was home when we arrived; she answered the door with a baby in her arms and a child on each leg.

She smiled when she saw the sheriff, but the expression faded the instant she set eyes on me. I was used to the reaction, but it still hurt.

"Mrs. Pruitt," Sheriff Adams began, "we're here to talk to you about Nadine. I understand she watched your kids?"

Mrs. Pruitt nodded, stiffly, clearly avoiding looking at me. Now what was that about?

"Was she watching them on Saturday?" he asked.

"No. My husband's off on weekends. I'm off Sunday and Monday. She only watches ours four days a week."

"So the last time you saw her was …?" Sheriff Adams prompted.

"Friday, at five thirty. She was happy. Said she had a great day with the kids and we chatted some about her wedding plans. She was planning a May wedding. Asked me to save the date."

"Do you know if she watched anyone on Saturday?"

Mrs. Pruitt shrugged and glanced quickly at me before looking away again. "I didn't keep up with everyone she watched."

"Mrs. Pruitt," I cut in, thinking I understood the problem. "Michael and Maya weren't there on Saturday either. They were at my house, celebrating their second birthday."

"Oh." She didn't look at me. "Well, I wouldn't know about that, would I? But I'm hearing strange rumors, and the Bakers aren't, well… they're not …"

"Witches?" I supplied.

Her face reddened slightly. "Neither are we. I did tell Nadine not to watch the twins. I worried what might happen to my kids. But... well, I understand she needed the money and your family paid twice as much as usual."

"Michael and Maya's powers are bound. Something like this, if it was an accident, is more likely to happen in a family without the knowledge or ability to do a binding." I don't know why I felt the need to defend myself or my family, but Juliana's words from Saturday kept haunting me: *Michael's gift keeps slipping its binding; it used to be every few months, but lately it's just about weekly. I'm terrified the house is going to burn down around us.*

"I'm sure I wouldn't know anything about it."

The sheriff asked Mrs. Pruitt a few more questions, but I mostly tuned the conversation out. Instead, I studied the two boys hanging on her legs, one of whom was staring at me intently. The older one, I thought. At least, the one who was bigger and taller. The younger one mostly seemed to be mimicking his brother's actions.

They could be tested for magic. But would their mother allow something like that? Especially after she'd said her kids weren't at Nadine's on Saturday? We would check with the resort, but actually, I believed her. It was too easy for us to verify her work schedule.

When we left, we drove straight to the Bakers' home, which was just down the street from Nadine and Jared's. Unfortunately, no one was home when we rang the bell. Some inquiries with the neighbors suggested that Mr. and Mrs. Baker were probably taking some tourists out on their fishing boat, so we headed to the marina.

The morning was half gone, but somehow the perpetual mist seemed to grow thicker as we drove along Lakeshore Drive towards the marina. The sheriff switched on his fog lights and drove on for a while, but finally the fog grew so thick that neither of us could see through it. Or pretend it was normal.

Sheriff Adams pulled to the side of the road and parked, probably half a mile from the marina. I lifted my hand, checking whether I could see it in front of my face. I could. Barely.

"Sheriff? I'm coming around the car toward you. Don't move."

"I'm right here by the driver's side door."

I edged along the side of the car toward the back, keeping one hand on the vehicle to guide me. Off in the distance, I heard a car engine and wondered if the driver was insane enough to try to navigate this fog or if it was a very localized effect.

"We're on Lakeshore Drive," Sheriff Adams was saying as I rounded the back of the vehicle, and I realized he was on the phone, probably talking to Janie back at the station. "Fog's thicker than I've ever seen it. Can't see my hand in front of my face."

I checked my view of my hand, gliding along the back of the SUV, but I couldn't quite make it out. The brown and white SUV was there, murky in the gray fog, but the detail of the hand resting atop it was lost to me.

"No, don't send anyone. I'm safe. We're not going anywhere." There was a pause before the sheriff added. "Okay, bye."

I had nearly reached him now, judging by the sound of his voice and the fact that I'd rounded the back corner of the vehicle.

"I'm not sure we should even walk in this stuff," I said. When I'd first begun moving, I'd thought we might finish our trip to the marina on foot, but now I wished I'd stayed in the car.

Sheriff Adams didn't answer. Apparently, he'd decided to make another call. "You told me to let you know if I thought there was danger."

I sighed. He was calling Evan, just as he'd promised to do. And maybe he was right to do so, but I couldn't help feeling annoyed. I could handle fog, even if I couldn't see through it.

"We're fine right now," Sheriff Adams was saying. "Fog rolled in so thick I can't see my nose. We've parked, but I've got an uneasy feeling."

I stopped moving and tried to look at my nose. It was hard to judge how well I was seeing it, since I didn't normally spend a lot of time looking at it, but the SUV I could feel with my hand was invisible to my eyes.

This was bad.

"You don't want to drive in this, son," Sheriff Adams was saying. "I can't even describe exactly where I am."

I grinned, despite myself, at the sheriff calling Evan *son*. It was the sort of term men used affectionately, but also to put younger men in their places. Evan didn't do other people's places.

I reached the driver's side door and my hand brushed against the sheriff's. Pausing, I drew in a deep lungful of air.

And wondered at the strange odor.

Had it been there all along? It reminded me of rotten eggs, but that wasn't quite right. Whatever it was, I didn't normally smell it here by the lake.

"It's getting worse." But how much worse could it get? I imagined the fog getting so thick I couldn't move in it, let alone see. Was that even possible?

It's magic, I reminded myself. *Anything's possible.* Nadine and Jared had frozen to death on a fifty-degree day, after all.

"Did Janie or Evan say if there was fog around them?" I asked.

"None by them. Seems to be pretty localized."

"Think we can walk out of it?"

"I was just going to ask you the same question. Magic fog is your department."

"Yes. Yes it is." I tried to gather my thoughts and my wits about me. This was unnerving. My heart was beating more rapidly than it should and I was drawing in shallower lungfuls of air than usual. Of course, there was still that smell...

"We have to move!" I grabbed the sheriff's hand, not wanting to get separated from him.

He resisted for just a moment, perhaps because the contact was unusual or because he wasn't afraid enough. But he must have sensed the urgency in my tone and manner, because he relaxed his grip.

"What's wrong?" he asked.

"I think it's poison." I wasn't sure what made me think so, since I hadn't felt any effects yet, but I'd been hit with poisons before that were so subtle I never knew I'd taken them.

I walked until I sensed I'd found the edge of the road, then began following it back the way we'd come, the sheriff a silent presence by my side.

"Say something," I said. "I can't stand the silence right now. I can't see anything. I don't want to think I've gone deaf as well."

"All right. What should we talk about?"

"Anything. Who's causing this?"

"The Bakers' daughter?"

That was my guess as well, but it was just a guess. And since we had no proof, I decided to change the subject. "Let's talk about your date with Jessica."

His grip on my hand tightened for a moment. "Who said it was a date?"

"What was it, then?"

"I just went to her place to ask her more questions about her brother. She was pretty upset when I arrived. Crying."

I tried to picture the woman I'd seen in tears, but the image wouldn't form.

"Anyway, she said she couldn't show weakness in front of you. Actually, I get the impression she doesn't think she can show weakness in front of anyone. She finished crying inside five minutes and then seemed to be trying to prove she was okay."

"Did she have anything interesting to add about her brother or Nadine?" I asked.

"Told me where she learned basic witchcraft seven years ago."

"Oh?" I kept walking, trying not to sound too interested. Failing.

"A group calling itself the Magical Underground was offering free seminars on-line."

I winced. The Magical Underground, run by Alexander DuPris, was attempting to unify the magical world under a single government. On the surface, it sounded okay. They had some good ideas. I'd even joined up for a while. But Alexander had gone too far and in the end, turned out to be a hypocrite.

Hopefully, Matthew had destroyed all the blood. I didn't like to think that I still had a sample on file somewhere. The harm a sorcerer could inflict on someone when he had access to their blood was beyond imagining.

One of the many things Evan was looking into now was how to destroy a link between a person and their blood. So far he had learned that the strength of the link diminished over time, although it was a matter of years, not months or weeks.

"That's awfully brazen of them," I said, thinking of the consequences of such a move rather than the fact that I still couldn't see my hand in front of my face.

One foot in front of the other. I felt my connection to the sheriff as the only solid thing in the world.

"It makes me wonder how magic isn't more widespread if they're putting it up on the Internet for anyone to see." The sheriff squeezed my hand, probably in reassurance. I didn't ask if he felt nauseous too.

One foot in front of the other.

"People stopped believing in magic a long time ago," I said. "After the persecution of the Middle Ages, sorcerers were quite content to help them stop, even to help them forget in some cases. And despite what you see around here, there's very little strong magic in the world. It's mostly smaller, more easily dismissible things. If a woman says there's going to be an earthquake tomorrow and there is, people think she's just lucky. That kind of thing happens all the time."

"So why are people so strong here?"

I didn't reply. The node was still a secret. So instead I changed the subject. "There's a lot of misinformation on the Internet too. I think it has to balance out. And while some of the herbalism can work for anyone, the magic itself only works for a select few. Anyone else who tries a spell will just think it was a joke."

"Is this fog getting thicker?" the sheriff asked.

I hadn't wanted to say it, but yes, I thought it was growing thicker too. It didn't seem possible, but I could almost feel the mist, not just see it.

And that wasn't the worst thing.

"Is it colder, do you think?" I asked.

Chapter 10

SHERIFF ADAMS STOPPED DEAD, PULLING ME TO A HALT AT HIS SIDE. WITH my free hand, I tugged my jacket closer around my body, but I wondered how much good it would do.

"Should we try to get back to the car and drive hell for leather out of here?" he asked.

I didn't know. We'd been walking for a good ten minutes. Another ten minutes could get us out, or get us killed.

"What does your intuition tell you?" I asked.

He didn't answer right away. He drew in a deep breath, coughing once. "I think we're screwed either going forward or back. We need to find another way."

"What, like up?" I looked heavenward, seeing only mist.

"Or down."

"The lake!" I turned my body, taking him with me. I couldn't see the lake through the mist, but it was maybe a hundred yards away. "It's December." I was thinking out loud. "It hasn't really gotten cold yet, and water takes longer to heat or cool than air."

"It'll still be damn cold in that lake." But the sheriff wasn't arguing, he was just stating a fact. He coughed a couple more times.

"You got a better plan?" The air was definitely below freezing now. And the temperature was dropping fast.

"Let's go."

We felt our way across the street then stepped off the other side, feeling our way blindly and hoping we weren't going in circles.

"You should call Evan before we go in," the sheriff said. "Tell him where you are."

"No need. He's got my blood. He'll find me anywhere on Earth."

"That's comforting."

"Right now? Yes, it is."

The ground began sloping sharply downward and I found myself wondering where, exactly, along the shoreline we were. This part wasn't exactly friendly to swimming, although there weren't tall cliffs we might fall from. There was just untamed wilderness, especially…

"Ouch!" The sheriff's hand fell away from mine and I stopped suddenly.

"Sheriff? Sheriff?"

"Here! I ran smack into a tree. Might have a bloody nose."

I followed his voice with my hands raised, carefully testing the air until I found him... and the tree, though I didn't run into it. "We need to be careful. There's a lot of undergrowth too. Would be easy to trip on a root."

"We also need to hurry. My fingers are numb."

I tried not to think about the fact that the tips of my ears felt like ice. My teeth began to chatter and I could barely feel my fingers.

"Hands out in front," I managed. "Slow and steady."

We continued to move, our joined hands and our free ones raised in front of us to feel our way. We found a few more trees, their bark iced over, but didn't have another collision.

Then my foot found a root and I went down, hard. My hand was wrenched once again from the sheriff's and I cried out before landing with a slight splash in weed-ridden water.

"Cassie! You okay?"

"Found the lake." And compared to the air temperature, it felt positively balmy, reassuring me that I'd made the right decision. Even if it was a desperate one.

"Keep talking. I'm going to crawl to you."

I guided the sheriff to the edge of the lake. He found my foot first, and I winced in pain when he put pressure on it.

"Cassie? You okay?"

"Might have twisted my ankle or something. Don't worry about it right now. We gotta move."

I offered him my hand and together, we crawled forward into the weeds.

The water was cold. But the air was colder. We half crawled, half swam until the lake floor fell out from beneath us. My teeth chattered so hard I thought my teeth would break but I pushed on. We dog-paddled, still clinging to one another's hands, still unable to see, although I thought the mist might be thinning here.

"We have to dive," Sheriff Adams said.

"I'm not sure I can swim holding onto your hand."

"Try."

We went under and kicked. Pain lanced through my bad ankle and for a second, I thought it would take me under. I tried to toe off my shoes, which were weighing me down, causing a pain so sharp I saw stars. The next thing I knew, I'd lost both the shoes and the sheriff's hand.

I scrambled to find him again, panic finally settling in where cool resolve had served me before. I'd let the sheriff be my rock, and now I had to stand alone.

My head broke the surface of the water and I gasped for breath. The air entering my lungs felt weaponized, like little shards of ice. And was the top layer of the lake starting to freeze? My toes were certainly warmer than my shoulders, although the water had to be about fifty degrees down there too.

"Sheriff!" I called.

No answer.

"Sheriff!" I dove again and kicked, just trying to move. To get away from the shore and the fog.

When I emerged, I once again called for the sheriff.

"Here." He sounded weak; the chattering of his teeth almost louder than his words.

I tried to follow the sound of his voice, but I kept having to dive to escape the worst of the cold and every time I came up for air, I lost him again.

"Sheriff!"

We were going to die. Right here, in this ice-cold lake, we were going to become human ice cubes. Just like Nadine and Jared. I'd never see Ana again. Or have a chance to meet her sister.

What would her gift be? Would she be a fire starter like two of my brothers? It ran in my family. If only I'd already conceived and had access to that gift now.

You have magic. You could pull off a heat spell. You know the theory.

"I can't create enough heat to warm the lake." I actually spoke out loud, but I was thinking too. Evan had struggled to get warm on Saturday, using a simple spell to warm himself. Could I even do that? Basic heat spells did little more than light candles, which wouldn't help me here.

You don't need to focus. You don't need restraint. Just make it hot!

I closed my eyes, found my quiet place, and spent a moment simply looking at the dancing lights filling the once pitch-black refuge. There had been more light when I was pregnant, but there was still quite a bit now. And also, there was the node beneath this very lake. I sensed it now, practically below my feet, offering me strength beyond my own.

The node called to me. I could hear it, almost like singing. It wanted me to take hold, to use it, to find the raw power I would need if I had any hope of survival.

"Hang on, Sheriff," I said.

Then I opened myself up to the node and let the magic pour through me, out of me, and into the world around me.

I didn't know what I was doing. Not really. There is a big difference between theory and practice, whatever the little voice in my head wanted to make me believe. Which meant that what I actually did was open a floodgate when I had no shutoff valve.

Power. Intense. Hot. Electric. I could no longer feel my body at all. I was the power.

Some dim part of me that retained awareness tried to will the power to form into heat, but I was simply overwhelmed. The power went out into the world to do whatever it would, with no form or focus.

I was at the center of an explosion. No. I *was* the explosion.

Pain crackled through me until I couldn't think. Couldn't breathe. Couldn't...

಄ഗ

I was warm. That was the first thing I noticed. Also, I was dry. That was the second thing I noticed.

"Come back to me, Cassie."

I was pressed against something firm and hot, but yielding. I nuzzled my face into it and tried not to think.

"Cassie."

Something touched my back, then began rubbing in slow, gentle circles. I relaxed further into the firm, hot, yielding thing.

"Come on, Cassie. Come back to me so I can yell at you properly."

Awareness returned in that instant, and I pulled away from Evan's chest even as my eyes blinked open to stare into his crystalline blue eyes. They were full of... anger?

"Where's the sheriff?" I asked.

"I'm here."

I turned my head to see Sheriff Adams leaning heavily against a gnarled, burned-out tree. He was alive. I was alive. The thick fog was gone, replaced with a faint mist.

My eyes were slow to work for some reason. There seemed to be a lot of blackness around us, like a fire had swept through the area. We were at the edge of the lake, not far from the road. Evan sat with his back against a large blackened tree stump, cradling me in his arms.

I thought about asking what had happened, but Evan's anger had me wary of that line of inquiry. So instead I ignored Evan and spoke to the sheriff.

"We definitely need to talk to the Bakers."

"Not without backup," Evan said firmly, returning my attention to him.

"I'm going to head back to my car." The sheriff pulled himself upright, away from the tree, with apparent effort and began walking a little unsteadily toward his vehicle.

"Can't you help him?" I whispered.

"He asked me not to." Evan turned his head and watched until the sheriff was out of sight and probably out of earshot.

"Well, that was different." I pulled myself away from his chest, or tried to. He kept me anchored there with one arm and possibly the force of his will. Hazard of being married to someone as powerful as Evan: If he didn't want me to move, I didn't move.

"Aren't you going to ask what happened?" Evan asked.

"No. I decided to assume I magically saved the day and then you came by just in time to save me."

"Wrong." His hand stilled on my back, and his eyes went cloudy. Even angrier.

"Oh."

"Almost two years," he began. His tone was hard. And as cold as the mist had been. "I haven't pushed you. You have your reasons for not wanting to use the magic you're channeling and I tried to respect that. But I also told you – more than once I told you – to come to me if you changed your mind. To learn how to truly use it and control it."

"The sheriff and I were about to freeze to death." I once again tried to pull away, and I felt my own anger rising inside me in an answering tide, particularly because I still couldn't move. "Let me go!"

He removed his hand and instantly, the pressure on my back eased, allowing me to sit upright and meet him as an equal. I suspected he hadn't realized what he was doing; his gift often acted up when he was feeling strong emotions. Unnatural winds were the surest sign of his distress, but it wasn't the only sign.

He'd never hurt me, though. When I was angry, like I was just then, I wondered if that meant he had more control over himself than he let on.

"We were about to freeze to death," I continued, speaking through clenched teeth. "I didn't have time to stop and consult with you first."

"Then you should have done it last week or last month or last year! Or hell, how about this afternoon? You want to work on it this afternoon?"

"Of course not! This was a one-time thing. You know how I feel about using this… this… temporary temptation."

"I know you're not your mom!" The wind began to stir, whipping my hair around my face and stinging my cheeks. As if I needed a reminder of his feelings.

"Why are you so mad? I'm alive. The sheriff's alive."

"You don't even realize what you've done, do you?" He laughed, the sound hollow and mirthless. "How can you not get it? Look around!"

I did, blinking up at the leafless trees and the clear blue sky beyond. I'd seen a few blackened trees before and assumed they'd been burned, but now I saw things differently.

They were black. All of the trees. Completely black. But not like they'd been burned, more like they'd been inked over.

I drew in a deep breath and took another look around, this time scanning the forest floor. Dead animals, also black as ink, littered the ground. By the lapping shoreline, I spotted dozens of dead fish washed up on the bank. The weeds that had tangled our legs when we'd first entered the water were now black tendrils, floating at the water's surface. More dead fish floated among the debris.

"What happened?" I asked, finally voicing the question I'd denied earlier. My anger wasn't gone, but bewilderment was working to undermine it.

"You opened yourself to node energy without having the first clue what you were doing. It nearly ate you alive. If I hadn't shown up when I did, you could have died!"

I swallowed, hard.

"There's a reason no one works node energy until they've mastered everything else. I didn't start using it until I was eighteen and Master Wolf took me on."

"Elena did something like this once," I said defensively. "Two years ago, she lost control of her magic on the playground and wreaked all sorts of havoc."

"I remember. But she literally lost control, which meant she didn't tap into node energy. That requires intention."

"Oh."

"You opened yourself up to powers you don't understand and can't begin to control!" The wind was stirring more forcefully now, rising in tune with Evan's outrage, which I was finally beginning to understand.

"I was just so cold and wanted to get warm." It was a last, feeble defense, but it was all I had.

"You didn't have to invite the node energy in to do that. You needed control, not more power, which you would have known if you'd ever taken me up on my offers to teach you!"

I closed my eyes and ducked my head, trying to protect my face from the stinging torrent of wind.

"You nearly died. You nearly killed the sheriff. You did kill most of the fish in the area, which could cripple the tourism industry around here for years! Not to mention the birds and the animals and the plant life!"

The true horror of what I'd wrought was finally sinking in. I'd destroyed an ecosystem. Or at least crippled it. I hadn't realized... but of course, that was no excuse. He was right. I should have realized.

"Can we – can't we fix it?"

"Fix dead animals and plants? I'm a sorcerer, not a god!"

"How bad is it?"

"I don't know. I'm going to have to spend time investigating. But I'd say bad. It would have been worse if I hadn't stopped you when I did."

"I'm sorry."

"Apologize to the birds and fish."

I felt a chill that had nothing to do with cold sweep over me. Had Evan ever been this angry with me before? If he had, I couldn't remember it. Worse, I might deserve it.

"How did the... what happened to the mist?"

"I dismantled it. The spell was powerful, but easily undone, which I believe I mentioned on Saturday." He paused. "What were you doing in the lake?"

"It was getting so cold, and the sheriff didn't think we could find our way out in time. So I thought... well, water doesn't change temperature as quickly as air."

"That probably bought you a few minutes." Evan's compliment was clearly grudging.

"I need to find the Bakers," I said, weakly. "That could happen again."

"I'm coming with you." His tone broached no argument, but I didn't plan to offer him one. As tense as things were between us right now, even I knew when to accept help. Usually.

I started to stand, but two things stopped me. First, I winced in pain when I shifted my ankle, and second, "I lost my shoes. Damn. I liked those shoes."

Chapter 11

THE INKY BLACKNESS HADN'T SPREAD AS FAR AS I FEARED AT FIRST. WITHIN half a mile, I spotted a sort of boundary marker separating the diseased area from a neighboring healthy area. On one side of a line, black; on the other, the natural colors of late fall. I breathed a small sigh of relief, although I didn't kid myself that the damage I'd done wasn't bad enough. I risked a glance at Evan, but he didn't look my way or say a word.

My ankle still throbbed; I'd told Evan not to take me home for healing or even for shoes. He hadn't argued, which either meant he agreed time was of the essence, or else he thought I deserved the pain, at least for a little while. Probably the former; angry or not, he still loved me.

The marina was deserted. There wasn't a lot of traffic in December anyway, but the only signs of life along the rows of boats were the gentle lapping sounds of water against hulls. I waited with the car while Evan and the sheriff milled about for about half an hour, checking every inch of the place. When they came up with nothing, we all headed to the nearby bait and tackle store. It was closed, though a sign on the door suggested its normal business hours were ten to six.

"I don't like it," Sheriff Adams said.

I didn't like much of anything. Evan's anger still felt like a palpable force and my own righteous indignation had long-since given way to shame. It was hard to think, with poisonous feelings like that.

"Where do they live?" Evan asked. "I could track them down with a hair sample."

"I'll have to get a warrant to search the house."

Evan didn't reply, but I knew what he was thinking: He didn't need a warrant to search the house.

"Wait for the warrant." The sheriff gave Evan a hard look. "I know you're inclined to rush ahead, and you don't think the rules apply to you, but I want to do this by the books. I should be able to get the warrant this afternoon."

"Better make it before nightfall, just in case." Evan began walking away, and I knew he meant that if the sheriff didn't come through with a warrant in time, he'd search anyway.

The sheriff seemed to understand this too, because he sighed. "Cassie, can you convince him to hold off?"

I shrugged. "Why? Two people are dead, you and I almost died, and there's a hell hound that almost killed Jim."

"Because I lose legal authority if we don't do this right. Neither one of us knows what's going on yet."

"I'll see what I can do." I glanced at Evan, who had paused by his car and turned to look back at me. "My car's parked downtown. I'll have to ride back with the sheriff."

"Can you drive with that ankle?" he asked.

"It's my left one. I'll be fine."

"Without shoes?"

"I'll buy new ones."

"Suit yourself." He got into the car and drove away, without so much as a "goodbye" or an "I love you."

"The lake going to be okay?" Sheriff Adams asked as he put an arm around my waist to help me limp to his car.

"I don't know. I'm not sure what I did. If it had been fire, that would be easy. Fires happen. But that's not …" I drew in a deep breath. "… that's not what I did."

"Hm." Something in my tone must have alerted him that this was not the time or the place, because he didn't ask me about it the rest of the way back into town. In fact, he didn't say another word until we returned to the station and then it was simply, "I'll call when the warrant's in."

I wasn't in the mood for shopping, so I bought the first pair of flip flops I found before driving out to my mom's place. The kids were all at school, except the twins, who were with Kaitlin, which meant I had no choice but to actually face Mom this time.

She wasn't in the living room when I walked in, or the dining room or kitchen. I headed upstairs to the library, finally spotting her draped across one of nine tall-backed chairs set in a square around a large table. One for each of us – before the twins were born and then Dad died. No one had bothered to reconfigure things since then.

She was staring at a thick leather-bound tome. I can't honestly say reading it, because there was something in her unfocused gaze that suggested otherwise. Plus, I could smell the pungent aroma of wine from the double-door entryway.

"Mom," I said. Then, when she didn't answer right away, I raised my voice. "Mom!"

She moved her head to the side and stared at me for a moment. She looked old. Not as old as forty-three, which was her actual age, but older than usual. She'd taken anti-aging potions for years that had kept her looking twenty-something. Before Dad's death, she and I almost looked like twins. Now, she looked more like her actual twin sister. Except with bloodshot eyes.

I stepped inside the massive room, designed as a place for a family of sorcerers to study together. A large fireplace, big enough to stand in, was centered on one wall, but no fire burned in the hearth. Around it and lining the rest of the walls were shelves and shelves of books on every subject imaginable. There was a fiction section, a large cookbook section, and biggest of all – the magic section.

I hadn't read one-tenth of these books. Maybe I should have. Maybe it would have prevented today from happening.

"What are you reading?" I asked, trying to sound pleasant. I probably failed; I didn't feel the least bit pleasant.

Mom flopped back in her chair and raised a bottle of wine to her lips, drinking deeply. She didn't even bother with a glass.

"I think you've had enough of that." I strode to her side and pried the bottle out of her hands, expecting resistance but finding none. Of course, the bottle was empty.

"Come to lecture me again?"

"Would it do any good?" I asked.

She sighed and looked down. I followed her gaze to the book lying open on the center table, then reached for it and tipped it so I could read the title: *Magical Transference*.

"What do you think you're doing with this?" I slammed the book shut and snatched it away. Evan had a copy of this book, but I hadn't known Mom had one. It was ominous that she'd gone to the trouble of getting a copy.

It was a book describing how to steal magic from one sorcerer and transfer it to another, a process that was so painful for both parties that it was said to tear the soul. People who were drained of their magic became shells of their former selves. I'd seen them, right afterward, empty inside. They could recover, but it wasn't a fast or easy process.

It's one of the reasons why I'd refused Evan's offer to restore the magic he'd taken from me, unbeknownst to both of us, before we were born. He claimed he could do it slower, make it easier, but I'd read that book and I wasn't convinced.

"Hey! I was reading that."

"I know. Why?"

"Just considering options."

"Options? What options? The man who stole your magic is dead. So whose were you planning to take?" I snatched the book off the table and clutched it to my chest, breathing heavily. "My God, what's the matter with you?"

"It's gone. It's all gone."

"Of course it's gone! You stopped nursing six months ago." Which was actually a lot sooner than she'd stopped nursing any of the rest of us. It is, of course, entirely healthy to nurse babies for at least two years, but she'd chosen to do it for selfish reasons. To prolong channeling magic. I'd expected her to nurse the twins until kindergarten.

"But you understand now, don't you? Now that you've had a baby. You get it."

I shook my head, not in negation, but in denial. "What's happened to you? Is this really all about losing direct access to magic?"

"I can't protect the twins."

"You could if you'd stop drinking. When did you ever send any of us to daycare?"

"Hypocrite." Mom pointed a long finger at me. "You work. You use childcare."

"This isn't a working mom vs stay-at-home mom debate. You don't work. You never have."

"I can't protect them. Can't bind their powers."

"You think a babysitter can?"

"I think you should talk to me with more respect."

"I don't know why I came here." I started to leave, taking the book with me. I had no idea what she wanted it for, but I was taking no chances.

"Wait!"

I stopped, but didn't turn around.

"Are you limping?"

"Yeah, I hurt my ankle."

"Why haven't you healed it?" She sounded strangely sober.

"Haven't had a chance to get home."

"There's salve in the lab."

"That's okay. I'm going home anyway."

"No, let me."

I turned around, not sure if I was going to stop her or not, but she was already up, wobbling slightly, but striding purposefully past me and out of the library. I followed, still limping.

"What are you doing?" I asked. She hadn't been a mother to any of the little kids for months, but suddenly she wanted to nurse my mildly sprained ankle?

"Getting salve." She clutched at the wall for a moment, as unsteady on her feet as I was on mine but for vastly different reasons. Holding the wall for stability, she made her way to the potions lab next door to the library.

"Why are you doing this?" I asked helplessly as Mom fumbled through several jars of ointment, finally finding the one she sought.

She turned, clutching the jar to her chest. "I love you."

I shrugged. She'd said that before and I usually believed her. But it didn't fix anything.

"Here." She opened the jar and knelt to rub the magical cream into my injured left ankle.

Instantly, I felt a tingling warmth. Within a minute, I was pretty sure my ankle was healed, but she stayed where she was.

"You're stronger than I am," she said, still rubbing. "You have no idea what it's like. I lost a piece of myself when I lost my sister. Then I lost another piece when I lost my magic. I tried to compensate by being a mom, by living through my children. Then I lost Edward..."

She kept her face averted, still rubbing salve into my ankle as if by fixing me, she could fix herself. I put a hand on Mom's arm to still her. When she looked up, I saw an expression of utter desolation on her face.

"I'm fine." I still held the book, clutched in my arms. "But I'm taking this."

She didn't say anything for a long moment, and when I finally left, it was with strangely mixed feelings. Who was my mom? She wasn't the woman I'd known growing up, but who was she now? Would I ever get my real mom back?

☙ℭ☙

The Bakers weren't home, which wasn't a surprise. They had clearly packed up and left, however, which was more surprising. Most of their clothes were gone, along with toothbrushes and hairbrushes.

They left no trace. Evan searched the house carefully for blood or hair, while the sheriff, Jim, and I searched for more mainstream clues. Evan found nothing – not in the shower drains or the sink. The hairbrushes were missing.

"There could be hair fibers in the carpet or bedding," Jim suggested when he realized what Evan was doing. He was much improved after his near-death encounter, although something dark lingered behind his eyes at odd moments.

Evan shook his head in answer to Jim's question, but didn't explain. I knew why it wouldn't work, though. Hair that falls naturally from a person's head loses its connection to that person. It truly dies. Only hair that is yanked out or agitated out, such as while brushing or washing hair, is useful for scrying. And even that didn't always work. Blood is much better.

"Too many people know to destroy hair and blood these days," Evan muttered as we gave up our search of the house and headed for Matthew and Kaitlin's place to pick up Ana.

It was my fault that so many locals knew not to leave hair and blood lying around. He didn't say so. He didn't blame me, at least not directly, but I knew he knew what I'd done. We'd never talked about it, but I wondered if he approved or not. His current complaint could just be annoyance, or it could be a real problem with the fact that some of his power was undermined by virtue of real knowledge being disseminated.

He had enough power. He truly did. He didn't need to use trickery and deceit. But it was something of a tradition among practitioners.

We didn't speak much during the drive from the Bakers' house to Mathew and Kaitlin's house. I started to say something several times, but couldn't decide if I wanted to apologize, defend myself, or complain about my mom again. In the end, I chose silence, and he joined me in it.

"You should stay for dinner," Kaitlin said as soon as we climbed the steps to her front porch. She already had the door open, and I could hear Ana chatting away in her usual baby babble inside. Kaitlin's own son, Jay, who was getting close to two years old, said almost nothing. I knew Kaitlin worried about that, and maybe she had a good reason at this point, but Jay had strength and speed years beyond his developmental level. He'd walked by the time he was four months old, and could run by six months. Now, at nearly two, he moved like a ten-year-old.

"Tonight isn't a good night," Evan said.

"It's six thirty. You really want to go home and then start cooking? Come on. I've got everything ready, and there's plenty. Most recipes don't scale well for three anyway."

I hesitated. On the one hand, I wasn't sure I would be good company. On the other, I wasn't sure I wanted to be alone with Evan just yet.

"What are you having?" I asked to buy some time.

"Enchiladas. There's avocado, plain white rice, and cheese for the little ones. Although Jay's starting to demand a serving of whatever we eat."

"It sounds great." I glanced at Evan, who wasn't offering any guidance, but I could still sense the anger simmering just beneath his neutral game face. Maybe he wasn't sure if he wanted to be alone with me either. That hurt, and it made my decision for me. "Thanks. We'd love to join you."

Kaitlin ushered us inside and Ana squealed loudly when she saw me. She wasn't walking on her own yet, but she could crawl like a champ and glide on the furniture. Within seconds, she was clinging to my leg, giving me her signal to pick her up.

"I missed you today," I said softly as I swung her into my arms.

She pressed her head against my breast. "Ma!"

"When we get home, baby." I wasn't opposed to nursing in public, but Ana could eat regular food now and I knew Kaitlin was sensitive about the fact that she'd had trouble nursing Jay more than a few months. I harbored no blame or judgment, but sensed she did.

"Ma!" Ana repeated.

"Let's get you some avocado." I bounced her and took her through to the dining room, where Matthew Blair was setting out a dish of Spanish rice on the oak table.

I stopped short. I didn't see Matthew often. For the longest time, Evan intentionally kept us apart, but since Kaitlin had started dating him, we'd come into one another's orbits more often. Still, I couldn't look at him and not remember that he'd once tried to reprogram my mind so I would marry him.

I trusted Kaitlin; I loved my best friend, but I still only tolerated Matthew.

"Hi, Cassie." He smiled, an expression that transformed his face from attractive to warm and friendly. I actually smiled back, before catching myself and remembering he could read my mind.

"Matthew," Evan said from behind me.

He put his arms around my waist in what I thought was an over-the-top mark of possession, especially since he was mad at me. I wrenched away from his grip, unwilling to humor him just then.

"Evan," Matthew said evenly. "I understand we've got some troubles. I'd like to talk about them over dinner. Informally, before we call a meeting of the White Guard."

I put Ana in the highchair Kaitlin had set out for her – Jay was in a booster chair nearby. While she played with some avocado, I helped Kaitlin bring two casserole dishes full of enchiladas out onto the dining room table. Evan and Matthew set out plates and forks and chatted about a new slave trading ring out of California that was giving them more trouble than usual because they had so few members there.

My mom had come from California. And been drained of her magic there, before being sold. I'd relived the experience alongside her once, deeply connected to her thoughts and memories. But I still didn't fully understand what was wrong now.

Kaitlin dished up a whole enchilada and a healthy pile of rice for her son. I looked at him dubiously, but he dug into it with an appetite as advanced as his physical prowess.

"It's delicious, thanks," I told Kaitlin when I dug into my own enchilada. "When did you have time to make this, looking after four kids?"

"It was no problem. Juliana came to get the twins right after school, almost three hours ago."

"Are you watching them tomorrow?"

"To the end of the week, for sure. After that, I'm hoping she finds someone else. The twins make me nervous."

"Why?" I asked sharply, offended on behalf of my youngest brother and sister. *They're a magical connection to Nadine and Jared,* came a most unwelcome thought. But they couldn't freeze people. Or make dense fog. And the Bakers had run, after all; they were the likelier suspects.

"So, hell hounds," Matthew said loudly, in an obvious bid to change the subject. "Tell me what's going on in my town."

"Your town?" Evan arched an imperious eyebrow.

"Sheriff Adams says he's seen three of them, or seen the same one three times. We just saw it once." Briefly I filled Matthew in on what had happened over the last couple of days and what we knew. Technically, I didn't have to say anything. I could think it, and he could read my mind. But it felt weird thinking at him instead of speaking to him and anyway, I tried not to remember that he could read minds. It made it impossible not to think about the things I most didn't want him to know. Such as the fact that I wasn't one hundred percent sure everything I'd felt for him had been coerced. I wanted to think that; Evan certainly reinforced the idea every chance he got, but in my most honest moments, I couldn't be so sure. Then Kaitlin had forced me to see a different side to him, one I probably would have been happier never to have seen.

Damn, I'd just thought about it.

"So what's wrong with Michael and Maya?" I asked Kaitlin while Evan and Matthew chatted about meeting logistics.

Kaitlin bit her lip and looked at Jay, who was trying to offer Ana some enchilada. She got her finger into some of the mildly spicy sauce and I stiffened, wondering what would happen. Ana lifted it to her mouth, licked it, and instantly made a gagging sound.

"Uh oh." I got to my feet and helped Ana wash the unwelcome taste from her mouth with some apple juice. When she was happy again, I returned to Kaitlin, who was being uncharacteristically reticent. Then again, she'd changed since she'd run away with a vampire and come home with a mind mage. She was still my best friend, but we were sort of rediscovering our roles in each other's lives.

"Never mind, forget it."

"Come on. You can't just tell me you find my brother and sister creepy without explaining why."

She sighed. "They're really attached to one another. I mean really attached."

"Juliana said the same thing." I hesitated, thinking. "In a way, they're the most consistent support they have. My mom was fine at first, checked out for months after dad died, then just when she started pulling herself together and being a real mom again, snapped and checked out entirely."

"How is your mom?" Kaitlin asked.

"Not good." I thought about what I'd seen that afternoon, and about the book I still had in the car. I hadn't mentioned it to Evan yet, but I noticed Matthew turn to look askance at me as I remembered the title. *Damn. Damn. Damn.* One of these days, I had to figure out a way to block him. Aside from singing, "Mary Had a Little Lamb" inside my head every second I spent in his company.

I also thought about what the sheriff had suggested. "Do you think someone or something could be making her act this way?"

Kaitlin glanced at Matthew and I followed her gaze. But I knew what she was thinking, even if I couldn't literally read her mind: The Blairs could work magic like that.

Oh God, what if my mom's been under attack for six months and nobody noticed because we were so mad at how she was behaving? Because we thought it was just part of her breakdown after Dad died?

"Maybe you should get an empathic healer to look at her," Kaitlin suggested.

Matthew cleared his throat and when I looked his way, he nodded. "I know just the woman to help; she's the best. Whether your mom's under attack by internal or external demons, if anyone can help, she can."

I hesitated, remembering as if it were yesterday the way it had felt to be under the influence of a mind mage: Normal. Completely and utterly normal, as if every thought had come from my own mind rather than someone else's.

"I understand." Matthew sighed. "Think about it, then. But don't take too long."

Chapter 12

EVAN WAS STILL MAD AT ME. HE DIDN'T SAY SO, BUT HE DIDN'T COME TO
bed with me, muttering something about having to do some
research – I assumed into the mess I'd made.

I set the dream catcher into place and tossed and turned for a bit,
wondering as I did how we were going to create my dream child if we
weren't even speaking. It was supposed to happen tomorrow night, a
mere twenty-four hours away. Just now those hours seemed simulta-
neously like forever and no time at all.

Well, technically, we didn't have to *talk* to make a baby... I had
never imagined making love to Evan angry, but what choice did I
have? Little Abigail's life hung in the balance.

I tried to recall everything I could about Abigail as I tossed and
turned, but when I finally fell asleep, I dreamed of another child. This
child was a boy, one who looked remarkably like his father. We named
him Henry, after Henry Wolf, who beamed with pride the first time
he held his namesake. Little Henry's life expanded before me, beginning with him hiding behind my knee as a toddler. In school he was
painfully shy and had trouble making friends. At home, however, he
was the biggest sweetheart, always helping out, always with a kind
word for his parents or siblings. He was clever and, as he grew into a
man, quite as handsome as his father. That's when the girls began to
notice him. He noticed them too, but he was frightened of what happened when he kissed one.

He hadn't inherited his father's power of telekinesis. But he had
inherited another gift.

When he graduated high school, he left Eagle Rock to tour Europe
and uncover ancient secrets of magic that would help him understand
the new magic better. He was gone for years, and when he returned
it was with an enchanting witch on his arm. I didn't like her at first,
because how could she be good enough for my son? But she eventually enchanted me too, right around the time she gave birth to my
first grandchild.

I saw his life in reverse once again, seeing his first day of school, his first steps, his first word – mommy – and returning at last to the moment of his conception. A moment three days from now that would bring my beautiful son into the world. Evan and I had been too angry to make love until just that moment, the perfect moment to create my perfect sweetheart.

ଓଗ

It was still dark when I woke, drenched in my own sweat as if I'd had some kind of nightmare. But of course, the dream catcher only allowed pleasant dreams to flow down to me at night, so that was impossible.

Flinging out an arm, I found the mattress next to me cold and empty and I nearly cried at the absence of my usual rock. I needed him right now, though I couldn't think why exactly. It had been a nice dream; I'd met my son. Gotten to know him. Just like I'd gotten to know Abigail…

Something tightened in my chest and I closed my eyes, trying to unsee the life I'd seen. The soul. The perfect little boy. The perfect little girl.

Choose, said some evil voice in my mind. *Quickly mend fences with Evan to create your daughter, or delay to create your son. Which do you love more?*

I reached for my dream journal out of habit, but let my fingers fall away from it. First, I needed to get up. Change the sheets. Change my clothes. Find Evan. Definitely, find Evan.

I found Evan sleeping in one of the guest rooms. I didn't wake him, but instead watched the rise and fall of his chest for several minutes before returning to my dream journal, trying not to think about the reasons why he had chosen to stay away from me tonight.

My hand shook as I wrote down every detail, somehow bringing my dream child more to life than he had already been. I stumbled over the concept of the new magic, which I'd run across in both dreams, but decided it didn't matter right now.

When I finished, I set the journal aside and checked my watch. It was near midnight, but I wanted to talk to someone. Needed to talk to someone. I considered going to Evan in the next room, but he had put that distance between us and I would have to bridge that gap before I could even begin to pour my heart out to him.

Juliana often stayed up late, even if she shouldn't. Even if she needed to get some sleep. She would take care of the family until they trickled off to bed, then still have homework to do at night.

I felt more than a twinge of guilt at the idea of adding to that burden tonight, but I had to talk to her anyway. She and I needed a better plan of action to care for the family while Mom was checked out. Plus, there had been things left unsaid between us that morning.

I threw on some sweats and an old pair of tennis shoes – seeing as how I'd lost the nice, new pair in the lake – and drove to the castle. The night was clear, the moon a bright sliver in the sky, but here on the ground the mist clung to everything. I shivered, feeling a sense of foreboding I found hard to ignore. I might not have intuition like Scott or the sheriff, but I did dream, even when I didn't remember those dreams. Some part of my subconscious did recall, and, I often thought, warned me of impending danger.

The castle was only about ten minutes from home. I parked in the front drive, stepped out of the car into the chilly night air, and took two steps toward the front door.

I heard it before I saw it – a low, guttural growl that seemed to come from everywhere at once. I sensed something to my right, near the corner of the house, by the north tower where my old bedroom had been.

I froze. Then, slowly, I turned. A pair of glowing red eyes peered at me through the mist, seemingly disembodied. But I had seen eyes exactly like that a couple of days ago, just before the hell hound had nearly killed Jim.

The sheriff had said he'd seen one around the castle, but somehow I hadn't believed it could be a danger to me. Not here, of all places, in my childhood home. Near my fortress of solitude – or what had once been my fortress of solitude before Elena had inherited the room and covered the jet-black décor with pure white.

The dog was that black – as black as my walls had been. I had the brief, insane notion that somehow the old paint had come to life in the form of a dog. Then the growling rose in volume and I backed slowly toward my car, praying the hound wouldn't attack. That I would be able to get inside before it moved.

The thing ran like the wind. If it wanted me, I didn't think I could stop it. The soft underbelly was its weakness, according to Henry Wolf, but if I could get to the soft underbelly then I would be between the monster's massive paws, probably crushed in its jaws.

"Nice dog," I whispered. I'd only taken two steps away from the car, hadn't I? It seemed to be taking more steps than that to get back. "Good dog. I'm just leaving."

I found the door handle and lifted. It was locked. I fumbled in my pocket for the keys, unlocking the door with a loud chirp that echoed through the night.

The beast lunged. I screamed. Yanking up on the door handle, I threw myself inside, but the beast wedged its head into the gap before I could slam the door shut.

Teeth sharp as knives pierced my left arm, just above the wrist. Pain slashed through me, radiating in waves to every part of my being.

"Evan!" I cried. And then, suddenly, I remembered someone else who might help. Who might even be able to see from far away. "Christina!"

Without warning, the jaw clamped around my arm let go and the hell hound disappeared as quickly as it had appeared.

I sat there for some time, too stunned to move, or even close the car door. What if it came back? What if I provoked it?

It was the pain that snapped me out of my terror. I think maybe the adrenaline rush kept me from feeling its full effects at first, but suddenly it was there, and when I looked down I saw blood streaming from multiple puncture wounds along my arm, dripping and beginning to pool in the narrow space between my seat and the car door.

I felt dizzy. Weak. Juliana could help in about a second, but I couldn't bring myself to get out of the car. What if that thing came back? What if this was just a warning?

I had no business driving home right now. I might black out at any moment from the pain or blood loss. But if I stayed here, frozen in indecision, I could die.

I had to use my right arm to close the car door because the left simply refused. Then, without pausing to fasten my seat belt for the second time in three days, I floored the accelerator and tried to breathe through the pain as I traveled the familiar road toward home. Toward Evan.

I more than half expected him to be outside waiting for me when I pulled into our driveway, but he wasn't. He couldn't read minds, or hear my long-distance call, not unless we arranged some kind of signal in advance. Spelled crystals had saved my life more than once, but I hadn't even thought about them when I'd gone out tonight. How could I have known that a drive to my childhood home would put me in such danger?

I had to kick open the car door and when I stood, I fell back to lean heavily against the side. It took a supreme effort of will to pull myself back off the car, stagger up the front steps, and stumble into the house.

And there he was. At the top of the curved staircase, looking down at me, blinking sleep out of his eyes. Evan.

"Help," I said, sounding small even to myself.

He was there so fast I knew he'd flown down the stairs. He could do that for short distances, levitate himself off the ground.

"I've got you," he said, then began muttering the incantation that would put me into a deep, healing sleep.

೮೦೧೮

"You get yourself in more trouble than anyone has a right to survive."

I blinked my eyes open and stared at Evan, leaning over me. Morning sunlight framed his face, making him look like he wore a halo, but he was no angel.

"Good morning," I mumbled.

"That's all you have to say for yourself? You ran off last night without even telling me you were leaving, or where you were going, and clearly it was someplace dangerous because you got your arm half chewed off!"

I winced. He was mad at me again. Or still. Probably still.

"I don't need your permission to drive over to my mom's."

The sunlight kept me from seeing his face, but I could almost feel a shift in his mood at those words.

"You went to your mom's house?"

"Yeah. Just to my mom's house. Thought I'd be gone less than an hour. Hell hound attacked."

"The sheriff said there was a hell hound around the castle. I didn't take it seriously."

At least I hadn't been the only one. I closed my eyes and felt for my left arm, where the thing had sliced its razor-sharp teeth into my flesh. The skin felt whole and unhurt, if a bit more tender than usual.

"Are you feeling all right?" Evan asked.

"Hungry," I said. "But you knew that, because I smell bacon."

"Sit up. I'll bring the tray over."

I propped myself up on some pillows while Evan floated a breakfast tray from the dresser to the bed, nestling it across my lap. He'd made bacon, eggs, pancakes, and orange juice. All my favorites.

Maybe he wasn't as mad as I'd thought. Maybe we could still fix this by tonight, so we could have Abigail. But then I'd lose Henry...

"Where's Ana?" I glanced at the clock on my nightstand. It was almost eight o'clock.

"She's fine. Kaitlin took her early so you could sleep in and recover."

"I didn't nurse her." I always nursed her in the morning.

"She did protest a bit, but she's fine. She can miss a morning."

"You're not going to make me stay in bed all day, are you?" I stabbed a forkful of pancake, trying to ignore the heavy, full feeling in my breasts.

"I doubt I could."

I arched an eyebrow, my mouth too full of pancakes to counter that obviously false statement. He could *definitely* make me stay.

"Okay, I could, but I don't have time to stay with you and I think we'd both prefer I not use sheer brute force."

"Where are you going?"

"Scott and I are going to McClellan's to see if we can turn anything up."

I'd almost forgotten about the fairy, with everything else going on. "I thought you'd need more evidence before breaking into a powerful sorcerer's shop."

"We're not breaking in, just looking around. Scott's going invisible and I'm handling the distraction."

I took another bite of pancake and chewed slowly, thinking. "Evan, do you feel like something big is going on?"

"Yes. Why do you think I'm going to McClellan's with so little evidence?"

"Is it possible it really is a fairy? I mean, hell hounds are real."

Evan sat heavily on the edge of the bed and stared out the window. "Who knows? It's like you said, something big is happening. I think I've been feeling it for a while, but I let myself ignore the warning signs until it was too late."

"Too late?"

"Two people are dead."

"That's not your fault!"

"Isn't it? If I'd paid half as much attention to the mist and the misery as the sheriff had, maybe I'd have figured things out months ago and we could have avoided this mess." Evan shook his head. "I'm the sorcerer, not him."

"You've been out of town a lot, and working hard when you're home. I should have taken it more seriously when the sheriff asked me about the mist. Or maybe I should have dreamed. I …" I trailed off, remembering the reason I'd left the house in the middle of the night to begin with.

"What?" Evan asked, a hard edge to his voice.

"Nothing. Just a — a bad dream."

Evan looked up at the dream catcher hanging over the bed. "A bad dream?"

"A good dream, but with horrific implications." I shook my head.

"You want to tell me about it?"

Again, I shook my head.

"Why did you leave the house in the middle of the night anyway?"

"I was going to talk to Juliana about it."

"Really?" That hard edge was back.

"Yeah. Really." I stared at the half-eaten food in front of me, but found my appetite gone.

"You went two miles down the road to talk to someone about a bad dream?"

"You were in another room."

"I was closer than two miles."

"Yeah, well, it felt much further." I pushed the tray away. "I need to get dressed. I should call the sheriff, tell him what happened, and find out if they found the Bakers."

"You're going to finish breakfast. You lost a lot of energy healing last night."

"I'll eat later."

"Why are you mad at me?" He stood, and for a second I thought he was going to force the tray back onto my lap, but he lifted it and carried it to the dresser. "I'm not the one who destroyed an ecosystem yesterday."

I winced. What was I supposed to say to that? I'd already apologized, and I'd be damned if I was doing it again.

Pushing the covers aside, I got out of bed, noticing for the first time that the sheets on Evan's side of the bed were untouched. Even after I'd come home bloody, he still hadn't slept the rest of the night with me. He'd pushed me away, and now he wondered why I was angry? He was barely even speaking to me, certainly not about anything important.

"You're taking a crystal with you today, wherever you go," Evan said.

"Fine."

"And you'll use it, if you even think there might be danger."

I bristled. I hated being told what to do at the best of times, and these weren't the best of times. I bit back a retort I was sure we would both regret later – barely. I tried to remember that he was scared and trying to protect me, but I mostly felt a surge of resentment.

How dare he treat me as an inferior? How dare he treat me as if I were a disobedient child? How dare he condemn me for an accident? It wasn't my fault!

"Cassie, will you use it?"

I stared at him, at his shoulder-length hair, his chiseled face, his blue eyes. I loved him, but also, right at that moment, I hated him too. It was the first time I'd felt that way since we'd been married.

Our daughter was doomed. And at this rate, so was our son.

Chapter 13

THE SHERIFF WAS STILL LOOKING FOR THE BAKERS WHILE HIS DEPUTIES looked for evidence of anyone in Nadine or Jared's life who might have wanted to hurt them. Or even anyone who might have been connected to magic. I decided to consult over the phone that morning because I still felt weak and magical healing saps a great deal of strength – unless Juliana does it. Her gift is truly miraculous.

By lunchtime I felt frustrated and restless, and I wanted to see Ana. So I headed to Matthew and Kaitlin's home, hoping to catch my friend alone this time.

I got my wish. Matthew had gone out to inspect possible office space for the headquarters of the White Guard. The organization had been too big to run out of his living room for some time but tradition, coupled with a desire for the movement not to turn into the Magical Underground's evil twin, had kept us in this smaller, more intimate environment.

The living room was now crawling with babies – mine, Kaitlin's, and the twins.

Ana crawled over to me the second I came through the door. "Ma!"

I picked her up and she tried to lift my shirt.

"Hey, easy there." I glanced quickly at Kaitlin, wondering if I should nurse in front of her, then decided Ana's needs were more important. I settled onto a recliner, grabbed a blanket, and then struggled for a moment to convince Ana to keep it over her head.

"Evan said you were hurt." Kaitlin went through to the kitchen, separated from the living room area by a long bar. She was also mostly behind me, at an angle where she couldn't see Ana nursing.

I gave up the blanket fight.

"I'm fine," I said, angling my head so I could see her. "He healed me."

"I figured." She began pulling out sandwich fixings, attracting the attention of her own son, who rushed to her side to beg for a piece of the cheese she'd pulled out. She was so distracted, it took her a moment to ask the burning question. "What happened?"

"A hell hound seems to have taken up residence outside the castle."

"It attacked?" Kaitlin paused to stare at me.

"You seem more surprised that it attacked than that it was there."

"Well, yeah. I mean, after what you said yesterday over dinner, I figured you thought the hell hounds were guardians."

"That's one theory, but who was Jim threatening when he was attacked? And who was I threatening last night?"

"Fair questions." Kaitlin returned to the refrigerator for some milk and began pouring glasses. "Another would be: How did you survive?"

"It backed off." I closed my eyes. "I'd yelled for Evan, kind of stupidly, and then I remembered Christina has farsight and I called for her. That's when it backed off."

"Do you think it's Christina's guardian?"

I shuddered to think so. Christina was a powerful sorcerer, daughter and sister of powerful sorcerers. She didn't need a guardian from hell; she had plenty of magic to protect her.

Or did she?

Ana popped up suddenly and I busied myself settling her onto my other breast for a moment. When she was comfortable, I stared at Michael and Maya, who were watching a cartoon on TV. They seemed to be floating on a sea of toys, likely thanks to Maya's summoning gift. If she could see something, she could make it come to her. It wasn't a sinister gift, but it could be a nuisance. I thought Juliana had been binding it too, along with Michael's more dangerous fire-starting ability.

They sat so close their arms, legs, and hands touched. It might have been a cute portrait, if it had been a snapshot. But sitting there watching them stay like that, barely moving for an extended period of time was a bit… well, I didn't want to say my brother and sister were creepy but I was struggling to think of another word.

Maya's eyes were closed. That was strange. Michael was staring avidly at the TV, but Maya could have been sleeping.

My presence meant nothing to either of them. It hurt, especially when I thought of how Adam used to cling to me when I returned from school or work. As the oldest, I'd been the role model, the support, the babysitter. Before Dad had died and Mom had checked out, they'd been the parents, but I'd been something of a caregiver too, for as long as I could remember.

Not to these two. They barely even knew me.

Ana popped fully upright and smiled at me, breaking my reverie. I smiled back and righted myself, then put her on the floor with the twins while I went to help Kaitlin finish putting lunch together.

I continued to watch the kids as I worked. Kaitlin let me, giving me the time to think and observe as if she knew what I needed. We had been that in-tune with one another once, but not lately.

Ana crawled to Maya, over the pile of toys, and sat next to her, watching her aunt rather than the TV. When Maya continued to act as if Ana weren't there, Ana began picking up toys and offering them to her, one at a time. Maya didn't look, didn't even turn her head in acknowledgment. Ana tapped her with a glow worm and Maya clung more tightly to Michael, who made a sort of angry grunting sound. Ana looked at me and seemed to be asking what to do next. I shrugged, as lost as she was.

"Lunchtime," Kaitlin called as she began carrying plates into the dining room two at a time. I took two as well, then returned for the adult plates, which were about the same size as Jay's.

Jay climbed right into his booster seat and I felt certain that if he were tall enough, he wouldn't need any help sitting at the table at all. He dug into his lunch with gusto, not waiting for the others to arrive.

Ana didn't immediately go to the dining room, but that wasn't surprising. She'd just nursed, and probably wasn't very hungry. She mostly played with her food, even now that she'd turned one. I knew that would change soon and that one day, I'd be caught completely unaware when she became wholly self-sufficient. I picked her up and carried her to a highchair, settling her in with Kaitlin's offerings – a deconstructed sandwich with crackers rather than bread, finely chopped chicken, cheese, and banana.

Michael stood when I returned for him, a bit awkwardly as Maya clung to his side. I hesitated, then reached down to scoop Maya into

my arms, figuring Michael looked more capable of walking on his
own.

She screamed the second she was parted from her brother. Michael
didn't cry, but he looked at me as if I'd betrayed him somehow.

"It's okay," I crooned, swinging Maya slightly as I walked her to the
table and set her in one of the booster seats. "Michael's coming right
over."

"Good luck with that," Kaitlin muttered.

"What do you mean?"

Michael crossed to the dining room on his own, his steps confident
but far more toddler-like than Jay's, despite being a few months older.
He had trouble getting into his booster seat, so I lifted him and tried
to help him settle in, but he continued to struggle.

"What's wrong?" I asked, not sure if I was talking to Michael or
Kaitlin.

"Scoot their chairs closer," Kaitlin advised.

I hesitated, then did as she suggested, butting Michael's chair right
up against Maya's so they were close enough to reach out and grasp
hands. They found one another unerringly, and Maya instantly settled
down.

"Juliana said it's getting worse." I was talking more to myself than
to Kaitlin.

"I don't know. All I know is if I separate them for a second, even to
change a diaper, I get tears. It's weird. I have no idea how they're going
to manage potty training."

"They were like that at the party too," I said. "Juliana had to hold
them together."

I took a seat between Maya and Ana and began to eat, though I
was paying far more attention to my brother and sister than my food.

They had disassembled sandwiches too, though Kaitlin had given
them slices of bread and bigger chunks of chicken than she'd given
Ana. Michael ate fairly well with his free left hand, but Maya struggled somewhat with her free right hand until Michael glanced her
way and some silent communication seemed to pass between them.

I shivered.

"They don't talk," Kaitlin said. "But they seem to understand each other."

"Juliana said they seem to have some secret twin language." I shook my head. I wasn't going to solve the mystery of Michael and Maya this afternoon. Besides, I had bigger mysteries to solve.

"Thanks for watching Ana today," I said. "I'm not sure how late I'll be. Will it be a problem keeping her late?"

"Nah. She and Jay play well together. Well, not exactly together. More next to one another."

I nodded. That sounded about right for kids their age, although I supposed Kaitlin, as an only child, wasn't as aware of these things.

"So," Kaitlin continued, "are you planning to tell me what you were doing at your mom's place in the middle of the night? You came over to talk about something."

I sighed and tried to decide if Kaitlin would make a good confidante. I trusted her completely, but she didn't understand magic very well, not even after having a magical son, running off with a vampire, and now dating a telepath. Would she understand that the dreams weren't really dreams?

Would anyone? It suddenly struck me that Evan might not entirely understand either. So I'd seen two possible futures and met two possible kids. Seers and dreamers must have been doing the same for centuries.

If only the town's two ancient seers hadn't both decided to die a couple of years ago, I could have asked them. I might even have risked going to Grace Blair, Matthew's grandmother, whose power-hungry ambition had ruled her family and threatened me personally.

"I'm practicing dreaming again," I began, deciding I needed to talk to someone before I exploded.

"That's good. Matthew's been asking about it."

I flinched. I owed Matthew ten years' worth of visions unless I learned to master my powers, in which case he'd knock it down to two. So far, he definitely couldn't think he was getting his money's worth.

Not remembering my dreams was my biggest problem, and it was purely psychological. I knew that. Everyone told me so. Matthew had offered to pair me up with one of his cousins, an empathic healer, but I'd refused for the same reason I had hesitated to have an empathic healer work with my mom. I wondered, briefly, if he was talking about the same person.

I should, at least, get an empathic healer to work with my mom.

"Anyway, I'm using the dream catcher so I'm only seeing the good futures, the happy times." I paused, but Kaitlin didn't add anything as I'd half expected her to do. Maybe berate me for using a dream catcher as a crutch? "So I saw the daughter Evan and I will conceive tonight."

"Tonight?" He face broke into a wide grin and she winked at me. "Oh, that's amazing. What's she like?"

I told her. I found myself reliving the memories and the moments I'd dreamed as I brought Abigail to life once again, though she'd always been alive in my heart.

"So what's the problem?" Kaitlin asked.

"Evan and I are fighting."

"Oh, well, you'll just have to make up."

"But if I do that, or at least, if I do it too quickly, I'll lose the son I dreamed about last night."

Kaitlin's mouth opened slightly, then she closed it again. Since she didn't seem able to talk, I filled in the silence, telling her all about Little Henry and the moments of his life I'd seen in my dream. Trying to show her in words, terrible, inadequate words, that for me at least, he was real.

"You could always have two more kids," Kaitlin said.

I shook my head. She didn't understand. "I can't have these two kids, not both of them. I think… there's something behind the nightmare shroud that's not coming through, but I know what it is. There are probably billions of unique babies Evan and I could have. Can you imagine? Twenty-three chromosome pairs from each of us. Do you even know how to do the math on that?"

Kaitlin shook her head. "Madison might."

She might; she'd minored in math and more importantly, she was brilliant. But I didn't really want to know. The number wouldn't make a difference. It could be a million or a billion or even more, and it would be just as unfathomable.

"I can have two kids. I can even name them Abigail and Henry. But it won't be the Abigail and Henry I dreamed about. Not both of them. It's not possible."

"Could they be twins?"

I shook my head; I'd never seen Abigail and Henry together, nor dreamed of having twins.

Jay finished eating and climbed down from his booster seat, racing back to the living room and making a racket I couldn't identify but which didn't alarm Kaitlin in the least. She took a sip of water and stared at me thoughtfully.

"What?" I asked.

"I don't know. I think – you only dreamed about them one night each. When you have the baby, you'll get to know that child. That's the one who'll be real. These two are just possible dream children."

She didn't understand, and I couldn't explain. They felt more real to me than dream children. And part of the problem – the big part – was that I knew how to make each of them. No matter what I did, I would be making a choice between two dramatically different children. I knew exactly the time and place and I even sensed, in both cases, that the position mattered. I felt my cheeks redden slightly at that last thought, which I didn't share with my friend.

"I didn't mean to make you mad," Kaitlin said, apparently misinterpreting my reddened cheeks.

"I'm not mad." It was true. I wasn't. I was just so frustrated. "But I have to choose. If I choose Abigail, I'll be saying, with my actions, that I'd rather have a girl, or an outgoing child, or a brilliant one. Or if I wait... I know Evan wants a boy. I do too. And Little Henry is so sweet and clever." I paused, struggling to find the point, to make her understand. "It's the choice itself."

"You could choose to have neither of them, refuse to make the choice."

My heart squeezed painfully in response to the suggestion. I almost wanted to lash out at her for making it, but I knew Abigail and Henry weren't real to her. She hadn't held them. She hadn't played princess monster truck rally with Abigail or taught Henry to shoot a bow. He'd become the junior state champion, just like me.

To distract myself, I glanced back at the twins. Michael had finished eating and was now watching Maya's tray intently. She held out her hand and summoned a grape from the tray; it disappeared from the tray and popped right into her closed fist.

"Maya?" I said.

Michael looked at me. Maya dropped the grape and let out a grunt of frustration. Michael rolled the grape back into her hand and she successfully got it into her mouth.

"Something's not right here." I still couldn't put my finger on what it was, but I thought maybe, "I think the problem is with Maya."

"Huh?" Kaitlin looked at me, then at Maya.

"Michael always seems to be helping her, not the other way around. He gets upset when they separate, but not as upset as she gets. I'm just not sure what the deal is."

What I didn't voice was my fear that whatever it was, Maya had something to do with the hell hounds. But what? Her summoning gift couldn't conjure a hell hound out of thin air; she could only call objects if she could see them. And where would she have seen a hell hound?

My phone vibrated and I reached into my pocket for it, almost gratefully. I didn't like my current train of thought.

"What's up, Sheriff?" I asked.

"The Bakers just used their credit card," he replied. "They're at a hotel up in St. Joseph. How soon can you and Evan start driving that way?"

"Very soon." I stood, even though I'd only eaten half my lunch. Evan was going to be upset with me for eating so poorly after a magical healing, but he was already upset. "Text me the address. We'll meet you there."

Chapter 14

ST. JOSEPH, MISSOURI WAS OVER FOUR HOURS AWAY FROM EAGLE ROCK. The prospect of spending so much time alone in a car with Evan just now was almost enough to make me ask to ride with the sheriff, but something told me that request would have put more distance between us.

I hated fighting with Evan. It rarely happened, and when it did, it was usually over little things. This was different. It wasn't anything like the turmoil that had preceded our marriage, when we'd both discovered the truth about what had happened to the magic that should have been my birthright but which, instead, made Evan more powerful than any one man had a right to be. Still, it was bad. And it struck me, as we began the long drive in silence, that I didn't even know how to begin getting past it.

Evan broke the silence. "Scott saw the fairy."

"There is a fairy? A real fairy?" I sat upright and stared at his profile; his eyes were glued to the road.

"I didn't see it. I was the distraction, remember?"

"Yeah, but what did Scott say?"

"He said he'd never seen anything like it. That it wasn't human, whatever it was, and he wasn't even sure if it was humanoid. It was moving so fast, he could only see a flicker of light before he had to back away."

"Did Cormack catch him?"

"No, he got away, but he tripped a ward. Cormack was already suspicious by then; it's not like I usually shop there."

I shook my head. No, Evan didn't buy dark artifacts. He had never used his power to seek more power, which was one of the things I loved about him. He'd even offered to give some of his power up, which made me love him more. That hadn't been an easy offer to make; the magic defined him, was part of him.

"What did you say to him?" I asked.

Evan hesitated. "I told him I needed more power than I had available to clean up your mess."

I froze. I felt as if he'd reached inside my chest and yanked my heart out. A moment ago, I'd remembered the reasons I loved him. Now, I could only think of the things that annoyed me or even angered me.

Arrogant. Controlling. Determined to get his way in all things.

"Everyone's heard about it by now," Evan continued. "Matthew called this morning to set up an emergency meeting about the problem. There are reports of dead fish up and down the entire lake, even into Arkansas, and other reports of mutations."

"No one's talked to me about it," I whispered.

"No one wanted to upset you."

"Glad you don't have that problem."

"Cassie." Evan sighed. "This isn't just about you."

"I know." I stared out the window, deciding that I needed not to be able to see him right now.

"Let me teach you," he said softly. "You're still channeling a lot of magic."

"Ana's a prodigy, all right."

"That's not the point."

I shook my head and continued to stare out the window, not speaking.

"Cassie, you know just enough about magic to be dangerous, especially if you ever got into another situation that threatened you or someone you love. We both know you'd use it again."

I tensed. I didn't want to admit he was probably right.

"If you were someone else," Evan continued, "if you were Madison or Kaitlin, I wouldn't worry so much because they never got much past grounding. You're different. You spent most of your life learning magic over your siblings' shoulders, hearing the theory of how to work powerful forces without the ability to practice. Now, you've got magic running through your veins and half-remembered theories through your head."

"You could bind it," I said, my voice shaking slightly. My gaze was still fixed out the window, but I was having trouble seeing through a haze of tears. And didn't that just make me a hypocrite? I didn't want to use the magic, but I didn't want to give it up either. I guess I'd wanted it for too long.

"You know I can't do that," Evan said, his voice harder. "It's not your power. I'd have to bind Ana's."

I shrugged. "The twins' power is being bound. It happens. Sometimes young kids can't handle their magic and it gets tucked away until they're older."

"Ana's not having trouble handling her magic. *You* are."

I closed my eyes, fighting back tears. Damn, I really was becoming my mother. In one stupid, selfish request, I'd managed to prove my worst fears. Excuses came to me – rationalizations. Binding Ana's magic, losing my access to it, might even help me dream. Abigail Hastings, during our brief mentoring relationship, had told me that there was no such thing as a seer-sorcerer. I'd never asked her what happened when seers had magical babies, but sometimes I wondered if that was my problem, rather than lack of confidence or other psychological problems. There were too many things I'd never gotten the chance to ask.

"Let me teach you," Evan said again. "This isn't going away anytime soon."

"Unless I decided not to have more children." I regretted saying the words the instant they were out. I didn't mean them; I knew they'd hurt him. "I'm sorry," I said, trying to backpedal. "You know I want more kids."

Evan didn't answer for a long time and I resisted the urge to turn and look at him, to try to read the expression on his face. I didn't want to see the anger.

The worst thing about this fight was that Evan was mostly right and I was mostly wrong. That made it much, much harder to move past.

"I know what the real problem is," Evan said.

"What's that?"

"The magic you're channeling now – it ends. Whether we have one more or ten, it ends. Now or in twenty years."

"Yeah." And more than that, I didn't want to make the choice my mom had made to prolong it to twenty years, at least not for the same reasons.

"It doesn't have to end."

"Huh?" I wiped my eyes on the back of my sleeve in case I decided to face him, but I didn't turn around.

"I saw the book in your car," Evan said, his voice barely audible.

"What book?"

"*Magical Transference*. I saw it there this morning, when I went to clean the blood. It was in the backseat."

I groaned. It wasn't his copy; it was Mom's. I'd never brought it inside.

"If you... if you still want ..." He drew in a deep breath and I finally turned my head. His expression was odd. Pained. Twisted. Raw. I'd rarely seen anything like it.

"It's not what you think," I said.

He glanced my way, then lifted one hand from the steering wheel to wipe a stray tear from my cheek. The moment shimmered between us, then he dropped his hand and left me feeling hollow again.

"Mom had it," I explained. "When I went to see her yesterday, she was reading it in the library. I don't know what she was thinking; she was drunk and didn't say much about it, but I took it away."

"Oh." He let out a long sigh and visibly relaxed, the tension leaving his face like a tsunami retreating back into the ocean.

"The sheriff asked if some kind of psychic vampire might be hurting her," I blurted.

"I've never heard of one."

"Me neither. But I've never heard of hell hounds. Or fairies. Things are changing, and I'm starting to think I know a lot less than I thought I did."

"You're changing the subject," Evan said, and I sensed the ocean crashing back into shore again.

"What was the subject?"

"Magic. You still want it. I keep wondering if I let the whole thing drop too easily two years ago, when I offered and you refused. I guess I was too relieved to question it."

I shook my head. I really didn't want to have this conversation again, especially not now, when I was feeling so raw.

"I mean, that's the problem, isn't it?" Evan asked. "You don't want to learn to use magic because it's temporary. When Ana finishes nursing… there might be another child, and another, but it does end."

"Mom kept having kids for the wrong reason," I said, voicing my real fear. "She doesn't even want Michael and Maya. She doesn't take care of them. They have to take care of each other, and they're two!"

"We can take care of them, if we have to."

I hadn't quite decided if it was that bad yet, but I was close. I needed to sit down with Juliana, then maybe some of the others in turn. Find out what things were really like at the castle.

"And I don't care what you think," Evan continued, "you're not your mother."

"My mother isn't my mother lately." I shook my head. "She fell apart when Dad died, and vampires had nothing to do with it." Left unsaid was my fear that the same thing could happen to me, if I lost Evan. Loss like that changed a person.

"All right, let's talk about something else." Evan paused for a moment, as if searching for a topic, then switched on the radio instead.

We passed the rest of the trip in relative silence, listening to music and making only the most superficial of comments. I thought about Abigail, the daughter of my heart and of my dreams, and the fact that tonight was the night – if I chose her. If I rejected Henry. If we could put this fight behind us. It was, in the end, a very long trip.

৩৩০৪৩

It was dark by the time we reached the shabby motel in St. Joseph. The sheriff pulled into the parking lot ahead of us, then double parked his SUV behind a couple of sedans. Evan followed suit, stopping just behind the sheriff.

We all got out and met between the two cars. The sheriff eyed the row of motel rooms, his gaze shifting to the small office at one end.

"I'm going to find out which room they're in," he said.

"Do we really want to go in at night?" I asked, glancing around nervously and half expecting to see another hell hound.

"I don't want to lose them," the sheriff said. "I can't guarantee they're here; I only know they used their credit card here around noon and we got a report they used it at a nearby restaurant too."

I glanced at Evan, wondering how he felt about the failure of magic to outdo good old-fashioned police work on this. His face was expressionless, much as it had been since we started listening to the radio several hours before.

"Any magic?" I asked.

He shook his head, slowly. "Nothing yet. That could change."

"Wait here." Sheriff Adams strode to the office, leaving us to wait in more uncomfortable silence.

"We need to talk about last night," Evan said after a minute or so.

"Why?"

He made a sound halfway between a snort and a sigh. "Come on, Cassie. What were you even doing there? And what was the hell hound doing there? You've got a theory; I can tell."

"It left when I called Christina's name."

"Do you think it was protecting her?"

The sheriff chose that moment to step out of the office, sparing me the need to answer. He strode toward us purposefully, his face set and hard. He held up both hands, with two fingers raised on the right and three on the left. Twenty-three.

I found the number near the end of the row and began walking that way, Evan right by my side. The sheriff beat us to it by seconds, then pounded on the door.

"Open up. Sheriff's Department!"

There was noise from within, a muffled sort of thumping, then silence.

The sheriff pounded on the door again. "Mr. and Mrs. Baker, I know you're in there. We just need to talk."

The door opened a crack and brown eyes peered out, just above the chain, which remained latched.

"Mr. Baker?" Sheriff Adams asked.

"We haven't done anything wrong," he said. "Go away."

"Then why did you run?" the sheriff asked.

"We didn't run. We're on vacation."

The sheriff arched his eyebrows. "You decided to head north in December to scenic St. Joseph, Missouri?"

"We have family here."

"I doubt it. Please let us in, or I'll have to arrest you for obstruction of justice." The sheriff's face was completely emotionless; I couldn't tell if he was bluffing.

Neither, apparently, could Mr. Baker because he closed the door just long enough for him to slide the chain loose and then open the door fully.

Mr. Baker was only a few years older than me, with dark brown hair and skin that maintained a golden tan even in December – probably because he spent so much time on the lake. He had a strong face that would have been handsome had his eyes not been narrowed in suspicion. He caught sight of me, then his gaze slid past me to Evan, standing just behind me. His face paled.

"What's he doing here? I don't have to talk to him. Just the sheriff. You two wait outside."

"They're consultants," the sheriff said, "and their viewpoint is invaluable."

"I know what he is." Mr. Baker didn't point at Evan; he didn't even look at him, but we all knew who he meant. "I won't talk to him."

"What about Cassie?" Sheriff Adams asked.

I tried hard to look nonthreatening. I'm not sure if I succeeded.

Mr. Baker drew in a deep, rattling breath, looked over his shoulder at something I couldn't see, then turned back, nodding. "Yeah. All right. She can come."

"If it starts to get cold in there," Evan whispered, "or you get nervous at all, just activate the crystal."

I nodded, feeling the reassuring weight of the purplish gemstone in my pocket. Then I followed Sheriff Adams through the doorway and into the dingy motel room.

I'd never spent a lot of time in rented rooms – traveling was one thing I hadn't had much of a chance to do. The few times I had gone out of town I'd spent the night in a nice hotel room. Nothing like this, which was well outside of my experience. I'd seen something like it in movies, but movies can't capture the dampness or the scent of mold.

Two double beds took up most of the space in the room, one with the sheets tossed, the other still made up in a threadbare orange comforter. A rickety table and single chair were crammed in near the window, where a heating unit rattled and hummed like it was on its last legs. A tiny flat-panel TV rested atop a dresser across from the beds, currently alive with the tones of SpongeBob SquarePants.

A small child – Haley, I presumed, sat amid the strewn covers on the bed furthest from the door, half hiding behind the sheets and her mom. I mostly had an impression of dark hair and a brown stuffed animal.

Mrs. Baker stared at me when I came in and I realized with a jolt that I knew her – not as Mrs. Baker but as Sydney Spencer, a member of my high school graduating class. We hadn't hung out in the same circles – I was a cheerleader and she was in basketball, I think – but we'd had some classes together and she'd seemed friendly enough.

"Sydney," I said.

"Cassie," she replied.

"Look, we're really sorry about Nadine and Jared." Mr. Baker went to stand next to his wife, as if he could shield her and his daughter from our view. "Really, really sorry. But we didn't have anything to do with it."

"Is there any magic in your family?" I asked, bluntly.

"No!" Sydney cried before her husband could speak for her. He glanced at her, but she didn't seem to see. "My family's not even from Eagle Rock. My parents moved to the area during the tourism boom. And Shawn moved here five years ago."

"You don't have to say anything," Shawn told his wife. "This is a fishing expedition. They don't have anything."

"We have two dead people and nearly two others," Sheriff Adams said.

"What do you mean, nearly two others?" Shawn asked.

"Someone tried to freeze us out on our way to talk to you. We barely escaped, then found you had vanished. Why?"

"I told you. We're on vacation."

Shawn and the sheriff weren't backing down, and this conversation was getting us nowhere. The Bakers were definitely hiding something, but what? Had little Haley caused the cold and the mist?

Her small head peeked out of the sheets and I caught sight of two wide, frightened eyes that looked just like her father's, even down to the emotions swirling within them.

The hairs at the back of my neck prickled. I felt something – it reminded me of last night, when I'd felt that hint of danger just before the hell hound attacked.

It was dark outside, once again. But we weren't in Eagle Rock. So surely...

"Where were you on Saturday?" Sheriff Adams asked.

"We were... we were taking some tourists out on a charter fishing trip." Shawn didn't look the sheriff in the eyes; he was a terrible liar, although I believed him about being on a boat.

"So where was Haley?" Sheriff Adams asked.

"With us on the boat," Sydney said, speaking for her husband. She was a much better liar, but it didn't make sense. They wouldn't have wanted a three-year-old on a charter trip with fishermen and Nadine would have been happy to watch their daughter – she'd needed the money, after all.

"Someone can corroborate that?" Sheriff Adams asked.

I glanced at the door, trying to figure out what was triggering my feelings of alarm. If only Evan were here. I felt for the crystal in my pocket, taking comfort in the reassuring bulge, but did not activate it. The second I did that, Evan would break the door down and our conversation would be over.

I drew in a deep breath, then wished I hadn't. The mildew was a bit overpowering, as was another scent... rotten eggs.

"Um, Sheriff," I said.

"What?" he snapped.

"Do you smell something?"

But before he had a chance to answer, I saw something too. The room was growing hazy with mist, partially obscuring the faces of the Baker family and fully obscuring the terrified eyes of little Haley Baker.

Chapter 15

"IT'S HER," SHERIFF ADAMS SAID.

"Get out!" came a frightened, little girl cry. "Go away! Go away!" The fog thickened and I shivered.

"Mrs. Baker," Sheriff Adams said, his voice pleading, "calm your daughter down before someone gets hurt."

"How can I, with you standing in the room?" Sydney's face was clouded over with mist by now, but the wringing of her hands gave me a clue to how she felt.

I backed up to the door and opened it, deciding against using the crystal. If I did that, Evan would probably blast the door apart and frighten the child more. But I needed him, and he was standing right outside, staring at me as if he'd been looking in through the door. X-ray vision wasn't something he knew how to accomplish, as far as I knew.

Fog escaped from the room through the open doorway and I coughed. I have no idea what I looked like to Evan, but before I had a chance to speak he was striding forward, yanking me outside, and taking my place within the room.

"Please," Sheriff Adams was saying. "This precedes the cold."

"It wasn't Haley!" Sydney wailed.

I couldn't see anything in the room now, but I could hear just fine. Someone was crying – probably Haley. The sheriff and Shawn started yelling so loudly I couldn't understand what they were saying. And underneath it all came the low tones of Evan chanting.

I held my breath and watched. For a minute or so, the fog continued to thicken and roll out the door. I tried to imagine how long it had taken Haley to produce enough fog to cover a square mile by the lake, or how scared she must have been to do it.

Then, suddenly, the fog dissipated. The rotten egg smell lingered, but was already far less potent. Evan stood between the sheriff and the Bakers, arms raised in what probably looked like a threatening gesture.

Sydney screamed.

Evan lowered his arms. "I was just dispelling the fog. It's okay."

"Haley didn't do anything. She wouldn't hurt anyone." Shawn's voice sounded weak now, almost hollow.

"I don't think she did anything on purpose," Evan said gently, "but she can't control her gift and neither of you can help her with it, can you?"

Sydney flung herself on her daughter, as though planning to use her body as a shield for whatever Evan had planned.

"A binding won't hurt her; it will protect her and everyone else." Evan said.

The Bakers weren't listening, though. They just kept sobbing that Haley was innocent, that she hadn't done anything. How they could be so blind in the face of overwhelming evidence baffled me. I mean, it had hurt to think for even a second that the twins might be involved, but I would have accepted it if it had come to that. These two weren't even willing to listen, to entertain the slightest possibility. Yet they had run, so they had to have suspected something.

The hairs on the back of my neck still stood on end. I'd almost forgotten my earlier sense of foreboding, given the danger that had already passed. Now I stiffened and glanced from side to side, looking along the brightly lit row of little motel rooms.

There, at the furthest end from the office, a dark shape crouched in a pool of lamplight. I couldn't see its form from here, but I could see the twin red, glowing eyes.

"Evan!" I cried.

He whirled and came out the door without a backward glance, standing by my side within seconds. No question. No argument. I called him and there he was.

"Get to the car!" Evan called.

I didn't wait to be told twice, though I did shout for the sheriff over my shoulder. A moment later, I heard his footsteps pounding the concrete outside the motel room and we both sprinted for our vehicles – his slightly closer than mine so that we each reached our driver's doors at about the same time.

A low, menacing growl filled the night. Once again, I felt the piercing sensation in my skull that was becoming all-too familiar. Goosebumps erupted on my skin and I recalled the feeling of having my arm trapped in its jaw, of dozens of knives piercing my skin.

"Evan!" I got the car started then reached across to push open the passenger door so he could easily get inside.

The car in front of me – the sheriff's SUV – peeled out of the parking lot and I pulled forward, watching the tableau before me through the windshield.

Evan had both arms upraised and was staring at the hell hound, as if sheer force of will could hold the creature at bay.

I couldn't immediately see the hell hound. It had left the pool of lamplight and lunged forward so that it was now mere yards from Evan.

Sweat beaded his brow. He couldn't hold the thing for long; I could tell. He had trouble holding vampires too.

"Get in the car!" I yelled.

"Go!" he yelled back.

I was facing the wrong way. He had to go around the car to get to the passenger side. So I pulled forward, did a quick three-point turn in the grassy area at the end of the lot, then returned to Evan's side.

"Get in!" The door had closed slightly, but I reached out and pushed it open again.

He let out a noise like a war cry. His concentration broke as he flung himself into the car and slid inside just as the hell hound bashed itself against the car, rocking it onto two wheels. For the space of a heartbeat, I thought we would topple. Then the world righted itself and I peeled out.

"I told you to go!" Evan cried.

"Can we fight about this later?" I glanced in the rearview mirror, half expecting the hell hound to be following us. It wasn't; apparently it didn't have vampire speed.

"It could have killed you!" Evan was clearly not backing down.

"It could have killed you," I retorted. "Don't I get to save you every once in a while?"

He didn't answer. For a minute or so, I could hear only the sounds of his heavy breathing as he wrestled with whatever internal demons tormented him. Finally, he spoke. "Thanks."

"You're welcome." It was my turn to draw in a deep breath. "We still have to bind her powers."

Evan nodded. "We could do it tomorrow. The hell hound only comes out at night."

"I doubt they'll stay at the motel; we'll have to hope they use their credit card again."

"Or we can use this." He held up a hand and I saw, pinched between his thumb and forefinger, a lock of dark hair.

"How did you get that?" I asked.

He lifted his eyebrows in an *isn't it obvious* sort of way.

"Right," I said. "But there's a more important question: When did you get it?"

"A split second before the hell hound attacked."

"That's what I thought. Evan, you do realize that we have bigger problems than one overpowered little girl with a strange gift?"

"Yes. Which is why we have a White Guard meeting tomorrow night."

⍚⍥

We spent the night in a hotel just outside Kansas City – close to the interstate in case we needed to get moving in a hurry. The sheriff wanted to return to the motel in St. Joseph and stand guard all night, but I talked him out of it. There was a hell hound ready to attack anyone who got too close – and the parking lot could easily be considered too close. So could the convenience store across the street.

"It could attack a civilian," Sheriff Adams argued.

"I don't think it will. I haven't entirely figured it out, but I don't think it attacks at random."

"We'll lose the Bakers. You know they'll run."

"Evan can track them," I assured him.

That ended the argument. He took rooms in the same hotel, but on a different floor, and we agreed to meet downstairs at sunrise.

There was very little comparison between the room the Bakers had rented and the suite Evan reserved for the night. It had a king-sized bed and living room area, separated by a half wall. While I unpacked our small overnight bag and called Kaitlin, Evan pushed the furniture aside to allow space for a casting circle.

"Of course we'll watch Ana tonight," Kaitlin said. "Will she be okay on a toddler bed? Jay can sleep with us."

I hesitated, torn between needs and wants. I needed to be here tonight, ready and able to track down and deal with the Bakers in the morning. I wanted to be with my daughter, especially if she was going to move into a big girl bed for the first time. She was one. She was ready. She could do it. I was the one having trouble.

"I've never left her overnight," I said aloud, even as the enormity of the fact struck me.

"She'll be fine. I promise. Moms can't always be there for their kids. It's not even good for them."

"I know. Maybe this would have been easier if I'd planned it. When I kissed her goodbye this afternoon, I told her I'd be back tonight."

"She'll be fine," Kaitlin repeated.

I wasn't entirely convinced, but I let Kaitlin go so she could finish fixing dinner. Evan was going to be a while, so I snuck out of the room and grabbed dinner for us as well – pasta and salad from a local place the hotel clerk recommended. Evan was just finishing his spell when I returned with food.

"Find anything?" I asked.

"They moved, but not far. They're actually closer to us than they were originally, about ten miles east. There are more hotels and motels in that area, so I think it's safe to assume they simply changed addresses."

"That's good. We can deal with this in the morning." I handed him a Styrofoam container full of pasta and watched him cringe as he took the non-biodegradable box from my hands.

"Were the Bakers telling the truth about their ancestry?" Evan asked, apparently choosing to let this relatively minor eco-disaster pass.

"I think so. I ran a background check this morning; I didn't get far before we had to come here, but I'm sure Sydney's family is new and Shawn moved to town five years ago. Of course, Eagle Rock isn't the only place in the world where magic exists. It's impossible to trace anyone's magical ancestry for sure, which is why you get magic users popping up in the most unlikely of places. The Magical Underground has a program to deal with that sort of thing."

"I bet that'll come up at the White Guard meeting tomorrow," Evan said thoughtfully. "Trouble is, despite our increasing numbers – ever since Matthew uncovered the truth about Alexander last summer – we still don't have the infrastructure to find and train random new magic users."

"They had trouble with it too, if I recall correctly." I thought back to the time I had spent with the Magical Underground in Pennsylvania. It had been an… educational time for me. But ultimately, not where I belonged, and that was before Alexander showed his true colors. "It was always more of an ideal than a reality. Unless you want to out magic completely and go around testing every preschooler across the country for gifts and talents, there's no way to track it."

Evan took a bite of his pasta and chewed thoughtfully. "We'll talk about it tomorrow. Right now, we just have one child to worry about."

I wasn't sure that was true, but I didn't say anything because there was nothing to say. Haley had proved herself capable of creating the mist and cold. And she had been with Nadine and Jared on the day they'd died. Still, something about the whole thing felt wrong. Or maybe not wrong, but… incomplete.

Haley's powers didn't explain the hell hounds, for one thing. Where had they come from? How? Why were they here? Were they protectors of children and if so, which children?

I thought of Michael and Maya as I had seen them that afternoon, strangely linked to one another but apart from the rest of the world. Their magic had slipped its bindings again.

Evan's magic used to slip its bindings, when he was a child, but that was because he had twice as much magic as he was supposed to and it kept leaking out all over the place. It had been a difficult childhood, because his parents had feared letting him be around other people.

Did Maya and Michael have that kind of power?

"What are you thinking?" Evan asked, drawing me to the present once again.

"I'm missing something. I don't know what, but it's right here... I can almost touch it."

"You could try dreaming."

I shuddered, remembering my recent dreams. The ones I hadn't shared with Evan.

"What was that?" he asked.

"Bad dreams."

"With a dream catcher?"

"Okay, good dreams with bad implications." I hesitated, but if I wanted to bring Abigail into the world, my deadline was tonight.

Was that what I wanted? What about Henry?

My heart began to pound as I glanced at the bed, then at Evan, then back at the bed. It wasn't the bed from my dream. Would that make a difference? Was it already too late for Abigail? For my clever, spirited girl who would take the world by storm?

I didn't know. I also didn't know if either Evan or I felt up to making her. I felt... raw. Not angry anymore, not exactly. Too much had happened and the danger of the hell hound attack had sharpened reality into a single focus for a while: life or death. But now that moment was gone, leaving behind the argument over what I had done and my refusal to learn to use the magic which currently pulsed weakly through my veins – I had only nursed Ana once today.

None of which was more important than Abigail, who *did* exist, whatever Kaitlin thought. She existed in my heart.

So did Little Henry.

"Cassie, what's going on?" Evan set his half-empty box of pasta aside on the desk and stood, crossing to the bed where I sat, not touching my own dinner. He hesitated, then took a seat next to me.

"If we don't have sex tonight, Abigail will never exist," I said.

"Oh." He withdrew slightly. "Um, well ..."

"Yeah, same here." I didn't need for him to stammer out a rejection. It would just humiliate me further. "Besides, if we do have sex tonight, Little Henry will never exist." And I explained about Henry.

"You know that neither one of them actually exists, right?" Evan said. "They're just possible futures, two of many yet to be written. We'll love whatever children come our way." He hesitated before adding, "and we can create them whenever it feels right. Not when it's a… I don't even know what this would be. A duty?"

He didn't understand either. Maybe no one ever would.

"I get it. Forget I said anything." I stood, not sure where I was going, but knowing I didn't want to be there.

"Cassie, look at me and tell me you want me right now."

I couldn't. We both knew it.

"I'm going downstairs to run on the treadmill for a while."

Evan grabbed my hand as I passed and I glanced at him. "I love you. That doesn't change, just because I'm mad at you."

"Yeah." But unfortunately he'd just said that he was, in fact, still mad at me. So that hadn't changed either. Which meant Abigail was as good as dead.

Chapter 16

I RAN FOR A FULL HOUR. TWO OTHER HOTEL GUESTS CAME AND LEFT THE tiny workout room during that time, the second taking one look at my face before backing away slowly and not returning – at least, not while I was there.

Sweat drenched my clothes, which weren't actually designed for working out – I hadn't packed that carefully. The blue jeans began to chafe badly, but still I kept running.

When I finally stopped and wiped the dampness from my face, I knew it wasn't all perspiration.

Evan had ducked out when I returned to the room, which meant I could sneak in and shower in peace. He didn't need to see my face right now; I didn't want pity sex anyway. But, as I glanced at my watch and saw the minutes ticking by, I sensed it was too late anyway. That my window had passed.

I flung myself into bed, hoping to be asleep before Evan returned, but he was back almost before my head hit the pillow.

"You're back," he said. "Did you have a good run?"

"Yeah."

"Okay." There was a moment of awkwardness during which time Evan crossed through the living room part of the suite and paused next to the bed. "Are you all right?"

"Yeah."

"Okay." He drew in a deep breath. "Do you think you'll be able to dream tonight?"

I bit my lip and thought, once again, of Abigail. She was lost to me forever, probably even lost to my dreams since she could no longer be. Maybe I would dream of Henry, or maybe yet another child I would have to play a game of life-or-death favorites with.

"I didn't bring my dream catcher," I muttered, frankly relieved at the oversight.

"I could cast the mind reading spell."

I shuddered. Not tonight. Not with the thoughts I'd been having about him lately. Luckily, I had a ready-made excuse to refuse.

"Mr. Wolf said that wasn't a good idea, that I had to learn to manip-ulate my own dreams."

"That's true. But after our talk earlier, I'd like to know anything I can."

"I'll try. I'll – I'll work on facing my nightmares like you and Matthew keep telling me."

He sat on the edge of the bed and rested a hand on my arm; I didn't pull away, but I was wary of the contact.

"I don't want you to have nightmares," he said, "but you're the best hope we have at figuring out what's going on."

Damn, but he did know how to push my buttons. "Yeah. I will try. I promise."

"I'll head downstairs for an hour or two so you can relax." Evan stood, but I clutched his hand.

"No, don't go."

"Are you sure?"

"Yeah, I'm sure."

He nodded and began stripping so he could join me in bed. I watched him, even as I fought to find the mental place that would guide me into dreaming.

He's right. You need to learn to do this. I pushed away my despair and resentment, focusing on what was at stake: More lives, if I didn't figure out what the hell hounds wanted and how to get rid of them.

All I had to do was face my nightmares – those from the distant past and the future. No big deal. Everyone had nightmares, right? I had to relax, focus, and accept.

The acceptance was the hard part. I'd spent my life relaxing and focusing as part of meditation, grounding, and centering. I continued to do that every day to siphon off excess magic. But acceptance was another matter. I had never been one to sit idly by and watch bad things happen. I tended to get involved, to work to change things.

Ironically, as a dreamer, if I could accept what I was seeing, I could do much more to change it. Still, acceptance felt too much like... surrender.

That night I was less relaxed and focused than I could remember being in a long time. I sensed, from my previous dreams, that something lurked on the horizon, waiting for me behind the nightmare shroud, but I didn't even know how to begin narrowing my focus to look for it.

Evan held me as I fought my way into sleep, neither of us talking or taking the simple contact further than what it was – a human connection. *You are not alone*, he was trying to tell me. And I knew he was doing his part to help me relax.

I tried. I really did. But relaxation doesn't respond well to brute force. Finally, I accepted that I was unlikely to remember anything tonight, and that I could at least use a good night's sleep.

I accepted…

The dream, what I could remember of it, wasn't a single dream. It was a series of images, feelings, and sounds. There was my mother crying – no, not my mother. Her twin sister crying over my mother's body. Mom was dead, but I couldn't see how. All I knew, somehow, was she'd taken her own life.

Flicker.

I saw another child, one conceived tomorrow night if Evan and I made love in the afternoon, at precisely the right moment. This was another little girl, but I refused to name her Abigail, even though Evan wanted me to. She was Belle, and she was never quite right. Her eyes were unfocused and we thought at first that she was blind, but then she demonstrated farsight more powerful than anything seen before on Earth. And she saw beyond Earth – to distant places where she spent so much of her time that she never really connected with those of us close to her.

Flicker.

I saw Juliana crying over Mom's body, her wig askew as her heart broke. Her fingers glowed with her gift of healing, but nothing she did made a difference.

Flicker.

Something was glowing beneath the lake. The node?

Flicker.

I saw another child, this one conceived next month. A little boy with both his father's gift of telekinesis and Nicolas's gift of fire. We tried to bind his powers, but they kept slipping until…

Flicker.

A hell hound, its red eyes inches from mine, its teeth dripping with saliva.

Flicker.

Another child. She looks just like me.

Flicker.

I woke drenched in sweat, around five in the morning. As gently as I could, I peeled myself away from Evan's still-sleeping form and made my way to the bathroom, where I spent a few minutes trying to drown myself in the shower.

Well, I'd remembered parts of my dreams. That was something. But I'd remembered dreams like that before – unfocused and flickering. I wasn't even sure if some of those images might not be normal products of my subconscious fears – i.e., real dreams – instead of visions of the future. It was just a jumbled mess.

I'd seen my mother dead twice, though. I shuddered at the thought. Whatever mistakes she'd made, whatever trouble she'd been in lately, I didn't want her dead. I wanted her better.

Evan was awake when I emerged from my bath, sitting upright against a stack of pillows, the blankets nestled around his waist. His chest was bare. So was mine, but I liked his better.

I focused on that chest as I worked to regain my equilibrium. The dreams might or might not be real, but that chest was.

"Bad dreams?" he asked.

I nodded.

"Anything relevant to little Haley?" he asked.

I started to shake my head, then stopped.

"Was there?" he asked.

Thinking back, I sorted through the flickering images – I didn't have my dream journal with me so I would simply have to remember as best I could. There had been children, half a dozen of them. My mom in multiple poses, but always dead. And then that strange light from the bottom of the lake.

It was relevant. All of it. I wasn't entirely sure how, but I felt suddenly certain of that much. It all fit, if only I could see the connection...

"The children," I said.

"You dreamed of more children?" Evan asked warily.

I tried to ignore him, as well as the ache in my heart as I considered all the children who would never be. I tried to think of them dispassionately, objectively. At least last night I had only gotten flickering glimpses; it was slim solace, but it was all I had. I knew I would always remember the children who might have been. Each one was unique, but they all had one thing in common.

"They're really powerful," I said.

Evan cocked his head to the side, and I sensed a flicker of pride under his confusion. *Of course* he would have powerful children, he seemed to be saying. Hadn't I been paying attention? Ana was a powerful child, too, although one with a naturally gentle gift. Not all of our children would be so lucky.

"More powerful than you," I clarified.

Now, Evan did frown. He was, after all, twice as powerful as he should be. Our children should simply be exceptional.

"What's more," I said, thinking out loud, "I think Maya and Michael are really powerful too. They keep slipping the bindings the family's been putting on them."

"I'm not sure what you're saying. What does this have to do with Haley?"

"Everything. Haley probably shouldn't have any magic at all, yet she does. She's more powerful than she should be too, don't you see? I wonder if there are others."

I paused, thinking. To his credit, Evan didn't interrupt.

"I think," I said finally, "that there's more magic in the world."

"Matthew mentioned something about this once." Evan stood and began pacing. "I can't remember what he said, exactly."

"If there's more magic," I continued, thinking out loud, "then that might explain the hell hounds."

"How? You don't think someone could conjure them?"

I shuddered. "I don't think anyone has the power of creation yet. Or at least, I hope not. But where does it end? Nobody should have had the power to make it so cold. What did Mr. Wolf say? The human body's usually warm."

Evan glanced at his watch. "I'd love to keep talking about this, but it's almost sunrise and we've still got a job to do."

I looked at my watch too: 5:32. The sheriff would be meeting us downstairs in less than half an hour.

"I'm still missing something," I mused aloud. Then I frowned, as the memories of my mom's dead body reasserted themselves in my mind. "My mom's in danger. I'm not sure when, but I think I need to do something. Now."

ဆၢ

I called Matthew Blair while Evan was in the shower. I told him about my dream, about seeing my mother dead, and asked him to send the empath to her.

"I don't care what it costs," I told him, desperately. That wasn't the sort of thing you should normally say to a sorcerer.

"Lucky for you, Belle has flat-rate fees clearly posted on her website."

"Belle?" I repeated. That's what we'd named one of our daughters. Did that mean – was it possible she'd be able to save Mom?

"She's my dad's cousin, actually, not mine, but she's the best. I won't charge for passing along the message. I think ten years of visions will continue to suffice."

"Thanks," I said weakly.

"And speaking of which, what did you see last night aside from your mom?"

I hesitated, but not because I didn't want him to know. He needed to know. I just didn't want to repeat myself. "I'll share it tonight, at the meeting."

"Fair enough. See you then."

I hung up just as Evan emerged, toweling his shoulder-length hair. He stopped, tossed the towel into the bathroom, then performed a spell to wring out the rest of the dampness from his hair. I heard a small splash in the nearby sink, and his hair fell in perfect waves around his shoulders.

"Showoff," I muttered.

He looked at me, his blue eyes alight with some emotion I couldn't identify. I swallowed, nervously; I could usually tell what was on his mind and I didn't think it was a good sign that right now, I really couldn't.

"I want to get downstairs quickly," Evan said after a long pause. Then, "You could do the same thing."

"That's not a simple spell."

"No. But if you tried, you could do far more than simple spells."

I opened my mouth, then closed it again and shook my head. We weren't going to have this argument again. Not now, at any rate. Later, I supposed, it would be inevitable.

We met the sheriff downstairs and he followed us the relatively short distance to the motel where the Bakers were now staying. I drove because Evan wanted to stay linked to the scrying spell in case they moved.

We arrived at about seven, then had to wait across the street for sunrise half an hour later. Finally, with sunlight brightening the eastern edge of the sky, we made our way to the correct door. This time, we didn't have to bother to ask the clerk. Evan's spell zeroed in on them, and we followed.

Evan knocked on the door, firmly. Someone inside let out a little shriek and I wondered if the room was, even now, filling with mist.

"You've got ten seconds to open the door or I'm coming in," Evan said.

There was a crash, a scuffling sound, and then the door opened, with the chain still attached.

Evan had no patience for the delay. With a casual wave of his hand, he ripped the chain in two and pushed the door open. Shawn Baker stood there in only his pajama bottoms, eyes wide, breath heaving.

Sydney lay in the far bed, her back to us, cradling something in a way that suggested she was protecting it with her body and her life – using herself as a shield.

I felt sick. Whatever had happened, whatever Haley had done, it had been an accident. These people were innocents, and they were being terrorized.

Evan started to step through the door, but I put a hand on his arm, urging him to stay put. Then I scooted past him, into the room.

"Please," I said, making my voice as gentle as possible, "we're here to help."

"You're here to make sure magic doesn't get loose in the world," Shawn said, his eyes still on Evan rather than me. "You're here to keep it for yourself, even if you have to hurt a little girl to do it."

"No," I said, still trying to keep my voice calm. I think I managed – barely. "We're here to help you – all of you. Haley can't control her magic and you can't help her with it. It happens; many children develop gifts and talents well before puberty and they can't always control it, even in magical families. My own brother and sister – the twins – have their powers bound."

Shawn eyed Evan warily, but his words were for me. "What about your daughter? Did you bind her?"

"No," I said, recalling with shame that I had suggested that very thing yesterday. "Ana's powers are gentle, passive."

"So are Haley's!" Sydney cried, though she didn't move. She kept her back to us, her body between us and her daughter.

"There are two dead people who might disagree," Evan said, and I shot him a warning glare. He wasn't helping.

"Mommy," came a pitifully small voice from Sydney's other side. "What's going on?"

Before anyone could answer, a veil of mist began to form around her, filling the room.

Evan was inside in a heartbeat, arms upraised, his voice even as he chanted the same counterspell he'd used yesterday.

I kept talking, ignoring the rotten egg smell filling the room and the fact that it was increasingly difficult to look anyone in the eyes.

"A binding is painless," I said. "It's as gentle as a hug. And it's not permanent. It can be removed at any time, or even outgrown if it's a temporary binding, like most children's bindings are. They slip off during puberty, when the child is more capable of handling their gift."

"She didn't do anything," Sydney said again. "It's like Shawn said — you're just afraid of magic getting out."

I stared through the mist and wondered how she could possibly believe that, with this evidence right before her eyes. But she was a mom, and she didn't want to believe anything bad about her child. I might feel the same way, if the situation were reversed. I only hoped I would face reality.

"We can do this with or without your permission," I continued, wincing at the implied threat. But I had to protect the town. It was more important than this family's feelings. "But I'd like your permission."

The fog dissipated. I blinked for a moment, then noticed Evan staring at me, frowning. I think he knew what I intended to do next, but I didn't care what he thought. It was the right thing to do.

"Let us bind her powers now," I said, "and when she's in high school, we'll teach her magic."

"Cassie!" Evan cried.

But Shawn had finally decided to look at me instead of Evan. Nice to know I existed, really.

"You would do that?" he asked.

Sydney, too, was sitting up and turning to face me. Her mouth was slightly open in shock.

"I don't think he's willing," Shawn said, nodding his head in Evan's direction.

"Cassie, can we talk privately?" Evan asked.

I almost said no, but I caught the look in his eyes and decided, wisely I think, that we needed a minute before I summarily outed hundreds of years' worth of magical knowledge.

"Sheriff, call us if anything happens," I said, then followed Evan back out to the car, well out of earshot of the Bakers.

"What do you think you're doing?" Evan asked.

"They're terrified," I said. "You saw their reaction. But I noticed it wasn't just about what they thought was going to happen to Haley – they were indignant that she be treated differently from other children with powers. Eventually, Michael and Maya's power will be unbound and they'll be taught to use them. Haley's will either need to be bound indefinitely or – and you know it can happen – if she ever slips her bindings she could kill someone else. You know it, and what's more, so do they. They're not stupid."

Evan ran his fingers through his hair, a nervous habit of his. He took several deep breaths, not saying anything for a long moment, and when he did, his words shocked me to my toes.

"You might kill someone someday too. Think about it."

He turned on his heels and walked back toward the motel room while I stared at his retreating backside. Damn. He was right.

Tears stung my eyes as I followed him back to the motel room. I only just managed to keep them at bay, but luckily, my part here was done. Evan took over the negotiations, agreeing to limited magical education dependent upon Haley's measured ability at the time so long as she agreed to a master/student blood bond and as long as they understood that certain closely held family secrets would not be disclosed.

He was a masterful negotiator, and in the end, I think everyone was happy.

Everyone but me.

I watched, dully, as Evan chalked the casting circle, lit some candles, and performed the ritual that would keep Haley from hurting anyone else.

You might kill someone someday too.

An ecosystem was bad enough; as a naturalist, Evan cared more than most and understood the danger such damage could do. But he was right. I could have killed someone. The difference between Haley and me was that I was old enough to know better. And a simple binding wouldn't help me.

Chapter 17

"ONE WEEK" BY BARE NAKED LADIES WAS PLAYING ON THE RADIO AS WE reached the outskirts of Eagle Rock. I don't think I had ever really appreciated that song before, but I suddenly knew just what it meant. I, too, had realized things were all my fault. And I, too, couldn't bring myself to tell Evan.

We headed straight for Matthew Blair's house where Ana had spent her first night away from home – and from mommy. I wondered if she'd missed me as much as I'd missed her, but pushed the thought aside as idle and useless.

Ana did give me a satisfyingly enthusiastic greeting when I walked into the living room. Her eyes brightened, her chin lifted, and she cried, "Ma!"

When I picked her up, she dove for my right breast, once again leaving me with the paranoid notion that she thought my breasts were called *Ma* and that she liked them more than me.

"Hey, I missed you too," Evan said, ruffling the baby-fine hair on the top of her head.

"Ma!" Ana insisted, smacking my chest with her open palm.

"All right, all right." I nestled into the same chair I'd used yesterday, and proceeded to give her what she wanted. What we both wanted.

"She did fine last night," Kaitlin said from the kitchen. A quick glance told me she was preparing snacks for the White Guard meeting that was due to start in only a couple of hours.

"She didn't fall out of bed?" I asked.

"Nope. Although actually …" She stopped talking and I craned my neck to look over my shoulder at her.

"What?" Evan asked.

"It's nothing, really. Innocent. But Jay crawled out of my bed sometime during the night and back into his own bed – with her. I didn't notice until this morning so they might have slept together all night."

I wanted to ask if she'd gotten a picture of it, but something in her tone suggested she was more disturbed by the incident than she should be. I'd always sensed that something dark lurked in her past; I only hoped she'd find a way to open up to me – or to anyone – sooner or later.

Matthew chose that moment to come downstairs. He ignored me and Evan, going straight to Kaitlin to gather her in his arms. I turned my head to give them some privacy.

I gazed down at my daughter, feeling the connection strengthen between us, feeling the magic grow within me. I had only nursed her one time yesterday, and the magic had dwindled almost to nothing. It stirred now as I recognized its presence, once again inviting me to use it, play with it, give it life.

Become like Mom.

"Did you talk to Belle?" I asked Matthew.

"She rearranged her schedule so she could see your mom tomorrow," he replied. "She's amazing. Your mom's in good hands."

Evan and I stayed until the meeting, helping Matthew and Kaitlin get ready and discussing the agenda. Finally, when the other members of the inner circle began to arrive, Kaitlin took Jay and Ana upstairs to watch a movie.

"Not *Frozen*," I found myself saying. As far as I knew, there was no connection between the Disney movie and what had happened. I didn't like to believe in coincidences but, looking back, I supposed it wasn't exactly a shock that the most popular Disney movie of the modern age had been recently viewed at a daycare. Maybe seeing it had inspired Haley, activating her sinister power – that could happen, when children weren't born with a gift – but if so, I doubted I would ever know for sure.

In the meantime, the movie remained unsettling. No use tempting fate.

The inner circle consisted of Matthew's family – his brother Robert, his mom, and his dad – plus Linda and Clark Eagle, Kevin Hastings, and Scott Lee. Scott was the newest member, and as he brought our numbers up to ten, probably the last for a while.

My role in the White Guard was ill-defined. I think in Matthew's view, I was the seer, but as I still hadn't seen very much, I wasn't always sure what to do. Evan had only recently let me come in person at all; he'd spent a long time allowing old resentments and jealousies get in the way of common goals. It probably hadn't helped that Alexander DuPris had stolen a blood sample – it still left us wondering what part of Evan's actions had been his, and what part had been manipulated. We would probably never know, although I privately thought that Evan didn't need to be manipulated to feel jealous. Especially where I was concerned.

I half listened as the meeting was called to order and old business was discussed. Evan reported on his progress – or lack thereof – with the latest slaver ring to pop up in the Midwest. Clark Eagle chimed in then with recruitment numbers, which were well up. Scott Lee had nothing new to say about werewolf pack alliances. And finally, Caroline reported that the Magical Underground Newsletter continued to print propaganda and outright lies about us.

"Two people were frozen to death a few days ago," Matthew said, finally.

I focused my attention back on the meeting.

"Evan assures me that the culprit – a little girl – has had her powers bound," Matthew continued.

"I've also agreed to teach her to use her powers when she's older," Evan said, shooting me an unreadable look.

"That's a good idea," Matthew said.

"It is?" This came from Kevin Hastings, Evan's uncle on his mom's side. Kevin's role in the inner council was more a unifying one – he was related, either directly or through marriage, to most of the powerful sorcerers in Eagle Rock.

"I'm not saying we need to let every magical secret get out into the general public," Matthew said, "but yes, people with power need to be able to use it. This has always been taken care of somewhat unofficially, by relatives, even distant ones, but not everyone can find a relative to teach them."

"Especially lately," Linda Eagle chimed in.

Matthew nodded, and I could tell he had spoken to her before the meeting. "Tell everyone what you told me."

Linda cleared her throat. "Babies are getting stronger. I've been a midwife for almost fifty years – I helped give birth to most everyone in this room. Kevin was one of my first."

Kevin gave her a wary smile and a nod.

"Anyway," Linda continued, "things have been changing. It didn't happen all at once. It happened so gradually I almost missed it, but people have been getting stronger. Every year, maybe, there's an infinitesimal change – the mamas are channeling more and more magic while they're pregnant. But in the last few years, the changes have been sharper. More noticeable. Why, little Ana saved her mama's life when she was barely an idea!"

I stiffened, then nodded, remembering that everyone in this room knew Ana was a healer. It had taken a great deal of trust to share that secret, but we had all revealed important truths about ourselves last summer, after Mathew returned from Pennsylvania, to help unite us.

"Cassie's mom had real trouble controlling little Michael's fire gift while she was pregnant," Linda went on, "and she'd done it before with Nicolas. Michael's stronger than Nicolas, although you'd better watch who you say that to."

I grinned at the thought of my brother being told anyone was better than him at anything, let alone the thing that personally defined him – fire starting.

"Kaitlin had trouble with Jay too, though she put her trust in modern medicine instead of me." Linda's tone clearly told us what she thought of *that* decision. "That might have been Kaitlin's own inexperience with magic, but my impression is Jay's a prodigy."

"He is," Matthew confirmed.

"And Michael and Maya keep slipping their bindings," I said.

"There are others," Linda said. "Possibly more babies born to the mundane community with magic, too, but most of those end up being delivered at the hospital so I don't have direct knowledge. What I do know is that magical talent has been increasing for decades, and lately it's increased sharply."

"I have more," Matthew said. "The seers in my family – and there is one every other generation or so – have been keeping journals for centuries. I've got records going back to the 1700s. Now, no one came right out and said that magic is getting more powerful, but it's clear by reading the accounts that over time, sorcerers have been able to do more. Each new generation seems stronger and more capable than the last."

"How much of that is knowledge?" Clark asked. "My family has records, too, which include spells that improve upon the spells of the previous generation. The potions, the rituals, the enchantments – we can use magic more efficiently than we used to and in that way, do more."

"And there's the node," Robert added. "This area wasn't settled until the 1800s, and it's the strongest node the family ever had access to. There was definitely a jump in power and potential when our family moved here – our great-great grandmother said so in pretty much those words."

"This is all fascinating," Caroline Blair said from her place in the corner. "But what, if anything, do we do about it?"

Caroline had a quiet strength about her that some people misinterpreted as weakness. I had been one of those people, years ago. Now I knew better. She'd had her magic stolen from her as a teenager, just like my mom, but she'd conquered her past to become a powerful matriarch. I almost hated to see what she'd be like when she had grandchildren – which might be soon. Matthew and Kaitlin were very serious, plus rumor had it Robert was seeing someone.

"I'm not sure there is anything to do," Kevin said. "We take each child as an individual, like always, binding powers when necessary."

"The powers aren't always staying bound," I said. "And with mundanes involved, it's easy to think more kids will slip through the cracks. I'd rather not wait for another death to find the next one."

"So what do we do? Institute a universal testing program?" Linda Eagle sounded half-serious, which was more than I expected.

"Maybe." I wasn't sure that was the answer – and it was invasive. There was no good way to measure a person's magical potential without a blood sample, and nobody was going to hand over blood in Eagle Rock. I'd seen to that personally.

"The Magical Underground educates young, unconnected sorcerers," Evan said.

"The Magical Underground also uses blood magic," Kevin said.

"Let's table this for now," Matthew said, perhaps sensing an argument on the horizon. That ability was one thing that made him so good at what he did. "I'll speak with each of you privately over the next week and we'll revisit it at our regular meeting. In the meantime, there's something about a fairy in McClellan's shop?"

Kevin snorted, apparently thinking it was a joke. No one else did.

"There is something in the back of that shop," Evan said. "Christina Scot called it a fairy; I'm just going to call it... unusual."

"Scott?" Matthew asked. "What do your instincts tell you?"

Scott's nostrils flared as he considered the question. "It's nothing I've ever seen before. I don't like it, whatever it is. It makes me uneasy."

"It makes me more uneasy that a man like Cormack McClellan has it," Evan added. "I haven't proven that he's taken over his brother's trade in soul magic, but the man's evil."

Scott nodded, once.

"All right." Matthew nodded, decisively. "Maybe we should steal the creature, and study it for ourselves."

Robert cleared his throat. "I'm not comfortable with that. Human or not, we can't just imprison it without a reason. Or was I the only one who went to law school?"

"The law doesn't apply to non-humans," Matthew replied, but he held up his hands when Robert started to say something else. "I take your meaning, though. Maybe we can try to befriend it."

"I'll join the rescue team," Robert said. "If we're going to try to make friends, having an empath along will help."

"Evan?" Matthew asked. "You're leading this team."

Evan nodded. "Robert's welcome to join."

"Anyone else want in?" Matthew asked.

"Me." I raised my hand.

"No," Evan snapped.

"I'm your distraction," I said. "I think I'll have much more luck than you did."

Evan arched an eyebrow. "How?"

"I'll tell him I might know who killed his brother."

Scott tensed. He had killed Cormack's brother, David, when the older McClellan tried to steal Madison's soul.

"I won't actually tell him," I hastened to add, "but it will be distracting."

"It's a good plan," Matthew said. "It's better than any distraction strategy I've come up with."

Beside me, Evan tensed. He hated sending me into danger. He hated it even more when I was right about needing to go into danger.

"I'll be fine," I assured him. "You and Scott and Robert will all be there to back me up."

He started to say something, but my cell phone vibrated between us. I dug it out of my pocket and glanced at the caller ID.

"It's the sheriff," I said before accepting the call. "What's up?"

"We've got another deep freeze. It's bad this time – two fishermen are dead and two others are in the hospital with severe hypothermia and frost bite."

"That's impossible." I shook my head. "Evan bound Haley's powers."

Beside me, Evan stiffened.

"Oh, it's worse than that," the sheriff said. "Haley and her family haven't returned to Eagle Rock yet. They're still in Kansas City."

"It wasn't Haley?"

"It wasn't Haley."

"But she made the mist …" I shook my head again, feeling far more than chagrin at my stupidity. I'd made a mistake that cost two more men their lives, and maybe two others. It was unforgivable.

The sheriff was talking again, but there was a sort of buzzing noise in my brain and I barely heard him. "I thought it was tied to the mist too. It was so thick, and then so cold… we almost died. It was an understandable assumption."

"Assumption, yeah." And we both knew what assuming did. I closed my eyes and leaned my head against the back of the love seat. "You suspected, didn't you?"

The sheriff didn't answer right away. "I... I felt like we were missing something."

"Me too. We both should have listened to our instincts."

Evan's hand came to rest on mine, offering me comfort I didn't deserve and support I didn't need. Numbness had me in its grip, but I steeled myself; I couldn't make this right, but I couldn't fall apart either. I still had answers to find and a culprit to stop.

"Who were the men attacked?" I asked. "Do we have names? Was there any connection to Nadine and Jared?"

"They're tourists. The two in the hospital – the only two we've been able to get to so far – have Illinois state IDs."

"What about rentals? Fishing gear? Boats? Any local connections there?"

"Looking into it," he said.

"But your instincts say that's not it, don't they?" I asked.

"Yes," he admitted, "but I also think that whoever's doing this, it's intentional."

"Let me think and get back to you." I hung up without saying goodbye, then turned to the eagerly eavesdropping council. "We've got a killer on the loose."

Chapter 18

E VAN DIDN'T SLEEP IN ANOTHER ROOM THAT NIGHT, BUT HE DIDN'T PULL me into his arms and make love to me either. We sat there awake for a long time, neither of us speaking, crushed under the weight of things left unsaid. I thought of Belle, who would not be conceived tonight, and of Little Henry, who still had a chance tomorrow.

I slept restlessly that night, burdened by images of frozen corpses I prayed were not visions of more death to come. At least I didn't dream of more children.

McClellan's store opened at ten o'clock the next morning. I was there at ten thirty, going straight in the front door, while Evan, Scott, and Robert snuck around back. My mission: To keep Cormack from realizing he had intruders in the back of his shop until it was too late.

I sauntered in with my sunglasses on, removing them the second the bright morning sunlight gave way to the darkness of the interior. The place always had seemed to want to live up to its nature. A handful of glass display cases along one wall were well lit, but the rest was as gloomy as a tomb.

I felt Cormack's eyes on me from the moment I entered the store. His brother had made some half-hearted attempts to control me before he'd died, but Cormack had only ever made one attempt – possibly because I married Evan shortly thereafter. I'd like to think I intimidated him, though.

I didn't go to him immediately. Instead, I wandered through the store, taking note of the items for sale. Most of the objects here promised power in one form or another – pocket illusions, simple potions, minor curses, and much more. I paused before a display of stones promising good luck, wondering if there was anything to them or not. I touched one and did, indeed, feel the faintest flicker of magic. They weren't powerful, and I couldn't be sure that luck was their true aim, but they really were magical.

I made my way past displays of rejuvenating drafts and beauty products, stopping again before a shelf of fertility aids.

"Looking for something in particular?" Cormack's voice came from directly behind me, startling me.

I jumped and turned to look into the dark, hooded eyes of Cormack McClellan. For a split second, I thought I was looking at his brother David, and then the differences between the two brothers became clear. Cormack was shorter and stockier than his brother, although they did have the same round face, slight nose, dark hair, and green eyes.

I swallowed, nervously. "I'm looking for truth."

"Ah, then you'll want these." He led the way past a bookshelf laden with tomes I barely had time to make out, although I wondered if *Magical Transference* might be among them. I almost hung back, but he was looking at me expectantly from beside a shelf of potions, rings, bracelets, and necklaces.

"We've got your basic truth serum, of course." He pointed to a vial with a clear liquid inside. "These are effective as long as you can convince the other person to drink it and if you know the right questions to ask."

"What if I don't know the right questions to ask?" Coming up with the right questions was often harder than eliciting the truth anyway. You could always watch a person's reaction for the truth.

"That gets much trickier. We've got the jewelry, which makes someone susceptible to suggestion and overtures of friendship – they become trusting. That can often lead to more truth, in the end."

"But you have to convince them to wear it," I said.

"True. That is the biggest downside of all of the less expensive options." He gestured at the collection, then turned toward the more brightly lit display cases. "Now, if you're interested in some real power, I've got a ring that *you* wear, which will allow you to detect the emotions of those around you."

"You captured the soul of an empath?" I asked, thinking of Robert lurking in the back.

Cormack snorted. "You're fixated on soul magic, aren't you?"

"I'm fixated on the truth, like I said."

He shook his head. "The White Guard has been after me for two years now, but they haven't found anything. Has it occurred to you that there's nothing to find?"

"How'd you make a ring of empathy then?" I asked.

"How does your family turn lead into gold?" Cormack countered smoothly.

"Touché."

"But you're not really here to buy anything, are you?" Cormack smiled, mirthlessly. "If you were interested in my trinkets, you'd have come years ago. It's not like you don't have the money."

"No, I'm not here to buy cursed or evil objects."

He shook his head. "One day, maybe you and I will come to an understanding."

"I doubt it."

"Me too, but life is full of surprises. Now, I assume you're here to distract me while your husband does something I won't like?"

"No," I said evenly. "I'm here to bargain for truth. I want to know how you make those powerful artifacts, and you want to know who killed your brother."

Cormack stilled, and I knew I'd gotten his attention. He might still suspect a trick, but he couldn't help himself; he was intrigued.

"You know who killed my brother?"

"I might."

"Don't play games with me!" He took a deep, shuddering breath, then let it out. "He's got a son, you know. I'm raising the boy now. He's got a right to know why."

"Don't try to pretend your brother wasn't a monster just because he had a kid. Anyone can have a kid."

For a moment, I thought Cormack might physically attack me. Maybe I'd gone too far. Then he reached inside his pocket, withdrew a key, and wound his way around the display case to open it.

"What are you doing?" I asked.

He slid the ring of empathy onto his finger. "Do you know who killed my brother?"

"Your brother killed your brother," I said. It was true – in part. The man's actions had led to his own death.

"You believe that." He sniffed the air. "And you're never going to tell me. So let's stop playing games."

He suddenly flung out his hand and I was sure, for a second, that he was casting a spell at me. Then I noticed his hand was pointing slightly to the right of me and the door leading to the back of the shop had burst wide open. I couldn't see anyone back there, but then, Scott was a master of illusion.

"Stealing from my shop?" Cormack asked. "When you can easily afford anything in here? What is the world coming to?"

"What are you talking about?" I asked. "There's no one back there."

"No, there's–" He stopped, suddenly, his eyes popping open in shock. "What are you doing?"

In a flash, he was back on this side of the counter, racing for the door to the back. I followed, slowly, wondering what had gotten into him. He'd seemed so cool and confident only a moment ago – part of the game, I thought, but now he'd obviously conceded.

He went straight for an iron cage set atop a tall shelf, now empty, with the door thrown wide open. His eyes darted around the room, skimming past the doorway where I stood, feeling a lot less smug than I thought I would at this moment.

"You have no idea what you've done," he said.

"I haven't done anything," I lied.

"It's inhuman. Evil."

"That's rich, coming from you." I felt uneasy, though. Just because an evil man kept something prisoner, didn't mean that thing wasn't also evil.

"The destruction it can cause..." Cormack shook his head. "You have no idea what you've done."

"Then tell me."

He opened his mouth as if to speak, then shut it again. "No. This is your fault. Your doing. If you want it undone now, I have a price."

I didn't ask, because I thought I knew what he wanted.

"Who killed my brother?" Cormack asked, apparently not feeling the need to wait for my response.

I shook my head and stepped back, hitting something hard and familiar. Evan.

"You'll want my help," Cormack said. "You'll need it. Believe me. And when you do, that's my price." He held out the same hand he'd used earlier and with another flick of a spell, the door to the back slammed shut in my face.

"I don't suppose Robert managed to befriend it," I whispered as I turned toward Evan.

"It flew off," Evan replied.

"I think we've made a mistake."

"So do I." This came from Scott, who appeared from beneath a veil of invisibility a little past Evan.

"Can we follow it?" I asked. "Find out where it's going and what it's doing?"

"Yes," Scott replied. "I think I can smell it."

஫ைസ

Scott followed his nose out of the shop and east along Main Street, pausing at the intersection that would take him south to Lakeshore Drive. Pausing, he nodded that direction and began running, while Evan went back to get his car.

Robert joined us in the car, though he didn't say much as we caught up with Scott and stopped to let him in. He couldn't smell anything from inside the car, but there was only one way to go along this road – it dead-ended at Lakeshore Drive.

When we reached the intersection, Scott got out again and I braced myself, sensing what was coming. He must have sensed it too, because he picked the trail back up almost instantly.

It was going toward the castle. It was headed for Mom.

Scott climbed back in the car and this time we didn't stop or speak until we reached the castle. When we arrived in the circular drive-way out front, everyone poured out, somehow sensing that this was the place. This was where the little creature had gone.

Scott sniffed the air once again before nodding at an upstairs window which, I noticed, was cracked open.

"It shouldn't be open," I said. "It's forty degrees out here."

"Who's home right now?" Evan asked.

"Probably just Mom," I said. "The kids are at school, except the twins, who are with Kaitlin."

"Can you get us in?" Scott asked.

"I hope so." The last time I'd tried to get inside my childhood home, a hell hound had attacked, but that was at night. This was late morning and, as far as I knew, I still had permanent resident privileges.

Moving quickly up the front steps, I had a sudden and vivid memory of Mom as she'd appeared in my dream – eyes wide and staring, face pale, lips blue. I'd never seen what killed her, but I'd sensed she'd taken her own life. Now, I wondered if I'd understood that vision correctly.

The door opened easily for me and when I stepped aside, Evan, Scott, and Robert all passed through the wards. They wouldn't be as strong on another sorcerer's home turf, but they were welcome here as my guests.

We paused in the living room, quiet, listening.

"I don't hear anything," Scott murmured. Since he had keen werewolf hearing, that boded ill.

"I feel something," Robert said, and his voice sounded strained. "Despair. Utter despair. Hopeless."

I glanced at him, at his strained face that only marginally reminded me of his brother's. Robert and I had never spent much time together, but I'd always gotten the impression that he was the gentler brother. Right now, his handsome face was twisted in pain and angled slightly upward, toward the ceiling.

"The library," I said, and led the way up the stairs, taking them two at a time as I raced to get to my mother before it was too late.

The library door stood open. Mom lay on the floor, motionless, an empty bottle of wine on its side by her outflung right hand. Something – I couldn't identify what – flitted around her head. It was more like a pulsing light than anything else, fleeting and ephemeral.

"Get away from her," I demanded as I charged across the room, kneeling at my mother's side. I drew in a deep breath and forced myself to look down at her still form.

Her chest rose and fell slightly. She was alive.

"Drunk again?" I asked angrily, lifting the bottle and tossing it aside.

Was this me? Was this my future? Broken and bleeding, unable to care for myself, let alone anyone else?

Behind me, Robert moaned.

"What's in her hand?" Evan asked.

I glanced at her left hand, which clutched a tiny vial I hadn't noticed before. Narrowing my eyes, my heart beating a little faster, I pried it loose from her fingers. It was unlabeled, but I sniffed the residue within the bottle.

"Death Sleep," I whispered. It was the gentlest, deadliest potion I knew – first putting you into a deep sleep, then ending your life painlessly. "Oh God, Mom? Mom?"

I turned to Scott and Evan, both standing there with mouths hanging slightly open. "In the laboratory next door, there's got to be a purgative!"

Scott moved first, Evan on his heels. Meanwhile, I propped my mother upright, wondering how long it had been since she'd taken the poison and how long she had left. It worked in minutes.

"Call your cousin, Belle," I said to Robert, who was still moaning. "She was supposed to come over today. Tell her it's an emergency."

He didn't speak for a long moment, but when I shot a look at him over my shoulder, he managed a nod. His eyes looked haunted, and his hands shook, but he pulled a phone from his jeans pocket and tapped the screen. He held it to his ear just as Evan returned with a stoppered vial.

"Lift her," Evan said.

I tugged my mom into a sitting position, propped against my side. Evan slid to his knees in front of her and forced her mouth open, then tipped the contents of the vial into her mouth.

"How quickly will this work?" I asked.

"Imme-" Evan began, but stopped when Mom jerked forward and began spewing liquid all over him.

It wasn't pretty. I won't go into details for the sake of the more stomach-sensitive reader. Suffice to say she spent the next five minutes vomiting, gagging, and dry heaving. The mess was impressive. The smell was worse.

Finally, the spasms passed and she blinked her eyes open, staring numbly at her saviors. Her eyes were dull, almost as lifeless as they had appeared in my dream, and she let out a soft sob as she closed them again.

"You should have let me die," she whispered.

"Is Belle coming?" I asked Robert.

"She was already on her way when I called," he said. "I-I can't stay right now. The pain… I've failed everyone, I know I have. Everyone would be better off if I were dead."

"Robert?" Scott asked.

"It's not him," I said. "It's Mom. But maybe he shouldn't be alone right now."

"Where's the fairy?" Evan asked, suddenly looking around.

I rotated my head slowly, scanning every inch of the library, finally settling my gaze on Scott, who sniffed the air.

"Gone," he said. "I think it's gone. I can track it again."

"No," I said, surprising everyone in the room with my vehemence. Three powerful men all looked to me for direction. It was an odd moment, not because it had never happened before but because it struck me that my mom wasn't the only one who'd felt like a failure recently. Maybe the fairy had been after me as well.

Yet these three men didn't see me as a failure, or at least, they still had faith in my abilities.

"No," I repeated, "not right now. We don't know what it is or how to capture it, but it did this to Mom. Probably others."

"Cormack McClellan knows how to capture it," Scott said gruffly.

"And all I have to do to get the information from him is start a feud between two powerful families." I shook my head. "I just ended a feud between two powerful families; I'm not starting another one."

Scott blew out a long breath. "So what do we do?"

"Spread the word: No one should be alone right now."

Scott nodded and started for the door.

"Take Robert with you," I said. "He needs to get away from Mom. Caroline Blair will know what to do for him."

Scott paused. "I didn't drive."

"Take one of the cars. Keys are on hooks in the kitchen."

He nodded, retreated a few steps, then urged the other man forward, out of the library. Neither said a word.

"He's right," Mom murmured. "Everyone's better off without me. I've failed everyone."

I didn't trust myself to speak. Part of me was so angry with her I couldn't see straight. Didn't she understand what she had? Nine children. Nine! Including twin toddlers who needed her. How dare she check out? Yes, she'd lost Dad, but so had I. We all had. And yes, she had made mistakes, but so had I. She was the only one falling apart.

But how much of what she was saying was truly her, and how much was that Fairy of Despair?

Chapter 19

I'M NOT SURE HOW LONG I STAYED ON THE FLOOR WITH MY MOM. PROBABLY not long, but it felt like an eternity. Finally, Evan's phone rang and he ducked out to answer the call. At about the same time, the front doorbell rang and I dashed downstairs to greet Belle, a seventy-something woman with long gray hair twisted into an elegant knot at the back of her head. It made me think of a crown.

She smiled the moment I opened the door, a smile that looked so genuine, that felt so real, I wanted to smile back. I couldn't quite manage it, but at least I wanted to smile.

She didn't ask questions, but went straight to the library where she told me to wait outside while she stabilized Mom.

"Was that Belle?" Evan asked as I stared at the closed door, wondering what was happening on the other side.

"Yes."

"Your mom's in good hands."

I turned to him, sensing he was about to leave me alone with this situation. "Where are you going?"

"Your Aunt Sherry just got back in touch with me about trying to heal the lake shore. She's willing, but it's best if we get started right away."

"Oh." I didn't look at him. I didn't want to talk about the lake shore right now, not after what had just happened.

"Will you be okay here?"

"Fine. Just fine. Go on."

He hesitated. "I can stay if you need me."

I shook my head. If he stayed, he'd make me feel worse. Besides, I had Belle, and she seemed to know what she was doing.

"Go on." I gave him a quick hug and then a shove toward the stairs. He took the hint.

I spent the next half hour pacing back and forth in front of the library door, wondering what was going on in there and what I would do next. What I could do. I wasn't willing to leave my mom alone, but I also wasn't willing to let the kids stay with her in this condition.

Sheriff Adams had mentioned a psychiatric hospital a few days ago, but that idea didn't sit well with me either. Who knew what mundane doctors would do with her, to her? Take her blood? Force her onto medication that might or might not help, especially given that a supernatural creature was at least partly responsible?

Finally, the library doors opened and Belle appeared, leading Mom out. I was almost surprised to see her on her feet. I started to say something, but Belle quickly shook her head and led the way to the master bedroom. This time, she allowed me to follow.

"Find some comfy clothes to change into," Belle said. "I'll need you to leave the bathroom door cracked while you shower."

Mom did as she was told, like some kind of obedient child, while Belle watched and maintained the utmost composure. It was almost surreal, watching the woman work. After the way Robert had cracked, I hadn't been convinced that an empath could stand up to the strain.

"What should I do with her?" I asked Belle in a low voice when Mom started the shower. "I don't want to leave her alone."

"No, she can't be left alone," Bell agreed. "This is bad, some of the worst depression I've ever seen. It's taking all I have to keep her stable right now."

Since she wasn't even breaking a sweat, I found that incredible, but I didn't say anything. Matthew had said she was the best. Apparently, she was.

"I'll need to cancel my other appointments or reschedule them with my apprentice," Belle continued. "I'm afraid I can't trust your mom around a novice."

"Robert looked bad," I said.

"I'm not surprised. He's good, but he's young, and he's never trained in empathic healing. Make sure Caroline gets a look at him before he's left alone."

"That's where Scott took him, I think."

"Good." She smiled, a tiny hint of weariness just showing around the corners of her mouth. "I'll take her back to my place tonight. She'll need some intensive work for a while; I can't say how long. Is there someone who can watch the children?"

"Me," I said instantly.

Belle eyed me up and down, making me painfully aware of the difference in our age and experience. We might both be moms, but she'd left the diaper stage ages ago and actually, had grandchildren now. I was just beginning.

"They'll be frightened," Belle said finally. "Would you mind if I sent my apprentice to work with you, maybe tomorrow or the next day? We'll have to check her schedule first."

"Thank you," I managed to say. Why had I resisted calling her for so long? Oh yes, because Alexander had used empathic healers as spies and reinforced my distrust of all mind magic.

"Your mom will be okay," Belle said gently.

"I know she will." I recalled my recent dreams and added, impulsively, "I'm going to name my next daughter after you." I knew it was true, too – it might not be the specific daughter I'd dreamed about, but there would be another daughter.

She blinked in surprise. "Really? Are you a seer, then? I'm surprised you're able to see much with you nursing right now... or have you weaned already?"

"No," I said, taken aback, "but I only catch glimpses."

"Not surprising." She smiled and I felt warm inside. "I'm glad to hear this will work out."

"Do you know... how do you know about this?"

"Seers are common in my family."

"But Matthew–"

"Is a man. The gift is rare in men. Aunt Grace used to say they lacked vision."

"I see." And I was beginning to understand. Abigail Hastings had once told me there was no such thing as a seer-sorcerer. Most people didn't know that, but apparently Belle was one of the few. There were so many things I'd never asked Abigail before she died.

"People keep telling me to relax and accept." I thought back to last night; I'd talked myself into thinking I'd done just that, but now I wondered if my improved visions had more to do with only nursing Ana once the day before.

"We can talk about it if you like," Belle said, still smiling. "Later, of course. You've got a lot on your plate right now."

I longed to do just that, but I had to ask, "What's the price?"

"My new granddaughter has the gift; I only had sons so there's no one left to help her if I die. If I share this with you, then you help her, when the time comes."

I didn't even have to think about it. "Done."

"Done." She glanced at the cracked bathroom door and then turned back to me, all business. I sensed a shift in her mood, and wondered if she'd planned to talk to me about this all along – maybe Matthew had said something to her. Had I accepted her offer too quickly?

"You can't help your mom right now," she said firmly.

"I can't?" Was I part of the problem, then?

"She'll need you in the coming days." Belle placed a gentle hand on my elbow and I felt a strange warmth infuse my body. A sense of hope and of purpose. "But not today. Today, she needs you to find the creature that did this to her and to so many others. If I'm not mistaken, you got at least a glancing blow from the creature yourself."

I had wondered if that was the case. Hearing it from someone else made me feel oddly vulnerable, and reminded me of the mental attacks I'd endured and overcome years ago. How could I ever truly know my own thoughts?

The sound of running water stopped abruptly.

"Go on, I've got this." Belle slid past me to tend her patient.

I hesitated for just a moment; there was so much more I wanted to say. More I needed to ask.

"Now isn't the time," she told me, and I knew it was true. "Go."

಄಄಄

Henry Wolf lives closer to the node than anyone else in the area, even if he claims that honor by about ten feet "as the crow flies," according to him. His house is old but sturdy, surrounded on all sides with vast swaths of lands – a buffer between himself and the rest of the world, or so Evan told me.

There was no way to warn Mr. Wolf that I was coming. He had no email, no cell phone, not even a land line. He was completely isolated. And liked it that way.

I shuddered when I drove through the wards marking the edge of his territory. They seemed to run along my body, testing me, feeling me out. This, I supposed, was the magical version of a doorbell. Hopefully, Mr. Wolf would welcome me in. Otherwise, I would probably find myself in a world of hurt.

To my surprise, Mr. Wolf came striding down the dirt path leading to his home before I made it all the way to his house. He walked directly toward me, hands raised in a clear indication that I should stop the car. I did, then stepped out to greet him.

"Cassandra," Mr. Wolf said warmly. "Where's Evan?"

Fixing my mess, I thought. "Busy. But I wanted to talk to you. If that's okay."

"'Course it is. Let's take a walk."

Mr. Wolf gestured toward an old walking trail that jutted away the road not too far from where I'd parked. It went straight for a few yards, then disappeared into the woods bordering the lake.

Wordlessly, I fell into step just behind him – the path wasn't big enough for two. He moved quickly for someone so old, navigating the forest with the gait of a man closer to my age than his. He even leaped over a fallen log, one that I chose to carefully step over.

He didn't say anything for a long time, and neither did I. Finally, we reached the shore of the lake and paused on a bluff overlooking vast swaths of water. It was a clear, cloudless day and I could see straight across to the opposite shore.

The blackened shore.

"What are we doing here?" I asked.

"Admirin' the view." He shoved his hands through his suspenders and stared out over the water. He was a naturalist too; he had to be as angry at me as Evan was right now.

"It's not misty anymore," I said on a sigh. If only it were, I might not be able to see the blackened shoreline. "I guess we really stopped the dangerous gift unleashing fog everywhere."

Mr. Wolf chuckled. "I heard about that."

"How?"

"I got my sources." He drew in a deep lungful of air and exhaled slowly. "Least it smells better."

"It does, doesn't it?" I had only noticed the rotten egg smell closer to what I now thought of as the epicenter of the mist, but there had definitely been something lingering in the air for the past few months.

"Wanna talk about it?" Mr. Wolf continued to stare out at the lake, and though his words were kind, I felt like his gaze was accusing.

"She's really got a powerful gift," I said. "Couldn't see my nose in front of my face the day the sheriff and I went to talk to her. And the smell... but that's not why I did that." I gesture at the lake shore.

"Why'd you do that?"

"The air temperature was dropping. Freezing. We still don't know who did that. I got scared and I... well, Evan says I know just enough magic to be dangerous."

"Huh."

I didn't look at him. Feeling suddenly fascinated with my toes, I spent a minute scuffing the earth with the point of my tennis shoe. "My mom tried to kill herself today."

"Heh."

I glanced up at him; he was still gazing out over the lake, but I sensed he no longer studied the blackened shore line.

"As if I haven't messed up enough, I decided to set loose a creature Cormack McClellan had locked up in the back of his shop. Turned out, it spreads misery and despair. I've decided to call it the Fairy of Despair."

"A fairy, huh?" Mr. Wolf asked.

"Maybe. Fairies vary from tale to tale quite a lot."

"So do real fairies, but no one's seen one since hell hounds disappeared. Damn, I shoulda figured..."

"Fairies and hell hounds are linked?" I asked.

He shrugged. "Neither's been seen for five hundred years."

"So what's going on?" I stopped scuffing the earth and instead looked out at the lake shore, forcing myself to see it. I shuddered. "Linda Eagle says magic is stronger in the new generation, and that

little girl who made the mist, well, she might not have been causing
the freeze but that mist is powerful enough — and she's not from a
magical background.

"I've got four people dead, frozen to death, a pack of hell hounds,
one fairy causing people to want to die, maybe even kill themselves
— the sheriff said there's been three suicides — and no better idea of
what's causing it all than I did when it started."

He didn't say anything for a minute and then, "You done?"

"For now."

"Good, now listen. You got it in you to figure this out. Just like you
got it in you to learn magic without turnin' selfish."

"Did Evan talk to you?" I asked.

"He didn't have to."

"Evan and I have been fighting."

"Happens." He paused. "He still loves you."

"I know."

"You still love him."

"Yeah."

"Then work it out."

"I can't fix it." I gestured to the blackness.

Henry Wolf didn't answer, but he lifted his hands in the air and
made a sort of complicated gesture I'd never seen before. Suddenly, I
was hit with a wave of vertigo as the blackened shoreline seemed to
zoom toward us. Or maybe we were being transported there. No…
I finally understood that we were seeing it in front of us as if it were
right there, though we hadn't moved.

"Is this farsight?" I asked.

"Close. Just watch."

I watched. Evan was there, amid the blackened stumps, with Aunt
Sherry at his side. She glanced around, and when her eyes came into
view I saw that they were puffy, as if she'd been crying.

Of course, her twin sister had just tried to kill herself. Maybe now
wasn't the best time to have her out working.

I started to say something, but of course she couldn't hear me. She
only looked like she was right here. She closed her eyes, lifted her

arms, and began to revolve slowly on the spot. I couldn't hear her, if she was saying anything, but I saw a few blades of grass poke hopefully through the ruined ground.

"It's working," I said.

Aunt Sherry suddenly collapsed; Evan caught her in a cushion of force just before she hit the ground.

"Too much too quick. She's gotta go slower."

"Slower? It was only a few blades of grass."

"Yep."

I turned away. I didn't want to see any more.

"Why'd you come see me?"

"To ask about fairies," I said. "Cormack offered to tell me how he captured one, but first I have to tell him who killed his brother."

"He's gonna figure it out, you know. Sooner or later, there'll be a reckonin'."

"Are you a seer now? I thought that was my job."

"Nope. Just seen enough of human nature to know."

"Fairies?" I prompted him. "How do I find it? How do I capture it? How can I send it back to wherever it came from?"

"What makes you think I know?"

"Don't you know everything?"

He chuckled. "No. Just been around a while." He started to walk back down the path. "Come on, we'll walk and you'll figure it out."

"Figure it out?"

"Yep."

He was already a good ways down the path when I got my feet moving, and I had to jog to catch up.

"Cormack had her in an iron cage," I said, panting slightly. "A lot of stories say iron hurts fairies. Is that true?"

"Never ran into a fairy myself. Could be true. Lots of folks say so. Course, lots of folks say a silver bullet'll do in a werewolf."

"The iron cage was working, though," I mused.

"Yep."

"But it moves so fast! How do I catch it? What's its goal, anyway?" I stopped short, then had to jog again to catch up. "What *is* its goal? Is

it just to spread misery, or is there something else? The hell hounds…
you said the last time the fairies were here, the hell hounds were too.
The hell hounds seem to be trying to protect kids – maybe not all the
kids but some of them. What are the fairies trying to do?"

"You're doin' great, keep talkin'," Mr. Wolf urged.

"Wait, is there just one fairy or more than one? There's been a lot
of misery lately. Plus the freezing …" I stopped again, abruptly, and
this time Henry Wolf stopped too.

He turned back to look at me, and in his gnarled eyes I saw the
light of comprehension mirroring my own.

"You said… you said the cold was a strange power, that the human
body doesn't create cold."

Mr. Wolf nodded. "Knew you had it in you to figure it out."

"A fairy of cold," I breathed. "I wonder if there are others."

"Best focus on what you know."

"Good point. But I still don't know how to find, corner, or capture
a fairy."

"You got it in you to figure that out too." Henry Wolf started walking again, and I followed mutely until we reached the car I'd borrowed from Mom.

"Thanks," I told him as I rounded the car to the driver's side door.

"Anytime. But do me a favor."

"What?"

"Stop being so damn prideful and let Evan teach you magic."

Chapter 20

I SPENT THE REST OF THE AFTERNOON PACKING CLOTHES AND TOYS FOR THE younger kids, then shuttling it back and forth and preparing the guest rooms at my own house. We had six rooms, apart from the master bedroom and the nursery where Ana slept, which meant the twins would have to share. But given their behavior, they wouldn't have it any other way.

At three o'clock, I called Juliana and told her to come straight home without picking up the twins – I'd pick them up along with Ana. Half an hour later, she drove the van with Isaac, Elena, Adam, and Christina up to the front of the house and got out, glaring at me suspiciously as I stood on the front steps.

"You guys are going to stay with me for a few days," I said, trying to project a note of cheer I didn't feel into my voice.

"Like a sleepover?" Christina asked.

"Yes, just like a sleepover." I ruffled her hair and shot a false smile at the others, who weren't convinced. Not even eight-year-old Adam. "I packed some stuff for the younger kids, but Elena, Isaac, and Juliana, you should decide what to bring. Adam, Christina, why don't you make sure I didn't miss something important?"

Christina went straight up to her room excitedly, Adam following behind at a more sedate pace. Elena frowned, her eyes glassed over slightly, though I knew she hadn't spoken to the dead in a couple of years. Our dead grandparents had, apparently, insisted that no one speak to her until she learned to cope in the real world.

"Out with it," Isaac said.

"What's going on?" Juliana asked at the same time.

"Mom's sick." I glanced at Elena, wishing she'd gone too. Eleven was really too young to hear this. Then again, eleven was too young for a lot of things she'd gone through lately. And I wasn't sure twenty-three was old enough either.

"She's not in the hospital again?" Juliana asked. "I can heal her."

"Not from this." I tried to look Juliana straight in the eyes. Failed. Looked at her bright white tennis shoes. "She tried to kill herself."

They stood frozen on the front steps.

"She's with Belle Wright, the empathic healer I mentioned last night. But I don't think this was her fault. She was attacked by something — a creature Christina called a fairy."

"Attacked how?" Isaac asked.

I told him what I knew, leaving out my private fears that the fairy hadn't created all — or maybe even most — of Mom's troubles. The blueprint for disaster had always been there.

"You two go pack," Juliana said when I'd finished. "Cassie and I need to talk."

I stepped aside so Isaac and Elena could disappear inside the house, both looking remarkably subdued. I wondered if they knew what I suspected — that they'd be living with me for longer than a few days — then I turned back to Juliana.

"I won't stay with *that man*," she said without preamble, reminding me with words and menace that we hadn't had this argument out.

"I've been married to *that man*, as you call him, for almost two years. The feud's over."

She shook her head. "Maybe for you it is."

"What's that supposed to mean?" I stared levelly into her brown eyes and she stared back, unflinching.

"You surrendered."

"Is that what you think happened?"

"I know that's what happened." She scowled. "He stole your magic! You might have forgotten, but I haven't. And I'll be damned it I'm going to let any of us move into that bastard's house!"

"Juliana!"

"What? You going to wash my mouth out with soap?"

"You have no idea what you're talking about." I clenched my hands into fists, keeping them carefully reined in at my sides. "And if you felt this way, why haven't you said anything before now?"

"You never asked me to move in with him before now. And I've thought about saying something a hundred times! But no, the feud's over, we need to keep the peace. Fine. As long as it's your life and your choice, fine. But not when it's my life or the lives of the kids I've been taking care of for over a year without your help!"

I glanced over my shoulder through the open front door. Adam stood there, staring at us, stunned. I took a step forward and closed the door on him, blocking him out.

"Evan didn't steal my magic, his father did," I said, even though I'd said it before. Many times. To many people. I was actually sick to death of saying it.

"And yet, he still has it."

"He offered to give it back." This, too, I'd said before.

She snorted. "Yeah, so you said. Sorry if I'm not buying it."

"Why wouldn't you buy it? Am I lying?"

"No, I just think he knew you wouldn't take it. I don't think he wants to give it up at all."

I froze, thinking of the look on his face when he'd made the offer – again – just the day before. No, he didn't want to, but that didn't make him insincere. It meant he loved me, even now, when he was mad at me.

"Hit a nerve, did I?" Juliana sneered.

"Not at all, I was just thinking about yesterday, when he told me the offer still stands."

It was her turn to freeze as mixed emotions played out across her face. "I don't... that can't be right. He... he kidnapped you and he put spells on you and... how many lines did he cross and you still forgave him?"

Quite a few. Some of them still rankled, when I dwelled on them, and I had dwelled on them lately. It's not like he'd changed personalities after we'd gotten married – he was still the same man, determined to protect me and get his way.

But I had forgiven him. He and I had compromised and found ways to work things out, because we loved each other.

"I love him," I said simply.

"He wouldn't really give you back your magic," Juliana said, almost desperately now. "Say yes. Go ahead, say yes and see what happens. See if he goes through with it."

"You listen to me," I said, feeling my temper rising yet again. "I don't want it. I'm a seer, and there's no such thing as a seer-sorcerer."

She frowned. "There isn't?"

"No. I can't have it both ways. I made a choice, and it was mine to make." There was more to the choice than that — far more. The truth was that I'd chosen to love him. I'd chosen to forgive him. But I'd said all that before, and apparently it wasn't penetrating, so maybe this would.

"Is that why you won't even use Ana's magic?" she asked.

"Yes," I lied. I wanted this conversation over.

She shook her head. "I didn't know that, about being a seer."

"Why should you? You're not a seer."

"I need to think."

"Think all you like, but you and the kids are coming to stay with me while you do it."

She shook her head. "Take the kids. Fine. But I'm staying with Aunt Sherry."

"Juliana," I began.

She held up her hands. "No. I need to think."

"It's my life. It's my marriage. It's my business."

"How can you forgive him? There are some things that aren't forgivable."

And that's when it struck me — none of this was about me or Evan at all. It was about her.

"Who hurt you?" I asked.

"Who do you think?"

"Mom?"

She hesitated. "And you. You knew how bad things were, and you abandoned us."

My stomach twisted with guilt. Is that what had happened? I had just been trying to live my new life with my new husband and new baby, but maybe to Juliana, it had happened just that way. And maybe she wasn't wrong.

"I'll drop you at Aunt Sherry's on the way," I said finally.

80 CS

We were a subdued group that night. I had no idea what to say to the kids; when the pizzas arrived for dinner, I put on a movie so we didn't have to make conversation. Isaac was the only one who asked after Juliana. He cornered me in the kitchen as I cleared away dinner; the others were still watching the movie.

"She decided to stay with Aunt Sherry instead," I told him.

He almost looked like he was in pain. At fourteen, he had truly become a young man rather than a boy. He was taller than me, with a tiny bit of facial hair, and when he opened his mouth to speak — well, he sounded exactly like our father. It was eerie. Nicolas might be the brother who looked most like Dad, but Isaac was the one who sounded most like him.

"I can't believe she didn't want to stay with the twins, at least," he said.

"She had some things to work out." I didn't want to tell him about Juliana's thoughts on Evan, in case he didn't know. Apparently, I needn't have bothered hedging.

"You mean because she hates Evan?" He shook his head.

"You know about that?"

"Of course I do. She and I have been the adults in the house for over a year. I think we've told each other everything by now."

I felt another pang of guilt at the idea that a fourteen-year-old and a seventeen-year-old had taken on these responsibilities.

"For what it's worth, I told her you could take care of yourself," Isaac added.

I gave him a hug, which he resisted for a moment before settling in. I didn't hang on for too long, but I appreciated his vote of confidence more than I could say in words.

"I guess I didn't realize how much she hates him," Isaac said.

Again, guilt twisted my guts. "I think she hates me as much as she hates Evan right now. She thinks I abandoned you."

This seemed to surprise him. "Really? Because every time I told her to call you, that we needed help, she was the one who said no, we could handle it."

"I think she wanted me to know." I laughed, the sound echoing mirthlessly around the room. "I should have known. I am clairvoyant."

He shrugged. "Maybe. Maybe Nicolas should have known too. Or cousin Robert. Or the school, when our grades dropped."

"You've gotten wise in the last couple of years." The transformation was almost hard to believe. Two years ago he'd been caught robbing banks because he felt inadequate due to his lack of a unique gift, even if he did have magic to channel.

"I'll show you how to do bedtime," Isaac said. "You can't read about anything real to Christina or she might try to see it with farsight; it's got to be totally make believe. And the twins take a bath together, unless you want Maya to scream the whole time and swallow half the bathwater. Elena and Adam are reading a chapter of *Harry Potter* every night – I usually read that to them while Juliana handles the bath."

"I'll manage the bath," I said.

He turned to leave.

"Thanks," I whispered to his retreating form.

I nursed Ana before starting the bedtime rituals. When I finished, Evan took her to the master bathroom while I filled one of the three other tubs for the twins. Elena helped Christina with her bath down the hall while Adam, who announced that he was plenty old enough to take care of himself, claimed the last free upstairs bathroom.

Bath time with the twins gave me another chance to watch them, this time with my full and undivided attention. I don't think I'd ever given them my undivided attention before – there were always other things going on. Even yesterday, when I'd watched them eat, there were distractions.

Now there was just me, a tub full of water, and two slippery two-year-olds protesting the need for soap. Actually, that wasn't entirely true. Michael was okay with the soap; Maya was protesting.

I tried to distract Maya with a bright pink rubber ducky while I slid the wash rag between her and her brother, angling for patches of skin I couldn't get with their bodies melded together. She stared right past the toy, almost as if she didn't see it.

"Find the ducky," I said in a sing-song, giving it a squeeze.

Michael stared at it and smiled. Maya looked at him and raised her arms in the air. The next thing I knew, the toy had disappeared from my hand, reappearing an instant later in hers.

"How did you do that when you weren't looking at it?" I asked, though of course I didn't expect an answer.

Summoners could only summon what they could see; it was actually a fairly limited gift and I sensed Mom was disappointed when she'd discovered what Maya could do. Having been a disappointment myself, I planned never to so much as hint at the possibility that summoning wasn't every bit as cool as fire starting or farsight or healing or any of the other gifts running through our family.

Kids were becoming more powerful, though. There was more magic in the world. Maybe I shouldn't assume her summoning gift worked the same way my great-grandmother's had.

"Can I have the ducky back?" I plucked the rubber duck from Maya's hands, meeting only slight resistance. Then I put it behind my back. "Can you summon it now? Go on. Get the ducky."

She smacked the water, splashing her brother, who scooted away. Predictably, Maya let out a screech and Michael returned to her side. He handed her a washcloth and she took it, dragging it through the soapy water.

"Peek-a-boo!" I cried, letting the ducky come out from behind my back for a moment.

Michael noticed and smiled. Maya didn't look; she didn't seem to be looking at anything, not even the washcloth. Her face was tilted toward the faucet as if she were staring at the taps.

"Peek-a-boo!" I cried again, letting the little pink ducky come out once again.

Michael and Maya both squealed in delight, but Maya still wasn't looking at the duck.

"Can you get the ducky?" I asked, making sure to keep it firmly behind my back.

She held her hands up, still facing the faucet, but nothing happened. I frowned, then let the ducky come out one last time. The second Michael squealed, the toy was gone from my hands, magically appearing in Maya's.

"What's wrong with you, Maya?" I whispered under my breath.

"She's afraid," said a small, childish voice from the doorway. I looked up to see Christina standing there, long hair dripping-wet enough to leave a large damp patch trailing down the front of her Disney princess nightgown.

"Let me help you dry your hair a bit better." I grabbed a towel from one of the racks and began toweling off her hair.

"Jules washes my hair better," Christina said.

"I'm sure Elena did the best she could." I finished toweling her hair dry and looked around for a brush, but didn't see one. Deciding the brush could wait, I went back to Christina's earlier comment. "Why's Maya afraid?"

Christina shrugged, again.

"Hey, listen," I began, thinking back to the other night when I'd been attacked by a hell hound in front of my childhood home, "the other night, there was a hell hound at the castle. I called your name, and it went away."

"What's a hell hound?" Christina asked.

"Big, black dog with glowing red eyes."

"You mean Max?"

I hesitated, then nodded. "Yes, apparently I mean Max."

"He's Maya's. But he listens to me too."

"He's Maya's? Where did he come from?"

Christina shuddered, her eyes lowering to the ground.

"Christina?"

Her eyes snapped back up, but they weren't looking at me. They were somewhere far away. I glanced at Maya, at the way she never seemed to be looking at anything, and wondered if she had two gifts instead of just one. Dual gifts didn't run in my family; they ran in Evan's, but not mine. Which didn't make it impossible. But when I looked back and forth between them, I decided they didn't have the same looks in their eyes after all. Christina seemed to be seeing something profound, but very far away. Maya didn't seem to be seeing anything, almost as if there was something wrong with her eyes...

"Christina?" I asked again. "What do you see?"

"An eyeball. Looking out at us."

"Where is it?"

"Not here yet."

"Okay, then where—?"

"Don't let it come in!"

"I'll try. But I don't know anything about it."

"Not you, her." Christina pointed at Maya, who had grown bored with the rubber ducky and was now splashing half the water out of the tub.

"Maya?" A sick sort of dread washed over me as I tried to understand what Christina was saying.

"There you are," Elena said, her soft voice barely audible over the ringing in my ears. She started to usher Christina away.

"Wait!" I said.

Elena froze, frowning.

"What did Maya do, exactly?" I asked Christina.

But my five-year-old sister was done, shaking her head and sobbing softly. "It's my fault. I'm the one who saw them."

Elena led Christina out and I let them go, my head buzzing with uncertainty. I stared back at Maya and jumped when I saw something silver flash across her eyes. She started to raise her hands and without thinking, I grabbed them.

"Let's get you out of this bathtub," I said, trying to inject some cheer into my voice. "We'll get you all dried up and read you a book." I kept talking as I lifted her, keeping her hands pinned so she couldn't do whatever it was she'd been ready to do.

She struggled to free her hands and didn't even cry when I parted her from Michael. Not good. Very not good.

"Evan!" I called.

I strained to hear if he was finished with Ana's bath in the other room. I couldn't leave Michael in the tub, but I also couldn't let go of

Maya's hands. I had no idea what would happen, or if it had anything to do with the eyeball Christina had seen, but I wasn't taking chances.

"Evan! Isaac! Someone!"

Isaac was the one to appear in the doorway, looking from me to the squirming toddler in my arms with a question in his eyes.

"Take care of Michael," I said as I walked past him and into the hall.

Immediately, Maya began to howl. She had apparently noticed the absence of her brother.

"You can't separate them," Isaac said. "What are you doing?"

At that moment, Evan appeared at the end of the hall, emerging from our bedroom carrying a wet Ana. "What's going on?"

"I need you to do a binding."

Evan looked from me to Maya, then back again. "I can try, but didn't you say Nicolas had already done a binding?"

"More than one," I confirmed. "Please, just buy us some time."

Chapter 21

EVAN DIDN'T ASK QUESTIONS. HE RAN STRAIGHT UP TO HIS LAB ON THE third floor and began arranging the binding circle just as he'd done for Haley. While he worked, I did my best to distract Maya, who was having none of it. Her screams grew louder and louder until Isaac shoved a damp Michael into my arms.

"Help Elena with Christina and Ana, will you?" I asked Isaac.

He nodded and was gone.

I juggled the twins a bit clumsily, half afraid I would drop them, especially because Maya hadn't fully calmed down. Her screams had turned into a series of violent, hiccuping sobs and she continued to struggle to get her arms free from my grip.

I could not let her get her hands free, whatever happened. I still didn't know exactly what was going on, but I knew she wasn't trying to summon the rubber ducky.

"I'm ready!" Evan called after an eternity that probably only lasted five minutes.

I placed the twins in the center of the circle; it couldn't hurt to bind them both. The real trouble was that I didn't want to let go of Maya's hands, but I couldn't be inside the circle with her and I definitely couldn't break the circle by leaning over it.

"I've got it," Evan said when he realized what I was trying to do.

I backed away and sure enough, Evan took over, using his gift to gently keep her hands still. Maya struggled against his hold, but with even less success than she'd had struggling against me. He would never hurt her, but his hold was iron. I'd only ever seen vampires and hell hounds break it.

"What is she trying to summon?" Evan handed me a fire stick to allow me to light the five white candles outlining the circle.

"I don't know." I bent over to begin my task, but my hands were shaking so badly I had trouble catching the wick.

I closed my eyes, drew in a deep breath, and opened them again. Michael, smiling proudly, pointed to each candle in turn, lighting the wicks.

"His gift isn't bound either." Evan sucked in a deep breath. "Who did the binding?"

"Nicolas." I knew Evan didn't have a lot of respect for Nicolas, even if he had come a long way in the past two years, so I hastened to add, "And Clark Eagle helped."

"Hm. We might need a full circle."

"Try," I said.

He hesitated for only a moment longer, then lifted his arms and began to chant. Maya's screams grew louder and as they did, the hairs on the back of my neck stood on end. Something was very wrong.

I became acutely aware of everything in the room, and everyone in it. Evan stood at the edge of his permanent casting circle, painted rather than chalked onto the floor. His wavy brown hair hung loose around his shoulders, moving slightly as magic stirred around him. He stared fixedly at the twins, his gaze never wavering, his lips forming the words of his chant.

Michael stared back at Evan, his happy expression gone as if it had never been, his gaze as intense as a grown man's. He looked like a miniature version of my father, and I had the sudden, eerie sense that he was somehow possessing Michael from beyond the grave.

Maya screamed and clung to Michael's arm, though he scarcely seemed to notice. Her eyes were open, and in them I saw that silvery glint I had observed earlier.

The candles began to shake. Beyond his workbench, littered with books, star charts, and spell diagrams, a window rattled. Evan didn't break concentration, but a bead of sweat formed on his brow and I knew he was close. He was feeling the tension too. I only prayed he could hold it, that he wouldn't be interrupted.

Interrupting a spellcaster mid-spell was a recipe for disaster.

Suddenly, the window burst open and a tiny ball of light zoomed inside. I was sure, for a moment, that we were being visited by the Fairy of Despair. But the quality of the light was different – more bluish, where the other was red. Then the room began to grow colder.

I saw the instant Evan's concentration broke. Diving forward, breaking the circle with my body even as I rushed to shield the twins from whatever catastrophe was about to befall us, I braced for impact.

It came suddenly and forcibly, a sonic boom that physically pushed me and the twins backwards against a wall and then through the wall – into the hallway. I felt a sharp impact point at the back of my skull, saw stars mixed with plaster and debris, and still tried to keep myself between the wall and the twins, taking the brunt of the damage on myself.

For a minute or so, pain was my whole world. Then I felt Evan's hand on my face and heard his voice, begging for a response.

"'m okay," I mumbled. "Twins?"

"They're fine. Barely a scratch. I put them in an enchanted sleep for now."

"Fairy?"

"It disappeared when I dispelled the cold. Cassie, you're bleeding."

His hand rounded the back of my skull to where I felt a goose egg forming, and I yelped.

"I'm going to put you in an enchanted sleep too," he said.

"No! Need to stay awake. Got to figure this out."

"Cassie, there's a lot of blood."

"Head injuries do that." I moaned softly, which probably didn't help my case, but I stayed firm. Now was not the time to sleep. Now was the time to plan. "Can you just stop the blood and numb the pain for now?"

He didn't respond right away, but when he touched my head again I felt the pain magically ease. I managed to sit up and push my way out of the destroyed wall, coming to a seat against an intact section of hallway.

Tentatively, I touched the back of my head. I felt only numbness and swelling.

"What happened?" Isaac had arrived from downstairs, along with Elena and Adam.

"Call Juliana," I said. "Tell her I don't care how mad she is at me, she needs to get over here now."

"There's blood everywhere," Adam said.

"Where's Michael and Maya?" Elena asked.

Evan gestured into his lab and Elena ducked inside, coming out with a sleeping Michael in her arms. He looked huge in the arms of an eleven-year-old; she definitely couldn't hold both twins.

"Is he okay?" Elena asked.

"He's just sleeping," Evan assured her. "Can you take him down-stairs for me?"

"I'll get Maya," I said.

"No," Evan snapped. "I'll do it."

"I can do it." Adam dashed past both of us and had gathered Maya into his arms before either of us could decide if it was a good idea or not. If Michael looked large in the arms of an eleven-year-old, it was nothing to how Maya looked in the arms of an eight-year-old. Still, he held her securely, as if he had done this many times before.

As Elena and Adam retreated down the stairs, Isaac pulled out his cell phone and ducked into the third-floor guest room we'd assigned to him. We'd offered another room up here to Elena, but she'd insisted upon sharing with Christina. I think she was afraid of being alone in a strange house, but didn't want to say so.

I started to stand, but Evan stilled me with his gift. I stared at him, but he just shook his head.

"If I can't heal you, I'll at least carry you."

"Okay."

"It must be bad, if you're not arguing," he said.

"I'm not *that* stubborn."

"Agree to disagree." He knelt at my side and gently, using a com-bination of physical strength and telekinesis, lifted me into his arms.

It was a bit of an awkward position, to tell you the truth. I wasn't sure where to put my head, and I felt simply too large to be car-ried around as if I were a child. I put my arms around his neck, not because I needed to hold on – his gift wouldn't let me fall – but because I had no idea what else to do with them.

"I saw Master Wolf today," I said as Evan began walking down the hall toward the stairs.

"By yourself?"

"Yes."

"Why?"

"To ask him what he knew about fairies."

"What did he know?"

"Not much. But he …" I paused. We'd reached the stairs and I braced myself for some jostling that never came. My ride down to the second floor and then into the master bedroom was as smooth as floating on air.

Ana squealed when we entered the master bedroom. She was in the middle of our bed, her extremely damp head on a pillow, but when she saw us she popped upright.

"I never got her to bed," Evan said. "When I heard you yell, I was just getting her dressed."

"Ma!" Ana cried as Evan placed me beside her on the bed.

"You just nursed half an hour ago." I tried not to cringe as my bloody head found a white pillow. It would have to be burned, to ensure all traces of blood were gone.

"Ma!" Ana cried again, and rolled over to nestle against me.

"All right." I started to lift my shirt, but didn't quite find the clasp of my nursing bra before Ana grabbed – not for my breast as she usually did – but for my head.

I felt suddenly warm and tingly. The numbness in my head vanished, replaced – not with pain – but with peace. I was whole. Undamaged. Healed.

"Ana!" I cried. It had all happened too quickly; I hadn't been able to stop her. Of course I knew she was a healer – she'd saved my life before she was born – but she'd rarely manifested her gift since her birth. It was special, it was powerful, but it was also draining, and I never would have wanted her to use it on me.

"Ma," Ana said sleepily, and, for the first time, I was pretty sure she meant me, not my breasts.

"I love you too." I kissed her on the forehead as Evan scooped her off the bed and cradled her in his arms.

"That's my girl," he crooned to Ana as he walked her next door to her nursery. "Just don't do that too often, okay?"

I sat upright and tried to figure out what to do next. I felt reenergized. Awake. Ready for anything. I definitely didn't need to be in bed, but I did need to clean myself off. Quickly, I slipped into the shower and washed away all the blood that was matted into my hair. Aside from the blood, my head felt normal – no goose egg, no swelling, no pain.

When I emerged, I quickly dressed and went downstairs to find Evan. He was in the den with Isaac, the two chatting quietly until I entered.

"Is Juliana on her way?" I asked.

Isaac nodded. "Any minute. As soon as I told her about the twins, she started heading for her car."

The doorbell chimed and I ran to get it, looking at the monitor to double check that it was Juliana before flinging the door open and pulling her into a hug.

"What are you doing?" she asked.

"I'm sorry I wasn't there to help you with the kids." I drew back and looked her in the eyes. "I'm here now. Okay?"

"Okay?" She made it a question, but she followed me into the den. "Are the twins all right?"

"They're both asleep," I said. "Evan tried to bind their powers—"

"Their powers are bound," she said. "Nicolas and Mr. Eagle did it last week!"

I shook my head. "They slipped again."

Evan stood when we entered the den, though Isaac remained slumped in a recliner. Juliana perched on the arm of a sofa, apparently not willing to make herself too comfortable.

"Would you like a drink?" I asked.

"Get to the point. If the twins are okay, what do you need me for?" Her eyes narrowed. "Wait a second. Isaac said you were hurt."

"I was. Ana healed me."

"Oh." Juliana frowned. "I was going to do that, you know, after you groveled a bit."

"What are we all doing here?" Isaac asked. "Can we stop with the chitchat and get to the point?"

I glanced at him, noticing how tensely he held himself despite his slumped posture. Nodding, I took a seat at the opposite end of the sofa from where Juliana perched. Evan chose a spot on the love seat.

"What do you think is wrong with Maya?" I asked Juliana.

"Nothing's wrong with her," she snapped, a bit too quickly.

"Juliana," I said as gently as I could, "you've been like a mother to her almost since she was born. Something's not right, and you know what it is. Or at least guess."

She shook her head, but I knew she was lying. She wasn't even trying very hard to hide the fact, which meant she had to be on the verge of talking. She'd never been this bad a liar.

"Maya's just a baby," Juliana said.

"Nobody's going to hurt Maya," I said. "But we need to know what's happening before someone else gets hurt."

Juliana licked her lips and looked at her hands; her fingernails had been chewed and one was even bleeding. She couldn't heal herself, I recalled, but biting her nails until they bled was a dangerous habit for a sorceress to develop.

"She's a summoner," I began, "but she can only summon what she can see. How's she summoning the fairies?"

"I don't think she can see at all," Juliana said in a voice so faint I scarcely heard her.

I frowned. I'd thought the same thing for a second, but she was a summoner – and a blind summoner was about as useful as a dreamer who couldn't remember her dreams.

"I know," Juliana added, "she's a summoner. She has to be able to see, right? And she seems to have visual awareness, but recently I began to wonder... she won't leave Michael's side."

"You think she's seeing through his eyes?" I asked slowly.

"Yes." She twisted her hands nervously. "I blindfolded him a few days ago, to test the theory. Showed her a picture book and asked her to identify a cat – she knows that word. But she couldn't, not until I took the blindfold off. I tried a few other similar experiments. I'm pretty sure I'm right."

"Why didn't you tell me?" I asked.

Her eyes flashed with anger and something else... fear? "If you bind Maya's powers, she won't be able to see."

I opened my mouth, then closed it again. I hadn't spotted that. Of course, Juliana would have. "But wait – you said her powers were bound. You said both of their powers were!"

She averted her eyes. "Her gift isn't dangerous; I only had Nicolas bind Michael's."

"Juliana–" I began, feeling the icy tendrils of dread creep over me once again. Maya's powers hadn't been bound; maybe they never had been. Which meant... what?

"What difference does it make?" Juliana snapped. "Maya's not doing this. It doesn't matter if she's seeing through Michael's eyes, Michael can't see fairies for her to summon either."

"No," I said, and the last piece of the puzzle finally slipped into place. "But Christina can."

Juliana sucked in a breath. "Christina? No... I mean... no, that's impossible."

"We might need to stop using that word." I glanced at Evan and at Isaac, both of whom looked utterly lost.

"Christina told me, not an hour ago, that there was a giant eyeball peering in at us, but it wasn't here yet. She was seeing something – with farsight. She saw it, then she looked at Maya and begged her not to let it in."

Juliana gasped, and I knew that she, at least, had followed my logic. Evan and Isaac still looked a bit lost.

"There isn't just one gift at work here," I explained. "That's why I wasn't seeing it before. That's what's so different. Maya's gift of summoning only works on what she can see. But she's also developed the power – I'm not sure if it's a gift or a manifestation of her talent – to see through other people's eyes. Maybe it was just Michael at first, but now it's Christina too. And Christina is seeing creatures in another world." I paused as I considered the enormity of that. Christina's gift was beyond any other form of farsight I'd ever heard of. Beyond anything, perhaps, save the potential daughter I'd seen who spent all her time gazing at worlds light years beyond our own.

"So Christina saw the fairies in another world," Isaac began, "and Maya saw them through her eyes and summoned them here?"

I nodded. Then I cringed. Had it all been right in front of me and I'd refused to see it? I'd disparaged Sydney for not seeing the truth when her own daughter was a suspect, but she hadn't been the blind one. That had been me.

But no... I hadn't guessed that Maya was literally blind. How could I have? I hadn't spent enough time with her to know, and Juliana had chosen not to share.

"So what do we do now?" Isaac asked.

"We do a binding," Evan said. "This time, with a full circle."

"No!" Juliana cried. "You can't. She'll be blind."

Evan looked at me helplessly, and I closed my eyes, feeling the same way he did. "Juliana," I said, not willing to look at her, "people are dying."

"Maybe we can find some way to heal her," Evan said.

"Don't you think I've tried?" Juliana shot back. "It must be something genetic. I can't fix genetic anomalies."

"Your gift isn't the only solution," I said. "We'll put all our resources into finding a solution. Nicolas will too. We'll talk to Henry Wolf and Mr. Eagle and—"

"Wait," Isaac interrupted. "You're forgetting something."

We all stared at him.

"Even if we bind Maya's power, how do we get rid of the fairies? Mom'll never get better as long as that fairy's attacking her."

I wasn't as sure as I should be that Mom would get better once it stopped, but I didn't say that out loud. There was also the matter of the other fairy. And the hell hounds.

"We need to capture them," I said. "And we can't bind Maya's powers until we do. She's the only one who can summon them."

Chapter 22

WE REACHED OUT TO THE WHITE GUARD AND SOON HAD AN EMER-
gency meeting in our living room, planning and arguing well
into the night. I forced Isaac up to bed but Juliana refused to budge,
not when we were discussing the future of her baby. I couldn't blame
her, but I did ask her to keep an open mind.

"The one thing I don't understand," Linda Eagle said shortly after
midnight, after I passed around mugs of a stay-awake potion stronger than coffee, "is whether Maya is controlling these creatures she's
summoning. You said the hell hound considers itself hers, but also
responds to Christina."

"That's what Christina said." I shook my head. "To tell you the
truth, I don't think there's only one hell hound. Not unless they can
magically disappear in Eagle Rock and reappear three hundred miles
north in the blink of an eye. Uncle John can shift place, but he can't
make a jump like that."

"But gifts are getting stronger," Linda pointed out.

I couldn't argue with that. The rules of magic seemed to be changing, and I was already behind the times.

"Maya isn't controlling them," Juliana said, almost defiantly. "She
wouldn't hurt people on purpose. Besides, she's a summoner, not a
mind mage." She winced as she shot a glance at the Blairs, though
none of them seemed to have taken offense.

"I agree, actually." I went to stand at Juliana's side, sipping from my
own mug of stay-awake potion. "I think these are wild creatures she
set loose, driven by their own impulses. The hell hounds have generally acted to protect children—"

"What about the one that attacked you at your own house?" Juliana
flushed. "I mean, our house."

"And the one that attacked Jim at Nadine and Jared's place," Scott
added.

"I think …" I considered my answer carefully before replying. "…
they're wild creatures too, driven by a need to protect. But I'm not
sure they always understand the danger. Nadine and Jared regularly

cared for five children. When the sun set the night they died, a hell hound, thinking to protect Maya or Haley or one of the other children, might only have sensed the fear and death without knowing what was to blame. And there's been a lot of fear going around, especially with two wild fairies on the loose."

Linda nodded slowly. "I wish there was a way to find out more about these creatures. If Maya can summon them, what's to say someone else can't do it too?"

The room fell silent. No one had an answer for that. And we still weren't sure how to either capture the fairies or send them back to wherever they'd come from. It was largely what we'd spent the last three hours arguing about.

"Cormack knows something," Scott said. "All you have to do is tell him the truth – that I saved my mate from his vicious, murdering brother."

"No," Evan said, for the third time. Though not as many people seemed to agree, judging by their downcast eyes. We were getting desperate.

"It's time to break for the night," Matthew said, rising to his feet and setting aside his stay-awake potion. He looked at it and shook his head. It would keep us all up for at least the next two hours, whether we stayed here to talk or not. "We're getting nowhere. We need to face this tomorrow with a fresh perspective."

"The fairies could attack again at any moment, though," Kevin said. "And Maya could summon another one."

"She'll stay asleep until I wake her," Evan insisted, although given how effective binding spells were on the twins, I wasn't so sure.

"You can't keep her asleep forever," Juliana protested.

"I won't, but Matthew is right." Evan stood too. "I'm tired. I worked a lot of magic earlier and while I'm feeling okay now, I don't think it's the right moment to start a fight."

Everyone grudgingly agreed and the group broke up. Evan and I showed everyone out, murmuring goodbyes and reminders of tasks each had been assigned. The Blairs were going to look through their seers' old journals for even so much as a rumor of a fairy or hell hound.

Linda Eagle was going to research magical visual aids – Juliana had refused to talk about anything else until she elicited that promise. Scott had some iron cages in his lab at home; I chose not to ask why.

Finally, we were alone. Well, Evan, me, and Juliana. She hadn't decided to return to Aunt Sherry's.

"I don't think I can sleep," she told us.

"Try. The twins will need you tomorrow." I paused then added, "and so will I."

I scooted past her up the stairs, Evan just behind me. A week ago, he would have held my hand as we walked. How things had changed. And all because of my damned pride.

Pride had always gotten me into trouble. Tonight, I had to swallow it. I'd started to say something earlier, but gotten sidetracked by everything that was going on.

When we reached our bedroom, we had to take a few minutes to change the sheets. Finally, the bed was made and we slipped into it, each on our own side. The distance between us felt like an ocean.

"I'm sorry," I said, and it took me a minute to realize that the echo I'd heard was Evan saying the same words at the exact same time.

We rolled over to face each other and Evan propped himself up on his elbow, letting the sheet fall to reveal his beautiful bare chest. He wore shorts to bed, in case an emergency woke him in the night, but never a shirt.

"What are you sorry for?" I asked. "I'm the one who destroyed the lake shore."

He sighed. "I was hard on you because I was mad at myself. You've been channeling magic for twenty months and aside from throwing around hints and suggestions, I never came right out and told you there was danger."

"Why not?"

"I convinced myself it wasn't that big a deal. That the risk wasn't that great. That you knew enough to protect yourself, at least." He shook his head. "I was half afraid that if you did learn, you'd never want to give it up. We were both afraid of the same thing, but for different reasons."

It was my turn to shake my head. "You did offer to teach me. All the time. If you weren't pushy about it, well, I can be a little stubborn. Pushy might have backfired."

"You are stubborn," he agreed, a little too readily.

"Hey pot." I punched him playfully on the shoulder. Then sobered. "When I was with Mr. Wolf today, he showed me you and Aunt Sherry by the lake shore."

"Oh."

"I really did mess up. And I – I need to learn. I want you to teach me. As soon as we have a minute." I looked at him, gazing into his blue eyes just a shade or two darker than my own. All our children had blue eyes, I thought. Every one I'd dreamed about. It was the one thing they all had in common.

"All right." He lifted a hand to brush it against my cheek.

"I won't ask you to drain your magic. Ever."

"I won't take the offer off the table."

"If you insist. But I want to be a dreamer, and I don't think I can do it as long as I'm channeling."

His hand stilled. "Oh?"

"It's something Belle said – I'm going to ask her more about it when I get the chance. She's a Blair, even if that's not her last name, and I think she knows something. Maybe something Grace never passed to her son and grandsons."

"Matthew's going to be pretty mad if it turns out most of the ten years you owe him will be useless because you're channeling the whole time."

I giggled at the thought, then suddenly sobered. "You're not seriously planning to keep me pregnant for the next decade?"

"Only if you'll let me." His hand trailed down my arm to my right hand, where I wore a ring to protect me against pregnancy. He paused with his hand on the ring, silently asking for permission to remove it.

I held my breath. Henry would be conceived tonight. I felt it. There were other children, other possibilities, all swirling in my subconscious, some a little more real to me than others, but only Henry would have a chance to live.

I felt a moment of panic at the thought of consigning the rest to death, but of course, they'd never all have the chance to live. It was never a possibility.

"What's wrong?" Evan asked sharply.

"Nothing. I-nothing." I let myself think of Henry for a moment, and only of Henry. Of my painfully shy, sweet-natured boy with his father's gift of driving a woman insane.

Then I thought of Evan, and smiled.

He slid off the ring and tossed it behind his head before leaning forward to kiss me.

I let my eyes slide closed as the world exploded into a thousand tiny points of pure pleasure. My body quaked and tears dampened my cheeks. Evan swallowed my cries as I moaned against him, inviting him in, begging him to join with me.

He must have needed the connection as much as I did because he didn't linger over the preliminaries like he often did; I'm not even sure what happened to our clothing but the next thing I knew they were gone and he was inside me, filling me, making me feel complete.

"I love you," I whispered just before another climax hit.

My body arched into his as I felt him begin to pulse inside of me. I cried out, momentarily stunned by the certain knowledge that we had just created a new life. The thought spurred me into yet another climax, and this time I cried out loud enough to wake the whole house. Evan bent down to kiss me again, swallowing my cries, and pretty soon we began making love all over again.

It was a very long time before we fell asleep.

Chapter 23

I DREAMED OF THE LAKE. AND ONLY THE LAKE. I REMEMBER FEELING DISAP-pointed, because I'd wanted to see Henry again. It was a sign that I was just beginning to have conscious control over my dreams, or at least the ability to separate a conscious part of myself from my subconscious. But that night, I merely felt disappointed. I wanted to see my son again. To feel solidly confident that he did exist. To take him from the realm of the hypothetical to the certain.

But I dreamed of the lake, and of the node glowing beneath the lake. Glowing brightly. Almost blinding me. I'd dreamed of it before, but now some part of me seemed desperate to tell me something.

Look!

I looked. And as I did, the surface of the lake began to freeze.

I woke up, blinking in the early morning sunlight. Evan still snored softly at my side; we could only have slept for three hours or so. He probably needed a full eight hours, but we didn't have time.

"Wake up," I told him.

"Huh?" He smiled at me, then frowned and sat upright in bed. "What's going on?"

"Call everyone and tell them to meet here as soon as possible. I know what we need to do."

ഇറ

It took an hour for everyone to arrive. I was dressed and ready to go within two minutes, not even bothering with my hair or makeup save to throw my hair in a long ponytail. I nursed Ana, threw together breakfast for the kids, then paced anxiously, checking my watch every two or three minutes.

Maya and Michael were still asleep when the first White Guard members arrived – Matthew, accompanied by Kaitlin and Jay.

"I get babysitting duty again," Kaitlin said on a sigh that made me wonder if we were all taking advantage of her a bit. I'd have to talk to her, when this was all over. I'd definitely offer to watch Jay for a whole week if she and Matthew needed some time away.

"Isaac can help," I told her. "He's surprisingly good with the kids, especially the little ones."

She nodded. "Can I just get some coffee?"

I led her into the kitchen and poured her a cup. Matthew followed, his eyes narrowed, as if in concentration. I smiled at him mysteriously, knowing I'd kept my thoughts to myself for once. It wouldn't last, but I had no intention of explaining myself or what I'd realized more than once.

Scott Lee arrived with two iron cages a few minutes later. Madison came with him, to Kaitlin's delight. She'd have company, at least, in the midst of half a dozen kids.

Clark and Linda Eagle were the last to arrive, bringing my brother, Nicolas, with them. I should have invited him personally, I realized, but I'd lost track of things. He didn't say anything about it, fortunately. He just settled himself in the den with the rest of the inner council and waited for me to start talking.

"We're going to the lake," I said, gesturing vaguely toward the back of the house, which was built maybe thirty yards from the edge. "We need to be away from other people, when Maya does the summoning. There's going to be a fight. I saw the lake freezing, and the node glowing – I think we're going to need its strength, too."

"You can't expose the twins to that kind of danger," Juliana said.

"We'll all be there to protect her," Matthew said. "If I'm reading Cassie's plan right, she wants you to be the one to take care of Maya, so you can heal her in an instant if anything goes wrong."

Juliana looked at me and I nodded.

"What about Michael?" she asked.

"He's staying here." I drew in a deep breath. "Evan will wake Maya up when we get to the shore, away from everyone else. If I'm not mistaken, when she realizes her brother isn't there, she'll get upset and summon her creatures to her, just like she did last night when we tried to bind her powers. As soon as she's summoned them, Juliana, you get her back up to the house and get ready for the binding."

Juliana looked pained, but nodded.

"Mr. Eagle, will you lead the binding circle? We'll need a full circle to make it work."

"Of course, of course," he said. "Linda, Nicolas, Kevin, James, Robert, and Scott – you're with me."

"Have your phone on you, Jules," I said, "so I can tell you when we've captured the fairies."

I looked at Evan, who hadn't spoken, not even when he realized I planned to go with him and Juliana to the lake. I'm not sure if I was going to back up him or Juliana, because as much as I tried to sound confident, I was terrified of putting Maya in danger. If anything happened to her, I'd never forgive myself. But if someone else died at the hands of the deadly fairies, either through suicide or cold, I'd never forgive myself either.

"Maybe we should have the full circle at the lake," Nicolas said. "We could help fight the fairies."

"Cormack didn't use a full circle to capture the Fairy of Despair, or we'd have heard about it." I drew in a deep breath. "I have a feeling that these fairies are skittish. They've always hit vulnerable people and left the moment they were challenged. We can't let them think they're walking into a trap, and having seven or more powerful sorcerers waiting for them …"

I shook my head. I'd seen the lake freezing and sensed the urgency; someone else was going to die today if we didn't get going.

"If there's nothing else," Matthew said, obviously having read my mind, "let's move."

☚◯☞

It was a crisp twenty-six degrees by the lake, even before the Fairy of Cold showed. At least the mist was gone. The sun shone brightly in the cloudless sky, illuminating the water clear across to the opposite shore. And somewhere beneath the lake – actually, I could sense exactly where, south and west of our location – the node pulsed with magic.

Juliana carried a still-sleeping Maya in her arms, glancing dubiously out over the water. She had Maya bundled up in a pink coat that made her look like a sleeping marshmallow. It also made her look a bit hard to hold onto, but Juliana didn't falter as we walked until we were well clear of the house and all the people in it. The nearest neighbors, sorcerers as well, though not connected to the White Guard, had been warned to stay inside this morning.

It was just Evan, me, Juliana, Maya, and the fish. Oh, and my iron fireplace poker. I'd grabbed it on the way out, when Evan had grabbed the cages. It couldn't hurt.

"Ready?" Evan asked.

Juliana and I nodded, mutely.

He passed a hand over Maya's face, murmuring the words that would free her from the enchanted sleep. I held my breath and waited.

Maya yawned, widely, and began to stretch her marshmallow limbs. Juliana held tight, crooning nonsense as Maya's eyes fluttered open. Did they actually see anything? Was she looking at anything? Maybe not, but it was hard to tell. Whatever was wrong with her eyes, it wasn't obvious from looking at her. Although maybe… maybe they didn't quite focus right. It was subtle.

A blind summoner.

Maya's hands began flailing to the sides and her face fell. I could tell the moment she failed to sense her brother nearby, although the scream took another half a minute or so to come.

"I don't think she's ever been this far from Michael," Juliana said as she continued to try to rock and soothe Maya.

My youngest sister would not be soothed. Her cries grew in volume no matter what Juliana tried, no matter how she danced or swayed or crooned.

"How long do you think it will take?" Evan's gaze swept past my sisters as he checked the sky for incoming dangers. He set the cages on the ground nearby and readied himself. He could dispel the cold if he had to, but I knew he wanted to trap the fairies first. The last time he'd dispelled the cold first, the fairy had scampered away before he'd had a chance to think.

"Is it getting colder?" I asked. I really wasn't sure, bundled up as I was in a heavy winter coat, gloves, and boots. It was all a bit overkill for mid-twenties, but I wanted to be prepared for anything.

"I don't think so," Evan replied, still scanning the air. "I thought they'd be here by now."

"Me too."

I shifted nervously from foot to foot, trying to block out Maya's cries as I helped Evan scan the horizon. In the bright morning sunlight, it would be harder to see the telltale flicker of light that was all I knew to identify a fairy by. I even thought I saw something out over the water, but it turned out to be a reflection.

Maya's cries made my chest ache with guilt, the longer we stood there. What was I doing? She couldn't see without her brother. Well, apparently Christina would work in a pinch, so maybe others could too, but right now it was mostly Michael. And when we bound her powers...

People were dying. They had been dying for days. No, months! The Fairy of Despair had apparently been in town longer. And I hadn't noticed. I'd blamed my mom instead of helping her. I'd refused to see the culprit in my own family, under my own nose, until it was too late.

And now I was about to curse my youngest sister with true blindness. It had been so clever of her, really, to borrow her brother's sight, but it had gone too far. Now, I had to bind her powers. What else could I do?

You could bind Christina's powers, then neither of them can see the dangerous creatures to summon. Why are you picking on Maya? Choosing between children, just like you chose between Abigail and Henry. Who did you kill last night? Who did ou carelessly dismiss as unworthy, perhaps because their gifts made them less convenient?

Belle, I thought. I'd lost Belle, with her sight fixed on distant worlds. There were others, too. So many others. Now I was choosing between children once again.

If only Mom were able to make this decision. She should be involved, at least. But no, she was off feeling sorry for herself while the rest of us tried to pick up the pieces. *I'm doing the best I can,* I thought.

But are you? whispered a nasty voice I didn't recognize as my own. *You used your baby's healing gift last night, too. Look at you, leaning on infants to feed that void of power. It will never be enough, though, will it? Learn magic, get addicted to it, or fail to learn and risk destroying something else? That's your choice.*

Hadn't I already worked through all this? I shook my head, a little wearily. Last night, when I'd apologized to Evan, when I'd told him I wanted to learn magic, I'd made up my mind. I might have lingering regrets, but this desolation was over thet op.

I glanced at Evan and saw, to my horror, that he was on his knees, weeping. I had never in my life seen Evan cry. The sounds of his sobs were lost over Maya's screams, but I saw the tears streaming down his cheeks.

No, frozen to his cheeks.

It was cold. My own cheeks stung with the bitter temperatures as I realized that we had been visited by both fairies at the same time. And they had slipped under our guard.

"Go!" I cried to Juliana. "Run!"

Juliana stared at me, and I saw tears frozen to her cheeks as well. She wouldn't be able to heal herself, but she had to get Maya to safety before it was too late for both of them. I ran at her and shoved with all my might. "Go! Run!"

Juliana looked at me blearily. "I tried so hard, but I'm not her mom. She knows it too. I'm not enough for her."

"Of course you are. Now get her out of here!"

Juliana shook her head and fell to the ground. I felt like falling too, but I didn't. Instead, I raced to Evan's side, kneeling by him and holding him tightly, trying to offer him both my support and my body heat.

"Come on, snap out of it. I need you to get the fairies. They're here."

"I'm sorry," he sobbed. "I'm so sorry. I know I'm selfish, but please don't leave me."

"What?" I had no idea what was going through his mind, and wasn't even sure I wanted to know. "I'm not going anywhere."

He clasped my hand in his and held on so tightly it hurt. "Promise?"

"Yeah. That's pretty much what our wedding vows were about, remember?"

"Promise again."

"I promise."

"Good." He started breathing heavily, and I sensed he was beginning to fight the Fairy of Despair. But not quickly enough. It was so cold, I could barely feel my fingers.

I felt something in my gloved left hand, the one not grasping his, and remembered the iron poker I'd taken from the fireplace. I looked up, seeing the tiny lights flitting above us, and could think of only one thing to do: I swung the poker at them wildly.

I heard little gasps and the lights fell back in a sudden panic. It was still cold. I still felt an aching sadness that wasn't entirely of my own making, but I had a little breathing room.

"Evan? Can you get them?" I tugged at him, urging him to his feet.

"Yes." He was still breathing hard, but I felt him coming back to himself. His face hardened and he stared at the tiny little lights in a way that made me shudder. No one wanted Evan Blackwood to look at them like that.

He raised his hands and the wind began stirring around us, adding to the bone-chilling cold. The flittering lights stilled for a moment, caught in his power, but I suddenly knew it wasn't enough. It wasn't right.

"No," I said. "You can't attack them directly. Bring the cages to them, not the other way around!"

He nodded, once, to show his understanding. The next moment, the two iron cages were in the air, flying toward the flitting lights. The cages closed with a deafening clang before being lowered to the ground.

Suddenly, the cold lifted. My mood lifted. And inside the cages flitted two frantic, angry balls of light.

"What happened?" Juliana asked.

"It's over." I rushed to her side to make sure she was okay.

Juliana's face was a little blue, but she was already offering healing energy to Maya, to keep her from succumbing to the cold.

"You need to get up to the house," I told her.

"No need." Evan pointed toward the house. "They're coming here."

I followed his gesture and saw he was right. Clark led the circle of seven to the lake shore, carrying the props they would need for the binding.

"We can always reverse it later," I told Juliana. "Or come up with a better plan. This can just be temporary."

She nodded, mutely.

When the group approached, Linda Eagle plucked Maya out of Juliana's arms and held her gently while the others completed the circle. I'll say this much for Maya: There was nothing at all wrong with her lungs. By the time Linda set her in the middle of the circle of candles, everyone was wincing or even covering their ears.

"Let's do it." Clark offered his hand to his wife first, then to Nicolas.

One by one, all seven members of the circle took his or her place, completely surrounding Maya and the candles. Then they began to chant.

Magic filled the air, hot and heavy, a veritable storm of power. I hadn't been able to sense magical currents for long, and in the time that I had been able to, I'd never seen a working like this. They drew on their own magic as well as magic in the nature around them. They also drew on the power of the nearby node, taking their combined efforts to even greater heights.

This binding would not fail.

Suddenly, I felt a surge from the direction of the lake. I whirled, as did every man and woman on the shore. The binding was complete, the circle broken, but something was still happening.

A light flashed, coming right from the node, sending power upward like a fountain. I was momentarily blinded; I covered my eyes, and when I opened them again, I saw the two fairies fly out of their cages.

"No!"

But they weren't free, not exactly. They were clearly struggling against something that was guiding them, pulling them inexorably toward that bright light. Toward that node.

Then I heard a howl and looked as, overhead, two – no three hell hounds, bizarrely black against the morning sky, unnatural in daylight, were pulled into the light of the node as well.

There was a rushing sound, a roaring, and then suddenly everything – the fairies, the hell hound, and the light – were all sucked back down into the water, disappearing as if they had never been.

No one spoke for a long time. Only Maya's continued cries could be heard as we stared, unblinkingly, at whatever had just happened.

"They came from the node," I said, finally realizing what my dreams had meant. "How-?"

No one else spoke. They didn't seem to have words.

"What the hell is at the bottom of Table Rock Lake?"

Epilogue

Mom still wasn't better when Belle visited me a week later to begin our lessons. I had only seen her once in that time, and then only for a few minutes while Belle supervised. It made me feel like a criminal, but Belle said it had nothing to do with me.

"Can I get you some tea?" I asked when Belle settled herself onto a chair in the kitchen.

"Chamomile, please," she replied. Did she look wearier than she had a week ago? More tired, perhaps?

"We can put this off, if you need to," I offered, though I had so many questions I was nearly bursting with them.

She shook her head. "This is important. Grace despaired of the fact that an entire generation of boys got between her and the next seer; she never even met Little Grace before she died."

"Grace?"

"Of course. The name has been handed down several times, through the centuries. The first one was born in England in 1602 and urged the family to move to Virginia."

I added loose chamomile tea to two infusers and poured hot water into the mugs. I offered one to Belle before sitting across the table from her.

"Where are the kids?" she asked.

"Ana's napping," I said. "Michael and Maya are with Aunt Sherry."

"Good." She nodded. "I finally convinced her to work with me too, and the first thing I told her was to get more involved with her sister's family. She put all her hopes in her grandson Jay, but she's suffocating poor Kaitlin. Your family actually needs her."

We did need her. We needed a lot of support, and I was beginning to understand that it couldn't come from Mom. Not yet, anyway.

It was easier to find people to care for the twins now that their powers were bound. The circle had bound Michael's powers shortly after the node had gone back to normal — or what passed for normal. Matthew was considering putting together a team of sorcerers to swim to the node and investigate further. I believed it was the right next step; my dream snippets kept fixating on the lake and the node.

"How's Maya doing?" Belle asked.

"She stopped crying." I played with the mug of tea in front of me for a moment to try to cover my feelings of guilt. Not that I could possibly fool an empath. "Linda's looking into it. Matthew is looking into it. Scott Lee, of all people, is looking into it. Someone will find something soon." At least, I hoped so.

"Of course." Belle sounded confident, but it might be an act.

"What about Mom? When will she be better?"

"When she's ready." Belle removed the infuser from her tea and gave it a quick stir. "I'm afraid we can't rush this. She's stable for now, but she's hurting."

"Why?" I let the question explode from me, frustration and confusion warring within me. "How much of this is the Fairy of Despair and how much of it is grief? Dad's death was hard on all of us, but—"

"Grief can do strange things to people," Belle said calmly, but firmly. "And your father was more than a husband do your mom. He was her hero."

"Oh." I deflated a little, not sure what to think. Mom had made plenty of mistakes even before Dad's death, having children for the wrong reasons and becoming addicted to borrowed magic. One day, that could be me. A small part of me still feared it, even though I had begun learning from Evan.

Now I would learn from Belle, and she could teach me magic that would be wholly my own. Which led me to my first question, one I had been positively bursting to ask for a week.

"I haven't dreamed about Little Henry at all this week," I told her. "At least, not that I can remember. I wanted to see him again, to reassure myself he was real."

Belle froze with her mug of tea halfway to her mouth. "You were dreaming of possible children?"

I nodded. "Why? What is it? What do you know?"

"Before Grace died, she told me a lot of things. She described lifetimes she'd lived in her head. She said her body might have been eighty-something, but her soul was eons old. She'd seen so much, some of it she could change. Some if it she had to learn, the hard way, that she had no power over."

"Okay …"

"You can't choose one of the children. They're all just possibilities."

It was my turn to freeze. I felt for a moment as if the Fairy of Cold had returned.

"But I was sure… I knew the day and the time and the place …" Not that I'd wanted to choose any one child over any other; I'd felt horrible about that part for a week and had planned to follow up with that confession, but I'd accepted Henry in that moment. I'd taken him into my heart.

"There were millions of possibilities even in that fraction of a second," Belle said softly. "It all came down to random chance, not time or place or any of the rest. It was chance. A roll of the die."

"But …" I shook my head. "When I first started dreaming, I dreamed of Ana. Of a little hearer who would save my life. I didn't see her in detail, but some part of me knew she'd be a healer."

"Gifts aren't entirely genetic. They might run in families, but they're tied to the soul. At that moment of desperate need, when your life was about to end, snuffing Ana's out alongside, what's to say her soul didn't make its choice?"

I shook my head, not wanting to believe it. I couldn't believe it. Little Henry had to be real. He had to be!

"Seeing isn't easy, and it's going to be harder for you because you're starting just when you're having babies, and seeing doesn't work at all well when you're channeling. That's why seers don't tend to have a lot of children."

"I want a lot of children," I said hollowly. I wanted Henry and Abigail and even Belle, bizarre farsight and all.

I felt a hand on mine just as a strange warmth began to infuse my body. When I looked up, Belle stood over me, smiling slightly, her hand resting lightly atop mine. *It's going to be okay*, she seemed to be saying. *Everything will work out in the end. You'll see.*

"I'm not dreaming about children at all right now," I said. Then a horrible thought struck me. "Am I pregnant at all?"

She closed her eyes and shrugged. "Too soon for me to tell."

"Damn." I shook my head. "All I keep dreaming about is the lake. I swear it's calling to me."

"Then let's see if we can't figure out what it's saying."

The End

Author's Note

When I finished *Stolen Dreams*, I honestly thought it would be the last Cassie Scot book. I wrote *Madison's Song* and *Kaitlin's Tale* because her friends had grown too big to be footnotes in Cassie's story, and that, I decided, was that.

Then I moved on to other things. Or tried to. What actually followed was the longest, darkest period of burnout I have ever experienced. I didn't write anything for eighteen months, between the spring of 2015 and fall of 2016, though I tried over and over again. Nothing would come.

Recovering from burnout and yes, depression, takes time. I did not wake up one day and feel better, though I noticed a sharp turnaround in August/September of 2016 due to some new treatments I was trying. My daily schedule now includes mindfulness meditation, walking, and yoga. Since Cassie has been meditating from the beginning, it might seem strange that it took me so long to work it into my daily schedule. I can only say that some part of me knew how important it was, but another part of me – the type-A part – refused to let go of the precious time. Now I know that taking time for me every day increases efficiency, focus, concentration, creativity, health, and happiness. All of which means I have more time in my day, not less, and the time I have is precious.

Between fall of 2016 and the end of 2017, I completed two novels and drafted two more. I have never written so much in such a short space and ironically, I did it by letting go of expectations. Years of focusing on goals, focusing on results, had kept me from enjoying the moment and from letting writing be the artistic outlet I needed. Now, I set myself daily word count maximums instead of minimums, to keep me from falling back into that race to the finish line that hurt me so deeply. I write first thing every day, putting "me first" ahead of all my other obligations, then I let it go to focus on freelance editing, marketing, correspondence, social media, household chores, and everything else that makes up my day.

Frozen was one of the two books I completed, obviously. It lived in the back of my mind for years before it made it onto the page, pretty much ever since I finished *Stolen Dreams* and swore I was done! But *Frozen* is not something I could have written while I was focusing on goals instead of on writing for me, and writing what I love. All signs suggest that a new series would benefit my career right now, and that a new Cassie book will only appeal to true Cassie lovers.

I happen to be a Cassie lover. :)

I know there are others out there as well. I've heard from some of you over the years, and I would love to hear from more of you. Nothing puts a bigger smile on my face than hearing from a fan with something as simple as, "I loved your book."

I wrote *Frozen* for me; I published it for you.

There will probably be more Cassie books, but I can't make any promises about when and how often. I am writing two other series at the moment, hoping to build my audience through new tales, and I'm enjoying the heck out of those too. Cassie fans should especially enjoy the new science fiction story *Metamorphosis*, even if you think you're more into fantasy than science fiction. There's a super fine line between those genres, and I like to straddle it.

For now, I'm brainstorming the next Cassie book and welcome your ideas. My current thought is that she needs an arch-nemesis. Not Alexander DuPris; she already beat him for all intents and purposes, but someone who could be a real challenge. It's got to be a woman, right?

If you liked *Frozen*, or any of my other books, please take a few minutes to post an honest review. I cannot overstate the importance of reviews.

For the latest news, including cover reveals, new releases, and progress reports, sign up for my mailing list at http://eepurl.com/dhZ4Cn. You can also visit my website at http://www.christineamsden.com.

Sincerely,
Christine

About the author

Christine Amsden has been writing science fiction and fantasy for as long as she can remember. She loves to write, and it is her dream that others will be inspired by this love and by her stories. Speculative fiction is fun, magical, and imaginative but great speculative fiction is about real people defining themselves through extraordinary situations. Christine writes primarily about people, and it is in this way that she strives to make science fiction and fantasy meaningful for everyone.

At the age of 16, Christine was diagnosed with Stargardt's Disease, a condition that attacks the retina and causes a loss of central vision. She is now legally blind, but has not let this slow her down or get in the way of her dreams.

Christine currently lives in the Kansas City area with her husband, Austin, who has been her biggest fan and the key to her success. They have two beautiful children, Drake and Celeste.

http://www.christineamsden.com/

Cassie Scot Mystery Series

Cassie Scot: ParaNormal Detective Book 1
Secrets and Lies Book 2
Mind Games Book 3
Stolen Dreams Book 4
Madison's Song Book 5
Kaitlin's Tale Book 6
Frozen: a ParaNormal mystery Book 7

Other novels by Christine

The Immortality Virus (SF suspense)
Touch of Fate (paranormal suspense)

What people are saying:

Praise for Cassie Scot: ~~Para~~Normal Detective (book 1 in the Cassie Scot series)
"In this entertaining series opener, Amsden (*The Immortality Virus*) introduces readers to the eponymous Cassie, a decidedly mundane member of a magical family. ...Readers will enjoy Cassie's fish-out-of-water struggles as she fights magical threats with little more than experience and bravado." ~ *Publishers Weekly*

Praise for Secrets and Lies: a Cassie Scot novel (book 2 in the Cassie Scot series)
"...Cassie, stubborn and proud, is bravely trying to live on her own after her family disowns her. ...The growing complexity of Cassie's world makes this an entertaining installment, focusing as much on the will-they, won't-they romantic chemistry between Cassie and Evan as on the primary mystery...." ~ *Publishers Weekly*
"Christine Amsden unleashes her brilliant storytelling magic as the adventures of Cassie Scot escalate to the extreme. Rife with betrayal and a debt too deep for money to clear, *Secrets and Lies* plunges the reader into an utterly believable world where villains and heroes spring lifelike from the pages. Brace for a whirlwind ride of sorcery, romance and knife-edge peril. A truly original urban fantasy. Not to be missed!" ~ Kim Falconer, bestselling author of *The Spell of Rosette*, Quantum Enchantment Series